THE APPLE HOUSE

APPLE HOUSE

GILLIAN CAMPBELL

Brindle & Glass Publishing Ltd.
brindleandglass.com

LIBRARY AND ARCHIVES CANADA CATALOGUING IN PUBLICATION
Campbell, Gillian, 1944–
The apple house / Gillian Campbell.

Issued also in electronic formats.
ISBN 978-1-926972-87-9

I. Title.

PS8605.A5435A77 2012 C813'.6 C2012-902559-3

Editor: Kathy Page
Copy Editor/Proofreader: Heather Sangster, Strong Finish
Design and cover illustration: Pete Kohut
Author photo: Gary Coward

Brindle & Glass is pleased to acknowledge the financial support for its publishing program from the Government of Canada through the Canada Book Fund, Canada Council for the Arts, and the Province of British Columbia through the British Columbia Arts Council and the Book Publishing Tax Credit.

The interior pages of this book have been printed on 100% post-consumer recycled paper, processed chlorine free, and printed with vegetable-based inks.

1 2 3 4 5 16 15 14 13 12

PRINTED IN CANADA

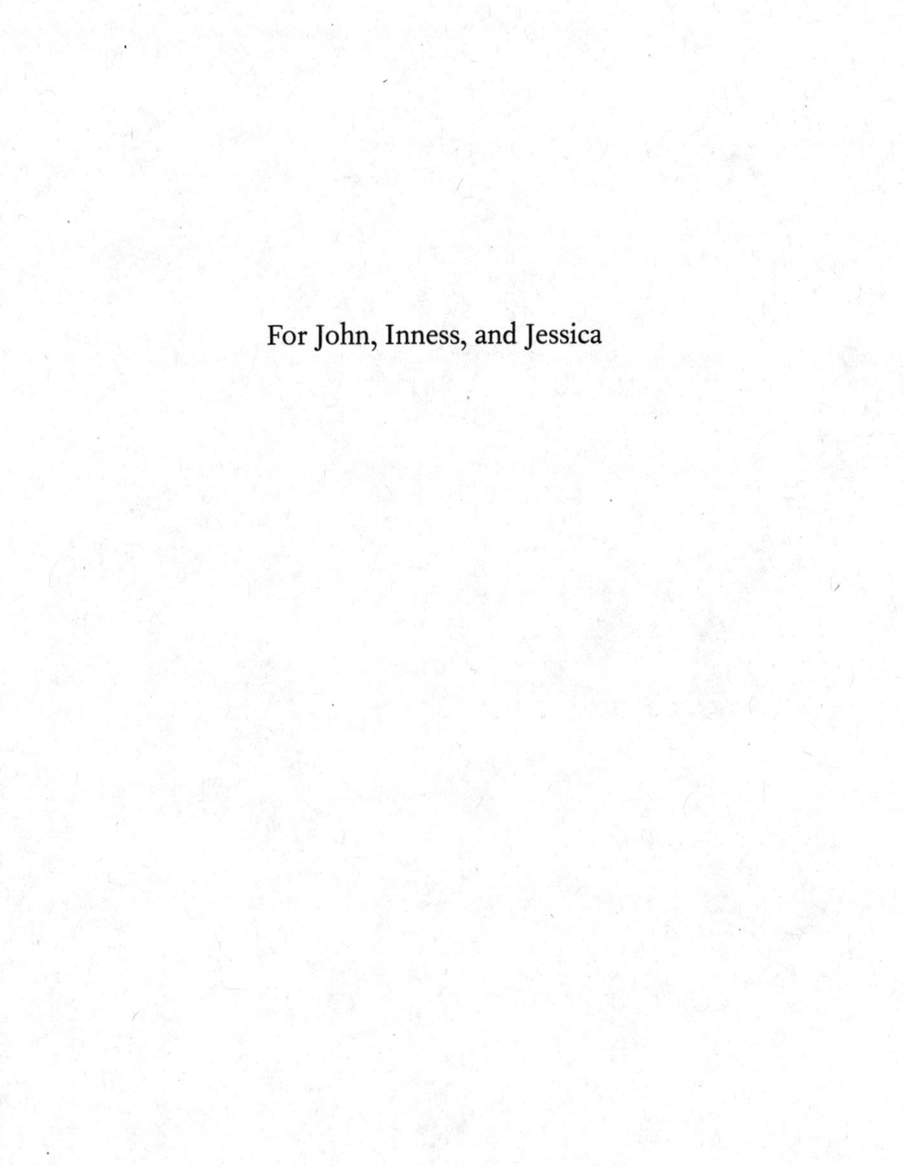

For John, Inness, and Jessica

The Road to the Village

You can go all the way to the village and back without touching the ground on the old stone wall that scrabbles along beside the road if you don't count the corner crossings and the gaps where the rocks have crumbled away or toppled into someone's yard and been planted with nasturtiums, if the toe of one of your raggedy runners doesn't catch in a crack and send you flying, if you don't jump off to poke a dead fish washed up on the public beach, if you're not afraid to go alone because the boys won't let you in their fort.

All along beside the lake, down the hill past the big stone barn where Charley lost his glasses jumping in the hay, past the workmen who sing out to one another in French from the roofs of houses newly risen in the field, around the corner past the crabby man in the green cottage who stands at his living room window shaking his fist, and on beyond the tree-lined drive that snakes its way to the big estate where rich people drink whisky on the lawn and a watchman stands guard over the apple trees with a rake.

The road would take you all the way to Toronto if you didn't have to go home for supper, but the wall falls away at the edge of the village where the shops jostle together against the sidewalk in a broad smiling curve, their doors clicking and clacking, coaxing you in.

First the wool shop with the little round window like a ship's porthole where tiny rainbow-coloured sheep graze endlessly on green felt grass without getting fat and a skinny lady with pointy elbows will knit you a toque as long your arm in any colour you like, with a tassel at the end too, if you have enough money. Then the café where you can buy a pickled egg from a big glass jar for twenty-five cents if you like pickled eggs; or if you don't, slip into Rossy's, where you can get anything at all except for the beautiful bead necklaces that are only for Catholics. Count the cracks in the sidewalk when the priest, who lives in the big stone church and sleeps in one of the pews, swishes by in his long black dress; everybody knows he doesn't approve of Protestants.

Down a little dip to the house of the man who fixes bicycles in his living room; spin the wheel on his gate to make a bell ring and run away quick. Hold your nose past the tavern in case the heavy wooden door opens and the beer smell comes out with a whoosh; only breathe again when sweet steam from the french fry wagon tickles your nostrils. Squish your nose against the big glass window at the Boutique de Bibelots to see the real live shrunken head all the way from Africa but don't dare enter without a grown-up, and skip aside quick when the old dame who lives above the IGA comes shuffling out in her pink pompom slippers. Then duck by the shoe shop in case the round lady who smells like shoe polish tries to chuck you under the chin, and nip into the pharmacy where they sell ice cream on Sunday and the parcels are wrapped in stiff white paper and tied up with thin red string that unwinds from a spool in the ceiling.

The door swings open with a warning jingle and closes again behind you with a bang. Dig in your pocket with a sweaty hand for your allowance; just enough to buy a Popsicle. Tear away the wrapper before it starts to melt, but try to make it last because it's a long way home and only beans for supper and you're not supposed to make a fuss.

The End of the World

I could have stayed home that Sunday, in which case the accident would never have happened. Thomas, who was swamped with repairs, had stayed up half the night to finish a pair of loafers for a customer over in Baie-D'Urfé with extraordinarily wide feet, quadruple F or some such impossibility, and he'd promised to deliver them the minute they were ready. The fellow had all his footwear made at Laviolettes' and never quibbled about the price or complained about the occasional delay, but he needed this particular pair in a hurry because he was flying out the next day.

We were already in the old taxi and about to set off when Thomas's former foster brother, Swen, appeared out of the alley.

By the look of him he'd been up half the night too, but that was nothing new.

"He's hung over again," I remarked.

Thomas put a hand on my arm. "Take it easy, Imogene, okay?"

"I'm just saying," I protested.

Swen ambled across the road, swaying slightly, putting each foot down with excessive care as if afraid the pavement might be scalding. He stuck his head in the passenger window and dropped a couple of joints in my lap.

"Going on a trip, Jackson? Better take something to help you relax." He always called me by my last name, which I found intensely irritating though at the same time I was glad of the distance it put between us. "What's the deal, anyway?" he demanded, peering past me to Thomas. "I thought we were going fishing."

"We're going to Ste-Anne's for lunch," I said firmly. I'd made a reservation at a tiny upscale café overlooking the locks at Sainte-Anne-de-Bellevue, just a few miles farther down the road from Baie-D'Urfé . La Fin du Monde, it was called. It seemed a fitting destination for people who never went anywhere.

My last memory of that day is of Swen's bloodshot eyes squinting at me through a thin screen of white hair that had escaped his ponytail, the sweet cloying heat of his breath, and Thomas in the long blue shirt that looked like a pyjama top, his dark hair still tousled from sleep, yawning as we drove away.

In my dream, always the same dream every night, the road winds under a leafy canopy and the lake slips by in glimpses. Shafts of liquid grey light spill out from the acute angles between the houses, old estates that have been divided and redivided and now stand shoulder to shoulder with brand-new stucco boxes, guarding the shoreline. The Man With The Wide Feet has a house on his own private peninsula with a lawn running down to the shore and a dock jutting out into the bay. As we pull into his driveway, he wheels up to us, pushing an old-fashioned reel mower, and I notice that he's wearing slippers, pink ones with pompoms on the toes, which is how I know it is a dream.

With a wave of his hand he indicates that he wants to cut one last swath. We wait for him on the dock: Thomas sprawled in a sagging canvas deck chair with faded blue and white stripes, taking deep slow drags on one of Swen's joints, and me pacing anxiously. The grass rises higher and higher until the mower is lost from sight.

"What's the rush?" demands Thomas. "I just want to finish this." And I know I should let him, but the joint is as long as his arm and growing with each inhalation.

"It's only a dream," he says, but I can't wake up.

The Man With The Wide Feet phoned a while ago, just back from his trip. On his way home from the airport, the taxi driver, who happened to be Thomas's cousin, told him about the accident.

"I can't believe it. I can't believe it," he moaned over and over again into the phone. "What happened?"

I couldn't tell him.

He sent a gift basket the next day, filled with fruit and chocolate and cashews, smelly candles, and a tiny white crock of Olde English Marmalade. It made a change from the endless bouquets of flowers that overflowed the shop and were now piled up in a makeshift shrine on the sidewalk. The card read, *In deepest sympathy, Gerard Johnson*. I couldn't think who it was from at first. In my mind he was The Man With The Wide Feet, and Johnson is one of those names in Quebec that could be either English or French. Almost all the cards were in English, out of respect, I supposed, though heaven knows the word *sympathy* is the same in both languages and just as hard to bear.

I wolfed down the chocolate in one go and took the basket over to the care home above the tracks. The duty nurse received it with a cry of delight. When I left she was rifling through the contents, looking for the chocolate, I expect. Her enthusiasm was a welcome change from the hushed murmurs and hooded looks that followed me around the village. Father Trepannier was the only one to look me straight in the eye. It was he, of all people, who broke the news to me the day after the accident.

I had walked away from the crash dazed but unscathed and in the ensuing confusion had not been admitted to the hospital or even given a physical examination. I spent the night in a barren waiting room next to the intensive care unit, waiting for Thomas to regain consciousness and making lucid conversation with a succession of interns and nurses. When, around ten in the morning, a young resident in need of a shave informed me of Thomas's passing, I appeared unaffected and calmly walked out of the hospital and climbed into a taxi.

By the time I got home all I knew was that I had survived a catastrophic event; I could hardly wait to tell Thomas. The hospital had phoned in the meantime, wanting instructions and signatures from the next of kin. Charmaine, who was minding the shop, had called my parents' number and spoken to my brother, Petey; then, worried that he wouldn't be able to cope, she had contacted Father Trepannier along with half the village.

When the taxi pulled up, the old priest was standing in the doorway of the shop, rosary in hand and a hole in the toe of one black boot. He led me inside and made me sit on a fitting stool while he explained exactly what I must do. The funeral service would be held in the church, he informed me, and Thomas would be buried beside his parents in the old cemetery. I could rest there too when the time came, should I choose to be received into the faith, in which case Thomas and I could be married posthumously though this was not a decision I had to make right away. I remember staring at his boot, which he kept sliding up and down the inside of his trouser leg, and fighting back the bubble of laughter rising in my chest.

After he left I waited till he was out of sight, then locked the door and called out to Thomas, a choked cry, half-laugh, half-sob that hung in the air unanswered. It was then I became aware that the shop was deserted, though the floor was a confusion of open shoe boxes. Supposing Charmaine had gone for lunch, I made my way to the backroom, where Thomas's workbench was cluttered with the usual jumble of broken-down shoes, winter boots, and a school bag with a broken strap, all carefully tagged for repair. He would be in the petit salon, the alcove that had served as a living room when the family still lived behind the shop. He had a habit of hiding out there to avoid aggressive sales reps and impatient customers. But his maroon leather armchair was cold when I sank down for a moment to catch my breath. He was playing cache-cache, I thought. We hadn't played it in years, not since we'd moved upstairs. I tiptoed through the old living quarters, listening for telltale creaks, a cough, or a snigger. When he didn't reveal himself, I crawled into our dilapidated old double bed. Let him find me, I told myself. My mother discovered me there hours later, half-buried under leather samples and yellowing invoices, sunk in a dreamless sleep.

Made to Measure

It's an odd situation, an anglophone inheriting a piece of Quebec's history. *Anglophone* is what they call us now no matter what language we speak. Back in the late sixties when I first moved to the village of Saint-Ange-du-Lac, I could hardly make myself understood, though I grew up only a mile away. Now, here I am, ten years on, the proprietor of a historic shoe store, Laviolette & Fils, Shoes for the Whole Family since 1892, and the unofficial curator of a tiny museum, Chaussures d'Antiquités de Québec. It's a modest collection housed on three shelves in a glass case mounted on the wall in the foyer. Some of the shoes are prized antiques and might well sell for a tidy sum if I were so inclined. Truly old shoes are not easy to come by, you see. They wear out and their stories get lost.

Both the museum and the shop belong to me now, or they will, once the will has been settled. Along with the business I've inherited the whole building. It's an old two-storey limestone house with a self-contained apartment on the second floor accessed by an outside staircase, a picturesque but treacherous wrought iron spiral that in winter ices up and defeats all but the most surefooted deliverymen. Tourists and members of the village heritage committee always stop to admire it, but most of them have never had to struggle to the top in a snowstorm with a sack of potatoes. Shoemaking has been in the family for generations. The Laviolettes are pure laine, as we say in Quebec. I'm a Laviolette too of course but only by marriage. When Thomas died, I don't think anyone expected me to stick around.

Thomas and I met over a pair of shoes. I was nineteen at the time with one undistinguished year of college under my belt, and young for my age. I had a summer job waiting tables at La Dolce Vita up in the new shopping centre. I had taken over the evening shift from a friend who had gone on to something she considered more sophisticated in the city. The uniform consisted of a black skirt, a white blouse, nylons, and black shoes; simple enough except for the shoes. I was tall for a woman, with impossibly big feet, well beyond the scope of the local shoe stores, which catered to the average French-Canadian foot, rarely stocking anything larger than size nine. The search for new footwear was always long and discouraging, and the result outrageously expensive. For months, unable to find anything I could afford in my size and unwilling to resort to the men's department, I had been slopping about in an old pair of sandals, my heels and toes protruding at either end.

To begin with I borrowed my mother's black pumps, which

were a size too small but broken in at least. They pinched my toes terribly and after half an hour of trotting back and forth to the kitchen, I wobbled with every step and even stumbled occasionally. The pain was excruciating. By the end of the first week my feet were red and blistered and I took to cooling my toes on the stone floor behind the bar whenever there was a lull. One evening the maître d', a pompous little man with a greasy comb-over, tripped over one of the pumps that I had neglected to kick out of the way.

"What's going on?" he demanded in a furious whisper at the sight of my stocking feet. "This is a restaurant, not a barn."

The next day I unearthed Petey's old canvas running shoes and coated them with black shoe polish. I was much steadier on my feet and proud of my ingenuity, but an hour into my shift I was brought up short by an outraged hiss in my ear.

"What the hell you got on now? This is a high-class joint!"

I considered quitting, but instead, at my father's suggestion, I took myself down to Laviolette & Fils, where for years there'd been a small, faded cardboard sign in the window advertising CHAUSSURES SUR MESURE. My father, whose outsized feet I had inherited, had all his footwear custom made, though not in the village. More than once he had suggested I do the same, even offering to pay for the first pair. Until that day I had rejected the idea out of hand, from embarrassment mostly. As children, Petey and I had all our shoes from Laviolettes', but I hadn't been near the shop since the September I entered grade eight, when to everyone's amazement and my utter humiliation, I had outgrown every ladies shoe they had in stock.

In seven years nothing had changed in the shop. Then as now the front door opened into a small foyer where the Chaussures d'Antiquités are displayed. It's the fancy ones that impress visitors. The platform heels date from the French Revolution, according to the little card. They look as if they've never been worn, but then it's unlikely that anyone could have kept them on their feet long enough to put a crease in the leather. My favourite item is a tiny black button boot with a child-sized buttonhook to match. Possibly the child died and one shoe was buried with the body, the other squirrelled away as a keepsake perhaps. The hollowed-out stumps in the corner are the remains of a pair of sabots that came to Canada in the 1600s with one of the filles du Roi, those foolhardy young women who sailed over to New France in order to marry strangers. This particular pair belonged to Marie-Josephine Vadeboncoeur, an ancestor of my mother-in-law, who inherited the same name. As a child my heart belonged to the glass slipper, but it turned out to be only plastic.

The shop itself is long and narrow, with a workroom at the back, partitioned off by a waist-high counter. The front wall is taken up with a bay window that juts out over the sidewalk, providing a commanding view of the main street. On either side the walls are lined from floor to ceiling with shoeboxes and in those days, before the wall-to-wall carpeting, there was a threadbare blue runner down the middle where my brother, Petey, and I could parade up and down without scuffing the soles of as yet unpaid-for shoes.

Thomas's mother, Marie-Josephine, tended the shop while his father, Joseph, and an assistant worked in the back, reheeling and resoling boots and shoes, replacing purse clasps and luggage handles, and generally repairing everything and anything as long as it was made of leather. Joseph was a quiet, sweet-natured man, though somewhat of a terror to his customers. When presented with a shoe in need of repair, he would turn it over in his hands, as often as not shaking his head with an air of resignation and despair, and point with blunt, accusing fingers to worn heels, unsalvageable soles, and cracked, scuffed leather, all witness to procrastination and inexcusable neglect.

As I stood hesitating in the foyer that day, inhaling the heady aroma of new leather, besieged by nostalgia and doubt, Madame Laviolette bustled out from behind the counter. She was a short round woman, with an unusually large head and thick blond hair that, to give an illusion of height, she piled up on top of her head in a sort of chignon held in place by a tortoiseshell comb.

"La petite Imogene," she exclaimed, throwing up her hands. "And so grown up!"

At once pleased and discomfited by this unexpected welcome, I asked diffidently about the possibility of custom-made shoes. She immediately called to Thomas, who was sitting at one of the work tables, stitching a child's leather schoolbag. He stood up, reluctantly I thought, and came out through the little swing gate beside the counter. I knew who he was, though we had never spoken. He was a boy from the orphanage up at Lac des Bois, a village in the Laurentian Mountains, north of Montreal, an old farming community, and one of the few towns without a saint or a ski hill. The Laviolettes had taken him on as foster child-cum-apprentice and later, having no children of their own, had adopted him. As a youngster he was short for his age, skinny and small-boned with a dark complexion and, according to my father, exceptionally clever with his hands and also very bright. I remember hearing that he had won a scholarship to L'École des Beaux-Arts in Montreal but had refused to take it up. He was ten years older than I was, but I always thought of him as "the boy" because that was how my parents spoke of him.

It was a shock to discover that the boy was well over six feet tall and a master cobbler. He stood smiling lazily down at me with his straight black hair falling over his eyes, his tall slim body dominating the little shop. He was wearing a long, loose, faded blue shirt of Indian cotton from one of the import stores that sprang up everywhere in the late sixties and a pair of black cotton trousers that barely reached his ankles. It was an audacious fashion statement for the village. I couldn't take my eyes off him. Despite the strands of thread dangling from the unfinished hem of the pant legs he seemed exotic. On his feet he wore leather thongs that appeared to have moulded themselves to his feet and that I learned later he had crafted himself. Madame Laviolette surveyed him with a loving if somewhat disapproving cluck, then stood over us both while he measured my feet, keeping up a running commentary in rapid French that I couldn't understand but that, from the set of his back and the lack of response, I assumed to be unwanted advice.

He traced each foot on a piece of paper, took a series of measurements, and then made me walk the length of the carpet in my bare feet. I felt very self-conscious, I remember, and only carried on because it seemed less embarrassing to stay than to leave. When I explained that the shoes were for work at a restaurant, Madame Laviolette suggested a lace-up. Beyond that there was no discussion of style. Comfort had become my main concern; even the least fashionable ladies shoe seemed out of my reach by then, and in any case what I really wanted was smaller feet. The price, a shocking seventy-five dollars, was high, Thomas explained apologetically, because he would have to make a special last to build them on. The next pair would be cheaper. If he had asked for a down payment, I think I might have backed out, but he didn't so I agreed and fled.

A week later when I returned, having survived the interim in Petey's runners, a stocky young man with white blond hair was minding the shop. It was my first meeting with Swen. He was sitting on a stool, unpacking a shipment of rubber flip-flops and tossing them haphazardly onto the broad ledge of the bay window. As I entered he turned toward me with a shout of "à vous" and lobbed one in my direction. It bounced off my thigh and flopped to the floor. Disconcerted, I looked around for one of the Laviolettes, but the backroom was deserted.

"You want something?" he demanded.

"I've come to pick up a pair of shoes for Jackson," I said stiffly.

He disappeared into the back and a moment later thrust a shoebox into my hands. Inside was a pair of black Oxfords with chunky leather soles and unfashionably rounded toes—the kind that nuns wore. They looked impossibly long and narrow and somehow funereal. My first thought was that he had brought out the wrong box, on purpose perhaps, and was playing a joke on me, but my name, Imogene Jackson, was clearly marked on the invoice taped to the lid. There was no way I could consider wearing anything so ugly in public, but I supposed I would have to try them on.

"Quite the clodhoppers," he remarked.

My face burning, I sat down and concentrated on removing my sandals. I would wear them to work and nowhere else, I decided.

It was years since I'd owned a comfortable pair of shoes and after Petey's runners, these felt oddly snug though for once my toes were nowhere near the end. Having laced them up, I rose and took a tentative step on the carpet, anticipating a familiar twinge from the corn on my baby toe or at the very least the bite of stiff new leather at my ankles. But these shoes, so grotesque-looking in the box, seemed to mould themselves to my feet. I walked the length of the carpet and back on a rising wave of euphoria, picturing myself dashing about La Dolce Vita, tossing out orders to the kitchen, raking in tips, and talking back to the maître d'. They looked better on than off, I told myself, not elegant, but nowhere near as disreputable as my brother's old runners, nor for that matter my bedraggled sandals with their frayed, sweat-stained straps sprawled on the carpet runner. Still blushing, I counted out seventy-five hard-earned dollars in rumpled bills, stuffed my sandals in the box, and left.

At work that night I operated with a new efficiency, zipping back and forth to the kitchen without stumbling or spilling or bumping against tables. The maître d' turned his attention to an older, somewhat cynical waitress with a permanent run in her stocking. And then one evening a few days later, as I was swinging out of the kitchen with a platter of antipasto for a table at the back, my left heel developed a squeak. It was barely audible at first, more like a soft whistle and hard to distinguish from the background buzz, but as the evening progressed, it escalated to a high-pitched squeal. By closing time an agonized shriek issued from my left foot with every step.

"What the hell you got on now?" demanded the maître d'.

"Shoes," I replied in a mortified whisper, drawing a laugh from a couple at the bar.

"Well, wear something else. You can't go around squeaking in a classy joint like this."

"I bought them specially."

"Take them back," he said.

Just then out the front window, I glimpsed Swen on the sidewalk leaning against a lamppost, though at the time I didn't know his name. The shock of white hair was unmistakable. He was wearing white bellbottom trousers and a bright pink shirt unbuttoned halfway to his waist and in the artificial glow of the lamplight his whole body appeared to shimmer. He was conversing with a man in a studded leather jacket, leering in the way I had found so disconcerting in the shoe store. His companion turned aside after a moment and disappeared from my sight. Then a customer entered and I turned on my heel with a loud squeal and retreated to the kitchen.

Any number of things can cause a shoe to squeak. Most often it's a flaw in the construction, but at the time I assumed it had something to do with the way I walked. For a couple of days I tiptoed around the tables, putting all my weight on the balls of my feet. When that proved too tiring, I developed a slight limp that reduced the pressure on the left heel and almost eliminated the squeak. I knew I should take them back—it was the only sensible thing to do—but I delayed, conscious of the seeming absurdity of my complaint and reluctant to encounter Swen. I'm not sure I would ever have returned to Laviolette & Fils if I hadn't received a phone call from Thomas.

"How are the shoes?" inquired a vaguely familiar voice with a faint but charming French accent.

"What's it to you?" I retorted, mistaking my caller for one of the regulars at the bar who the night before had drunkenly pestered me for a date.

"Excuse me, it is Thomas Laviolette, the cobbler. Perhaps there is some problem?"

"Can you do anything about a squeak?" I asked cautiously.

There was a pause. "A squeak?"

"It's a bit of problem at work."

"Perhaps the floor is wet?"

"It's only the left shoe. They fit fine," I added when there was no reply.

"You must bring them in right away, please. They are guaranteed."

Thomas told me later he had phoned for an excuse to speak to me. The idea of a squeak upset him even more than it did the maître d'. It was only his third commission and the first time he had tried his hand at a woman's shoe.

I went down on a Wednesday, forgetting it was half-day closing in the village. Thomas was locking up when I arrived, but he insisted I come in. He made me walk the length of the carpet and my left shoe squeaked obligingly though I had to make an effort not to limp. When I paused and waited for him to speak, he gestured for me to continue. After several turns, feeling foolish, I came to a halt in front of him. He knelt down and loosened the lace of my left shoe, then slipped a finger inside and prodded my inner arch. The sensation this produced was entirely unexpected. I stood frozen, fighting back an urge to flee until I noticed Swen saunter past the window.

"Your assistant is here," I exclaimed, jerking my foot away.

Thomas sat back on his heels, frowning. "You mean Swen? He's my foster brother. He was just filling in for a couple of hours the other day. Sit down, please."

Perching opposite me on the fitting stool, he removed each shoe in turn. After a cursory glance inside each one, he set them aside and lifted my left foot to his lap, cupping it in the palm of one hand while running the fingers of the other down the long bony ridge of the large metatarsal bone.

"It's the heel," he said finally. "I can fix it now. It won't take long. Come in the back."

I followed him into the workroom and sat at one of the work tables, my unshod foot propped on a chair because the plank floor was strewn with tacks. Within five minutes he had pried off the offending heel and reglued it, but instead of handing it back, he clamped it in a vise and announced that the glue would take two hours to set.

"I have something you can wear while you wait," he added before I could protest. From a row of cubby holes where items waiting to be picked up were kept, he produced a pair of pale green sandals in exactly my size. They were old fashioned in style with closed heels and toes and a strap that buckled high across the instep, something akin to the Mary Janes I wore as a child, though infinitely more sophisticated and obviously brand new.

"Straight out of *Vogue*," my mother declared when she saw

them and she was nearly right as it turned out. He had copied the design from an ad in one of Marie-Josephine's French fashion magazines. It was her idea I discovered later, and an infringement of somebody's patent, no doubt.

They're still with me, those sandals. When one of the buckles fell off a few days after the accident, I asked Thomas's assistant, Gaston, to sew it back on. He mumbled something I didn't quite catch and set it down on a pile of repairs. A couple of days later, I discovered it on Thomas's workbench anchoring a sheaf of invoices and handed it back to him, repeating my request. He gave me an odd sideways look and started muttering again. It was an easy enough task even for an apprentice, but he'd only been with us a couple of months and he's famously shy, so not wanting to embarrass him, I consulted Charmaine, who's known him since childhood.

She was out front at the time, clearing up after an influx of customers, sorting shoes into their proper boxes and sighing heavily as she replaced each lid; she'd been run off her feet since the accident. When the cobbler dies, it seems everyone needs new shoes. Friends, neighbours, long-lost cousins—and half the people in this village are related if not by blood then by marriage—one after another they all came shuffling in the door, unbearably solemn. The florist's boy in his tattered runners slunk in and out with his ghastly bouquets, old Madame Poulin shambled across the road in her slippers at least twice a day to view the living embodiment of tragedy, and every single real estate agent on the West Island tried on a pair of Italian loafers.

"The buckle is bent," Charmaine explained when I complained that Gaston had done nothing about my sandals "He couldn't find one to match so he's ordered some new ones."

"Why didn't he say so?" I asked, relieved by such a simple explanation.

She straightened slowly and turned toward me, her sweet blue eyes wide and worried. "He doesn't speak English and you're speaking English all the time now."

It can take a lifetime to master a second language and one terrible moment in time to lose it.

Garden Crescent

I was alone in the shop the day I decided to pack it in, perched on a fitting stool, sorting through a bunch of mismatched runners on the sale table, and wondering if I was about to lose my breakfast. I had been plagued with strange migrating pains, fits of crying, and bouts of nausea for days, but that morning it was worse than usual. Wanting only to be left alone, I had sent Charmaine home for a well-earned rest, insisting that I could cope. But when Madame Poulin appeared out of the alley beside the IGA and shuffled across the road, I stood up with a groan and made a beeline for the door. The old goat could easily afford to buy every shoe in the shop—she's tried on most of them and she owns half the village—but all she ever wears is slippers. Madame La Pantouffle, Thomas used to call her. Real estate is her passion; she's had her eye on the building for years.

Before she could plant even one pink foot on the sidewalk, I had pulled down the blind and turned the key in the lock. She rattled the doorknob for a good five minutes and then rapped on the window with a slipper, but there was no point letting her in. She would hover for hours, gabbling away in French while I nodded politely, not understanding a word. I made up my mind then and there to do what my family had been begging me to do for days, what children do when life becomes too much for them, to close up the shop and go home.

I grew up on a street called Garden Crescent, officially renamed Croissant Jardinier, which happens to be the Tuesday sandwich special up at the Saint-Ange-du-Lac Deli though not, as my father likes to joke, any relation. It's part of a suburban development carved out of a field that once belonged to my best friend Louise's great-great-uncle. Papa Chaput, we kids called him. My childhood home is exactly a mile from the village if you go by the old Lakeshore Road, once, back in the olden days, a thoroughfare for farmers' carts and summer visitors and the main road from Toronto to Montreal. It's the scenic route now and as you might expect, it winds along beside the Lake. Lac Saint-Louis officially, though if you consulted a map of Quebec, you would see it's not a lake at all, merely a widening in the St. Lawrence River where it sweeps past the south shore of the Island of Montreal. As a child I walked the road to the village many times and I know each curve and hill intimately, better perhaps than I know myself.

There are no longer any fields on Montreal's West Island and no farms either, just rows of houses squeezed onto smaller and smaller lots, and every year more traffic and fewer people on the sidewalk. These days I drive more often than I walk. I turned the corner onto

Garden Crescent at eleven the next morning, and though it was only Thursday, the street had that closed Sunday-morning look it has taken on in recent years, half the houses hidden by the branches of weeping willows and yellow maples that have outgrown the yards. The only sign of life was a rusty black pickup truck parked near the corner beside the old farmhouse that once belonged to Louise's uncle. Maison de Pomme, the old-timers call it because there was an apple orchard there once.

It's old, that house, seventy-five years at a guess, maybe even a hundred, but not historic, a higgledy-piggledy affair slapped together one room at a time. It's been rented out for years and neglected by the owner, who has allowed successive tenants a free hand with renovations. No one in her right mind would want to live there, but when, a few weeks before the accident, a FOR SALE sign blossomed on the ragged cedar hedge, Thomas persuaded me that we should buy it and fix it up. Our small down payment was still being held in trust by the lawyer, but the deal had lapsed and the place stood empty with the basement windows boarded up to discourage local teenagers from hanging out there in the evenings. Out of habit I slowed to check for signs of vandalism and noticed that the bed of the pickup was full of furniture. My heart began to pound. It seemed way too soon for someone else to be moving in.

I parked a few doors farther down the street in front of my parents' home, where the garden was gloriously overgrown. Chrysanthemums crowded the front walk. Two plum trees, my father's pride and joy, leaned onto the sidewalk offering their bounty to the neighbourhood, while a gang of leggy dandelions sprang out of the cracks in the paving stones and romped wildly across the thin grass, coming to an abrupt halt at the property line, overawed by the lush chemical growth on the neighbours' lawn.

Rita Dunster, who has lived next door as long as I can remember, has never allowed a single tree or flower to take root around her house, never tried her hand at a vegetable garden or berry patch. She's a specialist in grass, and sets the standard for lawns on Garden Crescent. The house, a mirror image of our own, still glows faintly in the peachy pink of my childhood, though it hasn't been painted lately and the wooden tulips under the dining room window have faded. There was an unfamiliar Honda in the driveway that day, and in the living room window a large hand-lettered cardboard sign I hadn't seen before, advertising the family exterminating business, Dunster Debug.

I climbed out of the car and was reaching for a plum when the front door opened and my brother, Petey, tumbled out and came charging down the walk. He's a short, stocky man and he walks with his head and shoulders thrust forward, swaying from side to side so that he appears to be constantly recovering from a stumble. Petey is mentally challenged. Retarded, we used to say, but he objects to that label and I can't say I blame him. The word has a host of nasty connotations that have nothing to do with him. He's a decent, kindly human being and his moral sense is more highly developed than most. It's just common sense he lacks.

He came to a halt in front of me, wrapped me in his gorilla arms, and planted a large wet kiss on my ear, a greeting we have prevailed on him to save for family.

"Hey, Petey," I said.

"Imo! Imo! Sorry, Imo, can't stay. See you later, eh."

"Where's the fire? Aren't you going to carry my bag?" Petey once aspired to a career as a bellhop and ever since it's been a tradition of sorts for him to carry the family luggage.

"Oh no, Imo, sorry, Imo. Can't be late. I'm going to work. I've got a job." He talks the way he walks, barely able to keep up with himself. As I watched him weave down the street toward the corner, I saw Swen emerge from a gap in the farmhouse hedge and saunter down the sidewalk to meet him.

"Hey, Pete, hurry up. You're late," he shouted, raising an arm over his head.

Petey speeded up and they came together with a high-five. For a split second, their bodies, alike in stature, merged and then my brother disappeared behind the truck. Swen paused to wave at me. I stared back at him in dismay.

I found my parents in the kitchen about to eat brunch. My mother, looking glamorous in a red silk jumpsuit she had picked up at the thrift store—her parachute, my father called it—was standing over the stove, her glasses slipping down her nose, frowning at something that looked like an omelette. Dad was ensconced at the drop-leaf table by the window, reporting on the antics of a cheeky squirrel at the bird feeder. He was wearing his gardening outfit, an old dress shirt and a pair of shiny grey wool trousers that he'd once worn to the office and that now strained at the waist, gapping slightly between the button and the top of the zipper. Our old spaniel, Tillie the Third, lay flopped on the floor at his feet with her head under the table, oblivious to the behaviour of the intruder. When I entered, she shifted her arthritic legs as if to stand but rolled over instead with an apologetic thump of her tail.

The kitchen was cluttered. Half blocking the doorway was a large ceramic crock filled with battered blue and white enamel tin dishes acquired months earlier at a garage sale. By the stove, dangling from the ceiling on frayed and faded ribbons, were five yellowing recipe cards with pictorial symbols, one of my mother's many attempts to teach Petey to follow a recipe. They had been there forever. The cupboard doors sagged on their hinges with the exception of one that had been removed entirely and sat propped against the wall beside the dog's water dish. The drop-leaf table, set with place mats, silver coffee pot and sugar bowl, and Petey's favourite cream jug in the shape of a cow, was an island of elegance.

"Your mother's making us an Italian breakfast. A frittata," my father announced with an air of adventure. "Petey was too excited to eat. You'd better have his."

My stomach felt queasy, but I ventured a cautious nibble. The frittata was a kind of glorified omelette rolled up with a soft cheese filling. It seemed a miracle that such a delicate flavour could have been produced in the midst of such chaos.

"Petey's got a job," said my mother, handing me my coffee in a cup that matched the others but minus the saucer that at the age of six I had broken on a furtive foray into the china cabinet.

"We're having a roast lamb to celebrate," added my father.

Tillie thumped her tail enthusiastically. Like all the Tillies before her she has a large vocabulary, mostly to do with food. She's particularly keen on red meat, but she's not fussy.

"He's working for Thomas's friend. You know, that Swen fellow. He came to your wedding," said my father. "He came round specially, asking for Petey, so we thought it would be all right. He's not such a bad chap."

"He's a drug dealer," I said.

"A drug dealer," echoed my father. "What do you mean?"

My parents, Ireney and Herbert Jackson, solid citizens that they are, hardly know what an aspirin is, let alone marijuana, at least that's what they'd have me believe. It's absurd that perfectly intelligent people should insist on remaining ignorant. And the truth is they can't possibly be ignorant. They read about cocaine addicts in the paper every other day. They've seen drug busts in actual progress on the evening news, for god's sake. And it's not as if Garden Crescent is an oasis of innocence. We've had burglaries, vandalism, any number of out-of-control parties, and more than one assault, though the usual scandals are related to alcohol and sex, not drugs.

"It's common knowledge in the village. Everybody smokes pot

nowadays. It has to come from somewhere," I said, trying and failing not to sound impatient. I knew because of Thomas. Swen had been supplying him with marijuana for years, but I wasn't going to say so and anyway Thomas was never into hard drugs.

My mother sat down with a jolt, producing her trademark groan, a low moaning sound that seemed to rise from the pit of her stomach. "He can't be. He's a landscape contractor. He told us so himself. He's bought the old Apple House and he's going to live there while he fixes it up. He's hired Petey to help him."

It was my turn to be startled. "He can't have bought the farmhouse. I haven't even got our deposit back yet."

"Well, he's got the key."

"You don't suppose he'd let Petey have any cannabis?" asked my father. Both my parents stared at me anxiously. Apparently I was the expert on the wicked world beyond Garden Crescent.

I had no doubt that he would, but there seemed no point saying so. I shrugged and changed to a safer subject. "I see Mrs. Dunster's got a new car."

"It's Charley's," said my father. "He's been back for a few days. He's giving Rita a hand. She's running the business from home now. Got in a bit of mess with the accounts, I gather."

"Maybe Charley can speak to Petey," suggested my mother, brightening up. "You can ask him when you get together."

Charley Dunster is, or rather was, the proverbial boy next door. As children we were inseparable, but our adult lives were worlds apart. He had an engineering degree from McGill, an elegant wife with a PHD in entomology or etymology—I can never remember which—and a fancy house in Westmount, while I had married the local cobbler and lived in the village over the shop. Except for a short chat at his father's funeral and the occasional neighbourhood holiday get-togethers, we hadn't spoken in years. It hardly seemed fair or even possible to shove the responsibility for Petey onto Charley. And in any case I wasn't ready to socialize, not even with an old friend. I had come home to get away from people.

I felt a wave of nausea and pushed my plate away. "I guess I'll go lie down."

"Oh dear, have you been feeling sick again?" My mother peered at me over her glasses. "What did Dr. Campeau say? Did he get the results of your tests?" She looked ill herself; her face sagged. "His office called the other day. They said you missed an appointment. You don't think you might be . . ."

"I'm fine," I said, cutting her off before she could finish. I'd been trying for over a year to get pregnant—it was our reason for buying a house—but the thought terrified me now. "I'm just tired," I insisted, discovering I was on the verge of tears.

I retreated to my old room and my narrow lumpy childhood bed, once overflowing with stuffed animals and cracker crumbs, nowadays squeezed in between a sprawling oak desk that my father used for his accounts and the ironing board, used by no one or so it seemed. I transferred a basket of wrinkled shirts to the floor, crawled under a familiar scratchy wool blanket, and buried my head under the pillow.

A Goat, a Victrola, and a Wooden Leg

They run in order of age in ragged single file along the whale-shaped hump of land that separates the housing development from the farmer's field, past the excavation for the new house and the stack of wooden forms that will be used to pour cement for the basement, around the contractor's truck that has been stuck in the mud for two days, over the sprawling pile of rubble waiting to be burned, all the way to the squat stone pillar that marks the limit of their territory. One after another they throw themselves to the ground and lie panting in the wet grass; first the two older boys, Rupert and Finney, then Charley, and finally Imo, who is only last because the others had a head start even though she is a girl. She leans on her elbows and surveys the forbidden terrain.

Chewing on an old mattress is a one-horned billy goat. It is not tethered and has chosen for reasons of its own to take its midday meal in the bed of a newly formed gully that cuts across the long, narrow field, slicing it in half before disappearing into a shiny culvert. Beyond the gully the land slopes gently upward past a spindly apple tree to the backyard of a ramshackle farmhouse with a ribbed tarpaper exterior and a high wide verandah propped on stilts that tilt backward toward the field. There are no railings, but long strips of metal screening trail from the roof posts and a still-functioning screen door leads to a set of stairs that descends into the side yard.

Spilling out onto the grass from underneath the verandah is a treasure trove of the farmer's possessions recently emerged from the winter snow: rubber boots, broken chairs, enamel dishpans, a tangled snake of a hose, a long wooden toboggan, a rusty witch's cauldron once used for boiling maple sap and small children—so say the boys—and a wonderful wind-up record player called a Victrola with a big metal funnel where the sound comes out. In the darkness under the porch there is almost certainly more, all of it apparently surplus to the needs of Old Man Chaput, the farmer, his wife, Madame, and the stooped, one-legged grandfather who is called Papa.

Everything is up for grabs, Rupert says, because the farmer, who has made a bundle selling his land to the developer, will soon be moving to a fancy new house of his own in the village where all the other French people live and he will buy everything new. The stone pillar, where the children are crouched, once marked the entrance to his farm. Two days ago its mate and the gate that swung between them were demolished. Cold brown mud oozes up from the caterpillar tracks, staining Imo's hands and knees.

Rupert and Finney are planning a raid on the farmhouse. They draw diagrams in the mud showing house, field, and goat, with arrows marking approaches and escape routes. The attack is to be carried out—*executed* is the word they use—with precision, and there must be no possibility of failure. At present the farmhouse is deserted, the enemy occupants having departed together in a taxi. It is unlikely they will return before noon, but such a possibility must be taken into consideration. Rupert, who is small and athletic, boasts that he can easily outrun the farmer. The others, he suggests in an offhand and superior tone, will have to duck into the culvert. The farmer, a heavy-set, lumbering fellow as broad as he is tall, will never be able to follow them there, and neither Madame, who is fat, nor the tottery old grandfather is considered to be a threat.

Finney, long-limbed and tall for his age, objects. "I cannot be a friend to small spaces," he asserts gravely. English is his second language. The others understand that he fears he won't be able to squeeze into the culvert.

A few months ago, newly arrived from Sweden with his family, Finney spoke in gestures and smiles. After two terms at school, his vocabulary rivals that of the other children, but still he struggles with the idioms of his new language. His oddly constructed sentences do not set him apart, however; rather, they give him an air of authority. His family is exotic, but Finney himself is no longer considered a foreigner. After a thoughtful pause he adds, "We will post a lookout. Maybe Imo. It is a good job for a girl, I think."

Rupert seizes on this suggestion. "She can stay here out of the way and whistle if someone comes, once for the farmer, two for the goat."

Imo feels her heart pumping. "I don't have to and you can't make me!"

She knows what she wants and it's there on the sodden yellow grass waiting for her. The Victrola is a beautiful thing, the first she has ever set eyes on, but she knows what it is because she has studied a picture in a magazine. The funnel is where the sound comes out, and sticking out the side of the wooden base, though hidden from her view, there is a metal handle for winding it up. In the pictures there is always a brown and white dog with an ear cocked to listen. Her own black spaniel, Tillie, can surely be persuaded to do the same.

Charley lays a restraining arm across her shoulder. He has his eye on the toboggan, a six-seater and the longest he has ever seen. Imo feels the heat of her friend's body against her own and the soft whistle of his breath as he whispers into her ear.

"Not yet, Imo."

But Imo has lost patience. She knows that Rupert and Finney don't care about Victrolas or toboggans or any of the farmer's cast-offs. They would be happy with an old boot for a trophy. There is nothing they would like better than to waste the day scheming and dreaming, and thinking up ever more complicated plans. Imo hates plans. They evoke the possibility that something will go wrong, that she will be caught by the farmer and dangled over the edge of the verandah or, worse, fed to the goat. Above all she is afraid of the billy. She knows too, deep down inside, that if she takes the Victrola, she will be stealing and it's better not to think about that.

In a burst of inspiration, Rupert says, "Maybe we could plant a flag."

"My sister can make us one," says Finney.

Finney has two sisters, both of whom are so much older than he is as to seem grown-up. Quite possibly either one of them could sew a flag, though Imo cannot imagine the process. It would take weeks, she is sure, and the Victrola has been sitting out for days. Already it has been rained on twice.

"Or Charley can draw one," suggests Rupert.

It's true. Give Charley a pencil and he can draw anything, though mostly he draws Superman and cartoon figures. Imo hears him sigh. It is clear to them both that the raid is about to be put off until another day.

Abruptly Imo shrugs off her friend's arm and stands up, snagging the sleeve of her new blue-and-green-striped sweater on the broken latch of the old gate post. She jerks her arm free and with a whoop hurls herself down the hill toward the farmhouse, her torn sleeve flapping at the elbow.

The startled billy looks up from its meal of mattress stuffing and eyes her balefully. Taking a step forward, it lowers its head as if to charge. Imo careens past it in a wide arc, splashes across the gully, and sprints up the slope past the apple tree to the farmer's backyard where she makes a beeline for the Victrola. But when she tries to pick it up, the funnel comes away in her hands and she discovers that the wooden base is hollow and rotten. Disappointed, she looks around for another trophy and sees that the goat has followed and is standing guard over Charley's toboggan. She heaves the funnel at it and then takes refuge under the stairs of the verandah where there is a suffocating stench of cat pee.

Ignoring the funnel, which lands well short, the goat takes an experimental bite of the toboggan. Imo picks up a boot and flings it as hard she can, following up with a canvas running shoe and then a blue tin teapot that bounces and skids across the grass, coming to a stop beside the beast's rear hoof. It turns finally and wanders back toward the field, pausing every few feet to gaze back at her with seeming malevolence.

Imo retreats into the gloom under the verandah where a musty odour mingles with the smell of cat pee. There is furniture piled everywhere: kitchen cabinets stocked with beautiful pale green china, a baby's crib stuffed with mildewed quilts and stacks of old magazines, a toilet with a cracked bowl, a chair with no bottom, and a wooden icebox filled with tins of rusty nails. Everything a person needs to set up house.

One of the supporting posts is hung with clothes, like a headless scarecrow: a lumpy cloth winter jacket, a red plaid shirt, and a pair of trousers dangling from elastic suspenders. Sticking out from between the legs of the trousers is a long cylindrical piece of wood with a shoe attached at the bottom. It is the grandfather's leg. She knows that immediately, though she has never seen anything like it before. For a brief second she imagines it to be his real leg, the one he must have lost in the war—so say the boys—but it is nothing at all like flesh and blood and much too short.

It's a peg leg with four flat sides, rounded at the corners and tapering down to where the ankle should be. Near the upper edge there are four leather tabs with metal fasteners and stuffed into a hole at the top is a piece of cloth. When she pulls it out, she sees that a family of mice have made a nest inside. There are five tiny pink babies, transparent and hairless as if they haven't been born yet. She can see their lungs pumping. The mother and father are not there. Most likely they are out getting food.

"It stinks in here."

"This place is a dump."

The boys crowd in behind her. Rupert elbows her aside.

"Hey, look at this, a wooden leg. Let's take it for a trophy."

"No, it's not ours. You have to leave it." She drops the cloth but it's too late.

Rupert flips it back and peers down at the nest. "Vermin!"

It sounds like swearing.

"Are these not mice?" asks Finney in a puzzled voice.

"That's what mice are," explains Rupert. "Disease-carrying vermin. We should kill them. The whole place is probably infested."

There is an uneasy silence. Both Rupert and Charley have experience of mice. Their beautiful new home, cleaned and shined daily by their mother, is under siege from field mice, and every night the brothers help their father set out elaborate traps along the perimeter of the foundation both inside and out. But these are only babies. They can't hurt anything, and anyway the mother and father mice will only make more.

"They are just born," says Finney in an awed voice.

"It will hardly make any difference if we leave them, not if the whole place is infested," declares Charley. Bold for once, he picks up the babies in his bare hands and places them in a fleece-lined overshoe at the bottom of the post.

Rupert shrugs and unhooks the leg. "The cat'll get them anyway."

"What's that?" says Finney. His body stiffens.

Imo becomes conscious of a knocking noise and the sound of heavy breathing. The billy goat is standing at the edge of the opening, glaring in at them. In its mouth is a boot. Rupert picks up a broken chair and, imitating a lion tamer at the circus, moves cautiously forward.

"Back," he growls.

Suddenly there's a shout from above. "Va t'en." A round brown object lands on the ground beside the goat's front hoof. Another glances off its rump and rolls under the verandah. With a snort the billy whirls around and canters away in a hail of potatoes.

"Come on. Let's get out of here." Rupert drops the leg and bolts out into the yard followed by Finney and Charley.

"Hey, you goddamn kids!"

The boys zigzag across the field. Charley lags behind, yelling for Imo to hurry, but the goat stands waiting for her by the apple tree. And then the barrage stops. She hears the slam of the screen door and the heavy step of the farmer descending the porch stairs.

She seizes the leg and, tucking it under her arm like a battering ram, she bursts out from under the porch and runs for her life. There is a surprised shout, a startled bleat, and then she is down the slope, across the gully, and up the bank, breathless but safe and brandishing her trophy.

A Pair of Wingtips

Our Wednesday afternoons at the back of the shop were the scandal of the summer in the village, though I was barely aware of it at the time. I was in love, not just with Thomas but with everyone and everything around him—with Marie-Josephine in her blue work smock that exactly matched the carpet runner, with Joseph in his leather apron, shaking his head over a pair of hand-tooled leather boots neglected beyond all hope of repair, with the rainbow of cheap plastic sandals on the window seat, the rubber flip-flops we couldn't keep in stock, and the expensive shipment of men's loafers imported directly from Italy, each left shoe cocooned in pale green tissue. The long lazy main street of the village with its dusty sidewalks leaning into the storefronts, and the spiral staircases punctuating the slow curve of the road, floated in a romantic haze.

Marie-Josephine welcomed me whenever I appeared, which was any day I didn't have a shift at La Dolce Vita, and set me to work in a backroom, out of sight I realized later, unpacking shipments and checking off invoices. Thomas was twenty-nine that summer, living in a mini-apartment behind the shop. His bedroom, the only room with a proper door, opened into a tiny kitchen with a half-sized fridge and an old coal-fired stove that had been converted to electricity. There was no counter, only a low table piled with scraps of leather, and not a single built-in cabinet. Apart from the few perishables that would fit in the fridge, any groceries were stored in a high wooden armoire balanced on spindle legs.

In his childhood the whole family had crowded in together, but when the tenant in the second-storey flat, a distant and elderly relation, passed on, his parents moved upstairs. Thomas and I, oblivious to anyone and anything but ourselves, spent Wednesday afternoons in their old bed surrounded by outdated cobbling equipment and excess stock. In the workroom, to the right of the service counter and out of sight of the customers, was an alcove that served as their living room, furnished with a maroon leather easy chair, a pale blue platform rocker, and a big square ottoman. Mounted on the back wall there was a small black and white TV that was rarely turned off.

On his very first weekend visit from the orphanage at the age of eight or nine—no one was sure of his birthday—Thomas had been given his own workbench and had amused himself making miniature animals out of scrap leather. He had always been clever with his hands; he supposed that was why they had chosen him. On his second visit he pieced together a pair of slippers for Marie-Josephine. He'd been designing shoes ever since. His sketches were everywhere, tacked up on the workroom walls, stacked a foot high on top of the armoire in the kitchen, and spilling out from under the bed where we spent our Wednesday afternoons and sometimes our evenings, sustaining our passion with tea and soda crackers.

His friend and self-styled foster brother, Swen, who was a couple of years younger, had spent his entire childhood at the orphanage, first favoured and then abused by one of the older monks. When the Laviolettes arrived to take Thomas home for good, Swen had hurled himself at Marie-Josephine, clamping his small arms around her legs and begging to be taken along. She would have adopted him on the spot if there had been even one square inch of extra space. Instead she arranged to have him visit once a month.

Weekends with Swen, which he and Thomas never tired of reliving, were notorious in the village. They unfolded in a series of disastrous escapades that included taking without permission an old wooden rowboat known as a chaloupe and filling it with rocks and sinking it in the bay, jamming the cantankerous heavy-duty sewing machine that no one but Joseph, not even Marie-Josephine, was allowed to touch, breaking the big show window at the IGA, stealing candy bars from the pharmacy next door, and a blissful afternoon spent hurling snowballs at cars and passersby from the landing of the outside staircase, an activity that ended abruptly when a particularly icy missile smacked Madame Poulin in the back of the head and knocked off her hat.

After the first year the visits had tapered off, but Marie-Josephine continued to send out care parcels full of cookies, toys, and clothes. Swen was a chronic runaway and always headed straight for the Laviolettes. Inevitably he would be sent back on the bus the next day, though not without a generous a supply of treats. When he left the orphanage for good at the age of sixteen, no one was surprised to find him on the doorstep with a duffle bag stuffed with his belongings and an expectant grin.

By then Marie-Josephine and Joseph were living upstairs, so Swen bunked in with Thomas. There followed a series of jobs around the village, all of which ended in disgrace. On the whole the locals were good-natured about his failings and when one business dumped him, another one took him on. Most of his behaviour was attributed to youth and an unfortunate childhood. It was well known that he had no family of his own. I suppose he was a child of the village as much as anywhere.

I came upon him one day helping himself to a pair of shoes. The Laviolettes, along with half the town, had gone to a funeral, and after considerable deliberation Marie-Josephine had left me in charge. The village was deserted, and knowing I'd only be a moment, I had nipped next door to the pharmacy for a chocolate bar without bothering to lock up. On my return I discovered Swen sitting on a stool lacing up a pair of black wingtips he couldn't possibly afford, his hair, white blond to the roots, veiling his face. I could have said hello or cleared my throat—I knew the shop bell was broken—but I stood in the foyer thinking I'd caught him out and unsure how to proceed. Hearing the door swing closed, he looked up with a smirk.

"Well if it isn't Long Tall Sally. Look what happens when they leave *you* in charge."

"I was just next door," I defended myself.

"There was a guy here, wanted to buy a pair of fancy hoofers. He said to tell you he didn't think much of the service."

"Where is he?" I glanced around in alarm, afraid I had missed a sale.

"Luckily it just so happens I know my way round." Swen gave me an exaggerated wink and I realized he was referring to himself.

"You planning to pay for those?" I demanded.

He leaned back with his hands clasped behind his head and stretched out his legs to admire the wingtips. His shirt was filthy, the armpits sweat-stained, and I saw with disgust that he had no socks on.

"I used to live here. I guess nobody told you. Thomas and I are like brothers."

I felt a tightening in my chest. His voice was slurred and I detected an odour of booze. He had helped himself to the petty cash a number of times before Marie-Josephine sent him packing, in sorrow rather than in anger. None of them referred to it as stealing. He still had a key, I knew that. I couldn't understand why they put up with him.

"Now my brother, he's got himself a nice English girl. I guess she's part of the family too."

"I'm not part of *your* family."

"Come on, Jackson, we got the place to ourselves. Might as well make peace." He stood up and held out his hand. I saw that he was offering me a joint. "All in the family, eh. You and me and Thomas."

I took a step backward, shaking my head. "No thanks."

His face reddened. My refusal had taken him by surprise. For a fleeting moment I wondered if he'd come in with the express intention of making friends but then dismissed the thought. I watched in silence as he unlaced the shoes and replaced them in the box, fussing with the tissue wrapper before closing it. I knew I should say something—he was Thomas's friend—but my mind had gone blank and my heart was pounding.

On his way out he turned to face me, his cheeks flaming.

"He plays the field, you know. He told me so. Don't think he's ever going to get hitched to some stuck-up English chick."

Before I could respond, the door slammed shut behind him. Lightheaded and mortified, I watched him swagger across the road and disappear into the alley beside the IGA. His words echoed around the empty shop. I distracted myself by reorganizing the shelves. It was a tedious job and I was relieved when I glimpsed a dark-haired woman in pale green slipping through the foyer with a shoebox in her hand. It took me a few seconds to grasp that I was seeing my reflection in the mirror. I was wearing a recent acquisition from the new import store, a blouse of soft Indian cotton with long flowing sleeves, finely embroidered in tiny flowers, and a divided skirt that came to just below the knee though on a shorter person it might have been mid-calf length. A skort it was called, and it was perfect for riding my bike back and forth to the village or for preserving my modesty while bending to retrieve a shoe.

I paused to assess myself and my eyes gazed back at me, dark green and startled. My hair straggled at my collar in an unsatisfactory way; Thomas had persuaded me to let it grow. I was tall for a woman with a youthful slimness that has deserted me now. Long Tall Sally stared back at me; or was I a stuck-up English chick? My mouth turned down in a scowl. I frowned a lot, apparently. The maître d' at the La Dolce Vita had once referred to me as Lady Doom and Gloom, and the day before, Marie-Josephine had admonished me to smile at the clients.

I grinned experimentally, admiring my teeth, which looked splendidly white against my summer tan. "Stupid jerk," I said out loud, sticking out my tongue and waggling it in the mirror.

"Do you do that to all the customers?" An arm circled my waist and my tan paled as Thomas's face appeared next to mine. His dark eyes sparked with amusement. He was Métis—half-Indian, half-French—or so he'd been told by the priests; he had no memory of either parent. More Indian than French, I suspected. He was brown all over.

"Only sometimes," I said, a little embarrassed by my performance but mostly happy to see him.

He nuzzled my neck. "So, who's the jerk?"

"Never mind."

"Maybe it was your new friend La Pantouffle? Better be nice to that one. Her feet are special."

I giggled. The day before I'd had my first encounter with Madame Poulin. To the family's great glee I'd spent the better part of an hour pulling down shoeboxes before I understood she was never going to buy anything. Her hobby, it seemed, was trying on shoes.

"Did she come back again and make you a little bit cross?" he teased, tracing my lips with his fingers. I was frowning again.

"Where are your parents?" I pulled my head aside and tried to wriggle free, but he clung to my waist and nuzzled my neck.

"Now you're changing the subject. Who was it, eh? Did he buy anything? Tell Toto." His free hand began to wander.

"If you must know, it was Swen. He was trying on shoes. I'm pretty sure he would've walked off with them if I hadn't been here."

His hand stopped. "Ah, but you were here so there was no problem."

A vision of Swen leaning back in the chair, smirking as he admired the wingtips, arose in my mind. "Don't you care if he steals stuff from the store?"

I felt Thomas stiffen and then a draft on my neck as his arms released me. "I was hoping you guys could be friends. I've known him all my life, you know that."

"He makes me uncomfortable," I complained. "He calls me Jackson all the time, and the way he looks at me. It's like he's eyeing me up."

"He doesn't know how to behave around women, that's all."

I rolled my eyes.

"He's English you know, the same as you."

"What do you mean, he's English?"

"His parents came from England. His name's Stephen Williams. He was embarrassed about it at the orphanage. That's why he called himself Swen. He wants to be friends"

I flushed. "Is that why he called me a stuck-up English chick?"

"Really, is that what he said?" Thomas's mouth twitched.

"It's not funny," I protested.

"No, of course, he shouldn't have said something like that." But he couldn't repress his grin. His arms encircled my waist again. "Give him a chance, okay. It's complicated."

It *was* funny in a way; even then a part of me understood that. Things might have been easier among the three of us if I could have let myself laugh.

One Sunday we went fishing in an old chaloupe which he kept in a neighbour's yard. He called it fishing, but I don't remember that either of us had a rod. He rowed out past the old stone church on the point, then let the boat drift. We floated around the bay with Thomas leaning on the oars, smoking a joint, and me in my bathing suit, sprawled in the stern, trailing my arms in the weedy brown water and wishing desperately we could go to bed. But there was no question of it, not on a Sunday afternoon.

"That is no way to entertain a girl," Madame Laviolette told him a couple of days later as I sat in the backroom, idly picking at my peeling sunburn and watching Joseph resole a pair of shoes. "At her age she should be out having fun! Take her bowling at least." She spoke in French, but I caught the drift of her words.

"I have to take you out somewhere," Thomas told me gloomily. "Old Trepannier's been talking to her at church."

On the evening appointed for our date Thomas picked me up at home in his cousin's taxi, which he had borrowed for the evening. He arrived half an hour late and came up the walk sporting a pair of Italian loafers that, to Marie-Josephine's chagrin, had turned out to be too expensive for the local clientele. He looked darker and thinner than I remembered, and wonderfully elegant in a suede jacket he had acquired that afternoon at a pawn shop in Montreal. My parents, who had been hovering expectantly, converged on the front door.

"You're the boy from the orphanage," my father declared, seizing Thomas's hand and pumping it vigorously. "Quite a change, living in the village, eh?"

I groaned out loud.

My mother gave him a nudge. "Really, Herbert, that must be twenty years ago. I'm sure he hardly remembers."

"Nonsense. Of course he remembers."

"We should go. It's getting late," I said, edging toward the door.

The conversation, if you could call it that, stalled. Smiling vaguely, Thomas stepped into the porch and stood without speaking, his head cocked to one side, gazing past us into the living room. He told me later that he had hardly heard my father's question. Intrigued by the house, which was newer and bigger than anything in the village, he had made up his mind on the spot to buy a place of his own someday.

His reverie was interrupted by Petey, who came tearing downstairs, hoping for a ride in the taxi. Thomas offered to drive him round the block. They were gone for nearly twenty minutes and on their return, my brother was in the driver's seat. My parents and I watched nervously as he inched the car into the driveway. He knew how to drive of course; he had badgered my father to teach him. They had practised for hours on Sunday afternoons in an empty lot up at the industrial park, but he couldn't read well enough to even attempt the written test and he had never driven on the road before. It took another ten minutes, but he parked perfectly and climbed out of the car, scratching his ear and grinning sheepishly. Thomas looked bemused by our white faces. He hadn't thought to ask whether Petey had a licence and Petey hadn't bothered to enlighten him. When I explained this to him later, he was amused at first and then indignant on Petey's behalf.

Despite Marie-Josephine's suggestion that Thomas take me bowling, I had assumed we would go to a movie. I thought he was joking when he grabbed my arm and steered me into the Bowlerama, the fancy new ten-pin lanes next door to the movie house in Dorval. But bowling, it turned out, was his passion. He had even made his own shoes. It was the atmosphere he loved as much as the game. He wouldn't go near the five-pin alley above the village tavern because the lingering odour of stale beer reminded him of the orphanage, where the dormitory had been permeated with the yeasty fumes of the monks' homebrew. By comparison, the Bowlerama, huge and brightly lit with its high domed ceiling and rows of long highly polished lanes, was antiseptic and otherworldly. The constant, echoing boom of balls rolling down the lanes and the distant crashing of the pin-setting machines put him in mind of the Greek gods. He had come across a book about them at the orphanage and had carried it around with him for months, sleeping with it under his pillow until one of the monks, concerned for his eternal soul, had confiscated it. At the Bowlerama, when the heavy, oversized balls vanished into that no man's land behind the pins, Thomas pictured thunderbolts hurtling down to earth from Mount Olympus, disrupting lives at random as his had been disrupted first by the death of his parents and later more happily by the Laviolettes.

I suppose you could say our date was a success because a week later he presented me with a pair of bowling shoes and for the rest of the summer we went to the Bowlerama at least once a week. More often than not, we took Petey along. Despite his poor balance and odd stance, my brother was a better bowler than I was. He'd been taken bowling by his school and his passion for the game was more than equal to Thomas's. On the way home, if there wasn't much traffic, Thomas let him drive the last mile or so. It made me nervous at first, but we were never stopped and Petey was in his glory.

In September, to everyone's relief, not least my own, I gave notice at La Dolce Vita, but instead of registering for my second year of college, I let the deadline slip by and continued to hang around the shop. Marie-Josephine shook her head in disapproval when I admitted I wasn't going back, but a couple of weeks later she hired me as a full-time assistant, somewhat against her better judgment, I suspect. I heard her arguing with Joseph about it. Perhaps it was a question of the devil you know because there were any number of thoroughly bilingual local girls who could have done the job better than me.

My parents were shocked when I told them belatedly what I had done, but they were distracted by Petey, who a few weeks earlier, on his thirtieth birthday, had quit his job at the sheltered workshop and announced that he was never going back. He was made for better things, he declared. What he had in mind was sleeping late and lolling about the house, listening to the Beach Boys at full blast on his new transistor radio. When my father tried to insist that he return to work, Petey barricaded himself in his room and refused to come out. The impasse continued for a couple of weeks with Petey sneaking downstairs at night to fortify his resolve with peanut butter sandwiches. Not that my mother refused to feed him. She took his meals up to him three times a day and left them outside his door, but my brother's a person who can only do one thing at a time and during the day he had to concentrate on his "revolution," as he called it.

It was Thomas who lured him out. He had driven me home one evening in one of his cousin's taxis and my mother invited him to stay for supper. When Petey refused to come down, Thomas went up to fetch him. He took the stairs two at a time, then pounded on Petey's bedroom door. My parents and I stood on the landing, listening shamelessly.

"Hey, Pete, I want you to check out this taxi."

"Don't want to," came the muffled refusal.

"Come on, man. I need your advice. See if you think I should buy it. Let me in."

"No!"

"It's got bucket seats, man."

There was a kind of a howling groan from Petey and then he must have opened his door because we heard it slam shut and after that their voices were muffled. Dinner was cold by the time Thomas reappeared, chewing on his thumbnail.

"I don't think he can go back there to that workshop place," he declared with a shrug.

We regarded him without speaking. Coming from someone outside the family, this statement seemed somehow unassailable. And by then we were into the third week of Petey's revolution. My mother pushed her glasses up her nose and sighed audibly, pressing her lips together.

My father drummed his fingers on the table. "What's he going to do?" he demanded, his voice rising with exasperation. "He's a grown man. He needs a job. He can't hang around the house all day."

"He hates it. He says it's worse than school." Thomas stood in the kitchen doorway, his palms held out as if was the most simple thing in the world.

I saw my mother's jaw clench. A palpable wave of guilt passed between my parents. Petey had been sent to boarding school for ten years, longer even than Thomas had spent at the orphanage. Their experiences were hardly comparable, but it was a bond between them all the same. The Bastion Training School for Retarded Boys had been more about giving my mother a break than educating Petey. Heaven knows, she must have needed one. The majority of the students lived there semi-permanently, only visiting their families a couple of times a year if that. The principal, seconded by the team of specialists that Petey saw periodically, recommended that my parents follow suit, but my mother had insisted on bringing him home one weekend a month and all the usual holidays as well as the summer. He fought tooth and nail against going back each time.

"It's not that we want him to be unhappy," she said now.

"He's getting paid at the workshop, you see," my father explained. "Not much, but he has money in the bank."

"Yes, of course, he's a grown man. He needs a job." Thomas tossed his head impatiently. "But a guy like Petey, he doesn't need to be in a little room sorting screws all day. He wants to do real work."

"We have tried," said my mother. And it was true, but the possibilities for Petey were limited. Thomas could have no idea how limited. In the village, because he couldn't speak French, they were non-existent. And the workshop was a safe place with a built-in social life, free from taunts and queer looks.

"You have to understand," my father began, but before he could elaborate, Petey, who must have been standing on the landing listening, charged down the stairs with a triumphant whoop. "Mum, Dad, I'm having a career! There's lots of stuff I can do."

"Petey, it's . . . we'll need to talk about this. You mustn't get your hopes up."

"Mum, Mum. Don't want to talk. Me an' Thomas are going in the taxi. I have to help him check it out. We're going for smoked meat sandwiches."

"Well, at least he's out of his room," my father commented as they drove off.

My mother didn't reply, but the next day when I returned from work, Petey was out on the Dunsters' lawn, pulling dandelions with gusto.

"I have to get the whole root," he told me when he came in. "Rupert and Charley never got the whole root."

A couple of days later he had a job cutting someone's grass, the Connibears', I think. He's been unofficial odd-job man for the entire street ever since, mowing grass in summer and shovelling snow in winter, still thrilled to think he's his own boss, though it's my mother who keeps him organized.

Mouse Relations

That first week at home, I spent the mornings in bed with Tillie. There hardly seemed any point getting up. My mother tiptoed in with tea and toast, and my father offered the morning paper and tales of the squirrel's latest escapades at the bird feeder. Half an hour later, after a long operatic shower, Petey would appear in the doorway, all spiffed up in a pair of white jeans identical to Swen's, hair slicked back and still dripping.

"Mornin', Imo, you gonna get up today?" he would inquire, helping himself to my toast. Between bites, he would rattle off his plans for the day. Swen was away for a couple of weeks and had offered him a paltry two bucks a day to keep an eye on the farmhouse and deal with an infestation of mice. He had a horror of cockroaches and small rodents apparently.

"Petrified, Imo, petrified. A grown-up guy!" Petey crowed, puffed up with pride at the responsibility.

It was impossible not to be pleased for him, and disapproving though I was, I took satisfaction in the fact that Swen, whom I found so overpowering, was terrified of something so small and powerless as a mouse. That Petey, who is a friend to all animals, had agreed to take on such a task at all, was a puzzle, and disturbing as well. My big, awkward, hulking brother is a Buddhist at heart. He won't even step on a spider, and years ago when Darwin Dunster offered to train him in the exterminating business, Petey fled in tears the first time he had to empty a trap. He's older now, of course, and desperate for a real job.

In his own mind, getting rid of the mice was the least of his responsibilities. I don't think it occurred to him that he would have to kill anything. He spent the first week scouring out the farmhouse. Following explicit instructions from my mother, he scrubbed the kitchen floor, wiped graffiti off the walls, knocked down the cobwebs, and one morning even donned the ear protectors he wears when he's using the gas mower and carted my mother's vacuum up the street and vacuumed the living room rug.

He was home again for lunch promptly at noon every day, and the first thing he did was to charge upstairs and fling himself on my bed. After a couple of such rude awakenings, I made a point of getting myself down to the kitchen in time to watch him eat his sandwich. I sat at the drop-leaf table, feeling nauseated by the smell of peanut butter, and listened with a combination of relief and despair to a blow-by-blow account of his progress, knowing it should have been Thomas and me doing all that work.

When he ran out of cleaning projects, he set a couple of token mousetraps in the kitchen, the humane kind that catch creatures alive, and he captured two unwary mice the very first night. He set them free a couple of blocks away, and when the next morning the traps remained empty, he concluded that he had dealt with the problem. But a few days later the mice returned with a host of friends and relations, gobbled up the peanut butter, and scarpered, leaving a trail of droppings that led to the top of the basement stairs and the depths beyond where Petey could not bring himself to follow.

The basement was pitch-black even in daytime because the windows were still boarded up. A bulb in the ceiling provided the sole source of illumination, but there was no wall switch, or even a string dangling down to tug on. The procedure for turning on the light, as outlined by Swen, was to go down with a flashlight, climb on a stepladder stationed at the bottom of the stairs for that purpose, and screw in the bulb. But even a footstool is a challenge for Petey, whose balance has worsened with age, and he has an abiding horror of the dark. On his first and only attempt the flashlight gave out and he had to grope his way back upstairs, fighting off a wave of terror.

"Pppitch-black, Imo, pitch-black," he sputtered that day at lunch, scrunching up his eyes as he relived the experience.

By then he was feeling panicky about the situation. Swen was due back at the end of the week and unlikely to be impressed by a floor littered with mice droppings, no matter how clean it was underneath. Eventually, at my mother's suggestion, he went next door to see Charley Dunster, who offered to cast a semi-professional eye around the place and at the very least turn on the light.

Until that day I hadn't spoken to a soul outside the family. Whenever the doorbell rang, I disappeared upstairs, never venturing into the garden if there was a neighbour within hailing distance. I had no intention of making an exception with Charley, but I was curious to see him and climbed out of bed mid-morning and stood at the bedroom window watching the two of them walk up the street together. From behind at least Charley still had the look of a gangly teenager, an impression due in part to the misalignment of his left elbow, which juts out at an odd angle like the arm of a child's action figure stuck on backwards, a souvenir of the time he fell out of a tree in our backyard. Dressed for the occasion in a pair of grey coveralls that drooped on his thin frame and an old crumpled fedora of his father's, he looked rather disreputable, as if at any moment he might disappear into a back alley and start digging through garbage pails. Petey, a head shorter and stocky, charging along beside him with his peculiar lurching gait, appeared distinctly odd but infinitely more respectable in his new jeans and a straw hat from Rossy's.

I was just out of the bath when they returned. Petey charged in and rushed straight through to the living room and flung himself into my father's wing chair. A moment later Charley put his head around the door. At the sight of me descending the stairs in Petey's old green-and-white-striped bathrobe, he started to back out again, but manners or conscience got the better of him and he hovered in the porch looking uncomfortable.

"What's the matter?" I asked Petey.

"Did a bad thing, Imo, did a bad thing," he moaned in the familiar singsong that he uses when he's upset.

"Of course you didn't," I assured him, assuming he had managed to dispatch a mouse. "Tell me what happened." But he continued to moan and started rocking back and forth. I turned to Charley, who had edged into the living room.

"I don't think Petey was supposed to allow anyone on the premises." They'd been checking the perimeter of the foundation for cracks where mice might be slipping in, he explained, when Swen pulled up in his battered black truck. He had been furious at the sight of Charley and ordered them both off the property.

"I have friends who can take care of people like you," was his parting shot to Charley.

"I did a bad thing, Imo," Petey wailed. "Not supposed to let anyone on the property."

"Charley isn't just anyone. He was trying to help," I said firmly.

"Lost my job, lost my job." Petey's voice rose to a shriek.

"He must have figured I was trying to steal stuff," said Charley. "Sorry, Petey. I guess I haven't been much help. He'll probably be on the phone to you in a couple of days, begging you to come back."

"Nothing to steal." Petey sat forward with a jolt and burst into tears.

"Something to hide maybe," said Charley grimly. "He had no call to behave like that."

It was years since I'd seen Petey so upset. We stood over him, watching the tears run down his face, at a loss to comfort him. It seemed an eternity before my mother appeared and elbowed us aside.

"Come along now, Petey. You know this doesn't help. I want you to get out of that chair and come into the kitchen with me. I'm going to make you a hot chocolate and you're going to tell me what's the matter. Come on now, stand up."

Still sobbing, Petey heaved himself to his feet.

"You mustn't mind Petey, he's going to be fine," my mother told Charley. "Don't you run off now. Sit down and catch up with Imo. It'll be good for her." It was an order not a request.

I took Petey's place in the wing chair and Charley perched on a seat by the door with the fedora balanced on his knee and one foot in front of the other as if prepared for a running start. We contemplated each other from across the room.

"I should have known better than to go up there," he said. "My father always had a strict rule only to deal with the owner, but I wasn't thinking of it as a job."

"We should never have let Petey impose on you."

"Oh, well, I was desperate to get out." He shrugged. "My mother's been driving me crazy."

"I think I'm driving my whole family crazy. I guess I haven't been very good company lately," I confessed, aware suddenly what a pall I must cast on the household. "I thought it would be good to get away from the village, you know." I broke off, betrayed by the tremor in my voice.

Charley leaned forward and put out a hand, a familiar gesture from our shared childhood, but I was several feet away and he let his arm drop.

"How's it going with the business?" I asked before he could say something about Thomas. "Dad says your mom's running it herself."

"If you can call it that. She's running me anyway, had me out doing calls this week." He grimaced. "Carpenter ants."

We could hear Petey in the kitchen, his voice pitched high with emotion, then my mother's, low and firm.

"Are you staying for a while?"

He shrugged and turned the fedora over in his hands. "Jennifer and I are having a trial separation. I figured I might as well spend a couple of weeks at home."

"It's probably nice for your mother," I suggested.

"It's a good thing I'm here, really. She gave up the office at the shopping centre without telling anyone, fired the manager, and moved all the stuff home. The basement's overflowing. Only trouble is when I went to renew the business licence, they told me that this neighbourhood is zoned one family residential. We've got a year to close down or move on."

There was a crash in the kitchen and a hoarse shout from Petey. Charley started to stand, then, seeing I made no move, perched on the edge of his chair again. I knew from experience that it would only add to the confusion if I went into the kitchen. One on one was the only way to deal with my brother when he was upset.

"What will you do?" I asked.

"We should sell," he told me, glancing toward the door. "We could get some money for the equipment anyway. But every time I bring the subject up, she phones Rupert in Vancouver, wakes him up at some godawful hour of the morning and tells him I'm trying to run her life. I suppose I am in a way. He just grunts and spouts whatever she wants to hear. I don't know how that Swen guy thinks he's going to get a licence to run a landscaping business."

"I doubt if he's going to bother with anything like that. He's never filled in a form in his life." I knew from our occasional interactions in the shop that Swen was barely literate.

Charley looked surprised. "I thought he was a friend of yours."

"He was a friend of Thomas's," I corrected him. "They were at the orphanage together."

"Petey told me you and Thomas nearly bought that place."

"We made a down payment, but it's off now because of the . . ." my voice quavered again.

"I'd say you're well out of it," Charley said quickly. "We didn't go down to the basement, but it's probably full of the same old junk. Half of it must be antique by now. Maybe that guy thought I was a dealer."

There was another shout from the kitchen and then my father appeared.

"Sorry you got embroiled in all this, Charley. Can I get you a beer?"

"No, no, don't bother. I better get going. My mother's making lunch for me." He stood up and sidled toward the door. "See you again, I guess."

Coward, I thought, as I watched him lope across his mother's manicured lawn, braving the sprinkler. I knew I was being unfair. We might be old friends, but he had his own problems to contend with. I could see Rita Dunster observing his progress from her front window. Halfway across he slipped but caught himself before he fell and stumbled forward, leaving a long muddy smear in the grass.

A Leg in the Culvert

There, in the yellow stubble at the bottom of the bank, lies the grandfather's leg, as stiff and dry as an old stick but full of possibilities.

"It is to hide under the bed and bop burglars over the head," suggests Finney.

"You could save it in case you get run over by a train and your leg is chopped off," offers Charley.

"Don't be stupid. She'd be dead as a doorknob if a train ran over her," says Rupert. "Let's make a bonfire and have a wiener roast."

The decision is Imo's and she knows exactly what she wants to do. Float it through the culvert on a string with a message tucked in the hollow part—"Come to the fort"—and then meet it on the other side to see if the paper got wet. But the fort is for boys only so what would be the point? And anyway the culvert is blocked with mud and no one wants to cross the road again in case the farmer is lying in wait. In the end they shove the leg as far into the shiny round pipe as they can until only the shoe is sticking out. Then they scramble up the bank to the road and head for home, giggling and shoving one another roughly and whistling as loudly as they can to show they don't care who's watching.

Finney's house, which is the closest, sits on a little peninsula encircled by a ditch overflowing with murky water and teeming with electric eels and water moccasins, so say the boys. Finney skips across on a sturdy plywood bridge built by his father with the help of Finney himself. His two older sisters are standing in the open front door, calling and clucking like two fat hens because he is late. His mother has been in the kitchen all morning making meatball soup to tempt the appetite of her sweet boy. And for dessert there will be his favourite, cherry pudding cake baked by his sisters.

For all his height, Finney is sickly. Twice he has had pneumonia, once in Sweden and once this past winter in Canada. Both times he nearly died. If his mother had her way, he would still be in bed, but his father insists that after all, a boy must be allowed out to play. The sisters gather their brother in, exclaiming over the muddy knees of his new Canadian jeans, which are hardly soiled at all compared to those of his companions. In her mind's eye Imo follows the trio through the house, an exact replica of her own though somehow nothing like it, through the wide empty front hall into the dark green dining room, around the long rectangular pine table and into the pale blue kitchen with its matching blue-and-white flowered curtains waving softly at the window. Finney sits down in his own special place at a table set with a sunny yellow cloth. Mrs. Finney dishes up the steaming soup in four yellow bowls with blue rims, four meatballs apiece, five for Finney.

"Such a boy! Where have you been?" she exclaims with mock horror in her funny Swedish accent when she sees his jeans. But really she is pleased that he is well enough to hold his own with his Canadian friends. What will he tell them about his morning? The farmer's field is off-limits to all of the children, the farmhouse too, though it has not occurred to any of the grown-ups that their darlings might trespass under someone's porch, let alone take something that doesn't belong to them. Finney is so upright in his carriage, so deliberate in his speech, that Imo cannot imagine him ever telling a lie. Perhaps he will distract them by asking for a second helping of meatball soup or cherry pudding cake. Imo has never tasted either, but as the door closes, she catches a whiff of something like beef stew and knows it must be the soup. Then the conversation fades to Swedish and her imagination fails her. She runs to catch up with Rupert and Charley, who have raced ahead to their own house, which sits high and dry on its cement foundation.

She watches the two brothers cross the yard on a haphazard collection of boards that float on a sea of mud, tilting crazily with each step. They jump from board to board, hooting with glee as the wet, warped wood sinks into the mud and then springs up again behind them with a loud sucking sound. They follow this rough boardwalk around the side of the house, past a neat pile of lumber stacked against the foundation, and disappear from sight.

As always they will enter their house through the back door, and without being reminded, descend to the basement where the familiar smell of raw cement mingles with the strange, disagreeable odour of vermin. When they have removed their muddy clothes and changed into cotton house pyjamas, blue for Rupert and green for Charley, they will mount the stairs to the kitchen to find their mother, a bright-eyed cowgirl dressed in baby-blue jeans, a pink blouse, and a dark blue denim vest, slicing wieners into a saucepan of tomato soup. The boys, hands freshly washed, take their places at the table. Rupert has a plastic place mat with a picture of an Arabian horse; Charley's mat has five puppies in a basket. On each mat, along with a spoon, there is a buttered hot dog bun that they will use to sop up their soup. Imo knows this because she is often invited over to play. She has even been given her own special set of pyjamas, green ones like Charley's, and once but only once because she doesn't like hot dogs in her soup and they have the same thing every day, she stayed for lunch. For dessert there will be chocolate pudding with a slimy skin on top that mustn't be wasted.

At her own muddy oasis Imo enters through the front door and trips over Tillie, who is cowering in the porch as far away as she can get from the howl of the vacuum rampaging upstairs in one of the bedrooms. Of all the terrifying sounds that assault her delicate ears—the shattering boom of jet planes, the reverberating claps of summer thunder, the vicious rat-a-tat-tat of Petey's cap gun, even the sudden unexpected crash of breaking china and the shouts of recrimination that linger in the air for hours—it is the vacuum, with its long writhing arm, that she dreads the most. It seeks her out and sucks at the soft quivering mass of her very being, leaving her prostrate and helpless.

"Never mind," says Imo soothingly, crouching down and covering the spaniel's long black silken ears with her grubby palms. Tillie wags her tail nervously and struggles valiantly to her feet, her body awash with vibration. It occurs to Imo that her beloved pet would not have liked the Victrola.

They go into the kitchen, where the counter is bare, the stove cold. Lunch will not be ready for ages. Imo climbs on the counter and forages in the cupboard for the soda biscuits. Inside the big blue oblong box she finds a long tube of wax paper with a few broken crackers at the bottom. Petey has been here before her. The peanut butter jar is empty too. Yesterday he sneaked downstairs before breakfast and scooped out every last lick with his pudgy fingers. He's gone now, back to the Bastion Training School for Retarded Boys, and he won't be home for a month. He left only last night and his mother, Ireney, who is also Imo's mother, made him two honey sandwiches to eat on the way and gave him all the leftover chocolate cake and a tin of peanut butter cookies to keep in his cubby. Daddy said he was a lucky fellow to have so many treats, but Petey didn't think so. He was crying when they drove away, and this morning Ireney stayed in bed late and now she is vacuuming. It's what she always does when Petey leaves. What would she do if Imo went away to school? The dusting maybe, and then instead of hiding in the front porch, Tillie would run around in circles sneezing. The house is always dusty, even in the winter, and if all the mud ever dries out it will be even dustier, that's what Ireney says. But by then it will be summer and no one goes away in summer, not even Petey.

Petey has been at the Bastion School for three years. He is bigger and older than Imo, who only started at the local school last fall, but he still can't remember all the letters of the alphabet and he's hopeless at arithmetic; he hardly knows what two and two make. Already Imo can read the back of the cereal box and she reads the funnies to Tillie every day, and to Petey too when he's home. She knows exactly how much money she has in the jar on her dresser and how much more she will need if she wants to buy a *Little Lulu* comic. Sometimes it seems to her that Petey is growing backwards and that soon she will be older than him though she doubts that she will ever be able to eat as much as he does.

She and Tillie retreat to the cupboard under the basement stairs where the sound of the vacuum barely penetrates. With the door closed, it is pitch-black inside but there's a string you can pull to turn on the light. Then you can see the sloping walls lined with cans of baked beans, mushroom soup, and watery vegetables, all lined up in order of size and every single one upside down. Petey was in here all day Sunday and he wouldn't come out when it was time to leave for school. He kept the light on the whole time, but Imo doesn't mind the dark as long as she has Tillie to keep her company.

They snuggle together on a lumpy cushion, and Imo shares out the remaining crackers one at a time but Tillie is impatient. She sticks her nose right inside the box and gobbles up everything that's left. When she has licked up the last crumb, she makes a burping noise and neatly coughs up a ball of wax paper. Then she lays her head on Imo's chest with a rumbling sigh of contentment. Imo puts an arm around her pet's neck and rumbles back. They lie together in the dark, sharing the events of the morning in a series of grunts and growls. It's called Tillie-talk, and Petey can speak it too, better than Imo and better even than he speaks English. When he's home from school, Tillie sleeps on his bed and the two of them stay awake late into the night grunting and growling to each other and sometimes yipping and howling along with their favourite cowboy song, "Cool Water," so loudly that they keep Imo awake even though her room is at the far end of the hall.

But today Tillie dozes off, exhausted by terror perhaps. Imo can feel her pet's heart pumping, and she remembers the racing of her own heart under the farmhouse verandah, the choking stink of cat pee, the belligerent snorting of the goat, and the baby mice squeezed together in their nest. She tries not to think about the cat. She wonders if the grandfather will miss his leg. Surely not. He has a better one that flashes in the sun like a silver sock. It's made of aluminum, Rupert says, and it's hollow all the way down. At mealtimes it fills up with all the food the old man doesn't like and at night, when he takes it off to go to bed, he empties it into the toilet. It's a terrible thing to waste food, even vegetables. Imo gives all her Brussels sprouts to Tillie, but only when no one is looking. It would be better if Papa Chaput emptied out his leg in the field for the goat, but then it might eat the leg too and Madame would find out. The farmer would have to fetch the old one from under the verandah and if it isn't there, he will know who has taken it. Imo sees herself running across the field again in a hail of potatoes, splashing through the stream and squeezing into the culvert. She hears the boys calling to her from the far end, but it's too dark to see them and she can't move because something warm and heavy is pressing on her leg. And then suddenly there is a light and a bright familiar voice.

"So this is where you've been hiding! I've been looking all over. It's after one and we haven't eaten. My goodness, you're covered with mud!"

For lunch they have lovely yellow grilled cheese sandwiches with the crusts cut off for Tillie, a special treat to make up for the nasty old vacuum. And for dessert there is hot chocolate for Imo and coffee for her mother and they sit together at the drop-leaf table for the longest time, reading the funny papers out loud to each other while they wait for their drinks to cool.

A Silver Jukebox

I was well out of it, Charley had said, and I knew he was right, though the thought felt disloyal. It was Thomas's idea to buy Maison de Pomme. I wanted a house, there was no question about that. Our apartment was tiny, and the outside staircase, so admired by the local heritage committee, was treacherous in winter. But I loved living over the shop with the grocery store, the pharmacy, and everything we needed close at hand. From the bedroom we had a view of Father Trepannier's old stone church and the lake beyond. Most days we could see all the way to the south shore, which more than made up for the lack of yard; we were too busy in any case to tend a garden.

We lived directly across from Madame Poulin's tiny suite above the IGA, and I observed her comings and goings with a curiosity that matched her own. She patrolled the main street daily, checking up on her various tenants, overseeing any repairs that were carried out by one of her many grandsons, and collecting rents. She could have easily afforded a house on the lake or one of the new condominiums above the tracks, but her apartment, which was accessed from the back alley by a steep, albeit covered, flight of stairs, was even smaller than ours. Not that she ever carried anything up those stairs herself; she had her grandsons for that, and a granddaughter, Françoise, to deliver her meals three times a day and collect her laundry, or most of it. For reasons no one in the village could fathom, she insisted on rinsing out her own undergarments, which she hung in full view of the street on a makeshift clothesline strung across her balcony, long lumpy wool vests and voluminous once-white bloomers, all huge and shapeless and yellowing with age. "Just right for an old bag like her," Thomas remarked when I commented on their decrepit state. The Chamber of Commerce discussed L'Affaire des Culottes regularly and even delegated an unsuspecting new member to broach the matter with Françoise, but no one, least of all her own granddaughter, was willing to bell the cat.

We had been living upstairs for most of our married life. Marie-Josephine suffered a minor heart attack a few months after our wedding and Joseph, worried about the outside staircase, had rented a small bungalow at the edge of the village before she even came home from the hospital. Thomas and I, who had been more or less camping out behind the shop, took over their apartment.

After a short convalescence Marie-Josephine was back at work, wrestling with the accounts and badgering us to have a baby. We carried on that way for a couple of years and then on our third wedding anniversary, she collapsed in the middle of cooking dinner and never regained consciousness. Six months later Joseph died in his sleep, of a broken heart everyone said. The official diagnosis was malnutrition. I cooked him dinner every night those last months, but he rarely managed more than a mouthful.

Thomas and I were in the dinette, lingering over coffee one morning before going down to the shop, when he had his epiphany, as he called it. He was checking the real estate listings in our weekly paper, squinting a little because his hair, which as usual needed cutting, was falling over his eyes. I knew something had caught his attention because his foot was doing a heel-toe under the table but I was thinking ahead to supper, debating whether to use up the leftovers in the fridge before it was too late or to pick up a couple of chops at the IGA. Glancing over at the plate-glass window where the weekly specials were painted in big red letters, I saw that Madame Poulin's clothesline had slipped and an enormous pair of dirty-grey bloomers was flapping against the window just above the lettering. In the night some wag had crossed out the word *côtelettes* and written in *culottes* instead. One of the grandsons was already up on a ladder, preparing to scrub out the offending word, supervised by Madame Poulin, who was peering down at him from her balcony.

"Spéciale de la Semaine. Culottes de porc," I read out gleefully. "Thomas, look at this. You've got to see. Culottes de porc!"

He gave a perfunctory glance across the road. "Never mind that. Imogene, listen, you know that old house at the end of your parents' street? It's for sale. I think we should talk to Jeanette." He pushed the paper across the table.

Jeanette Lauzon, a distant cousin and high-powered real estate agent reputed to be responsible for half the house sales on the West Island, occasionally stopped by with hot housing tips. She'd steered us away from a number of handyman specials, but we'd been looking for a couple of years by then and hadn't been able to scrape up much of a down payment. Neither of us wanted to mortgage the shop.

I wrinkled my nose. "The old Apple House? That place is a dump. My dad figures it's a miracle it hasn't collapsed."

"It's going cheap, I mean really cheap. We can fix it up."

"I was in it once. It gives me the creeps, you know that."

"But that was years ago. You were only a kid. The place is historic, it's even got a name. It's called Maison de Pomme." Thomas reached over and grabbed my hand. "Come on, let's look at least. You know we need some privacy."

Before I could answer, he was on his feet, heading for the phone. Glancing across the road, I saw that Madame Poulin was eyeing us from her balcony.

In the end, curiosity got the better of me. The original structure had undergone a series of metamorphoses over the years, on the outside at least, and as a child I had been intrigued by the changes. After the original owners, the Chaputs, departed, a young couple moved in and spent weeks scraping down the siding before repainting it a shocking pink with bright green trim. At the age of eight I remember admiring the effect tremendously, especially in the winter when the trees were bare and all the other houses on the street seemed to fade to ashy grey along with the snow. But it was considered an appalling breach of good taste, and the neighbours, my parents included, breathed a collective sigh of relief when the couple did a midnight flit. The next tenants toned things down with olive-green aluminum siding but the respite was temporary. Their successors reinforced the old screened-in verandah and walled in the space underneath; then, having presumably run out of capital to pay for more siding, they painted the new addition the old brilliant pink. No one had ever bothered with the yard, which was eternally strewn with broken toys and rusty bicycles.

It was an eyesore still, though the verandah no longer threatened to collapse into what was once a pasture and is now the Connibears' back lawn. The fields disappeared years ago under truckloads of fill, and where the apple tree grew, the Connibears' tired-looking bungalow sits surrounded by patchy grass and through some mysterious process of osmosis, its own tumbledown verandah and a modest collection of junk.

The house was basically sound, Jeanette told us the day of the showing. We'd have to fix it up, but she'd had it inspected by an engineer.

"It's a little musty. You have to remember no one has lived here for nearly a year," she warned us as she unlocked the door. I saw Thomas wrinkle his nose. The telltale odour of mice was unmistakeable.

She led us straight to the kitchen, which she characterized as "ripe with possibility." Along one wall there was a set of scarred wooden cabinets painted pink and a tall, new-looking fridge. The only counter space was an old corrugated wooden draining board that slanted into a wide, shallow sink. The stove was uniformly black inside and out with eons of grease. "A touch of oven cleaner, maybe," she suggested when she saw my appalled expression.

The most prominent feature of the room was an old restaurant-style booth with padded seats in what was once pink plush—threadbare now and ripped in several places and leaking stuffing—complete with napkin holder, sugar dispenser, and a shiny silver jukebox mounted on the wall. I had a vague memory of it from my childhood visit and slid across the seat to try the jukebox, but it didn't work.

"The booth goes with the house," said Jeannette. "It's vintage, you know. You could get a thousand dollars for it if you don't want to keep it. A lot of people are putting them in their basement rec rooms."

Despite myself I wondered if we could get it hooked up.

"I like it right where it is," said Thomas. "Anyway, you'd never get it down the stairs,"

I saw Jeanette smile. "I know it's a mess, but this place is going for a song. Make a low offer and then you can afford to renovate," she suggested.

"It just needs cleaning," said Thomas. "Petey and I can do that. We wouldn't need to do a big reno or anything right away."

"Before we move in," I said firmly.

"Yes, I think so," said Jeannette. "Really, Thomas, I couldn't recommend it otherwise, not if you're planning to have a family. It needs more than a coat of paint."

Looking back, I suspect that if Jeanette had been pushier, we might have backed off, but there's a reason she's won the Salesperson of the Year award five years in a row. Further inspection revealed mice droppings in the bathroom and, despite Jeanette's attempt to distract me with the heritage light fixture in the living room, a small brown corpse at the top of the basement stairs.

"Save us another thousand," Thomas exclaimed with a gleeful snort.

We debated the pros and cons endlessly over the next few weeks. We couldn't lose, Thomas maintained. The price was so low, it could hardly fail to rise, which meant that we could move on and up at any time. The West Island was trendy again; three new boutiques had sprung up in the village in the past year. And we'd be doing our bit to preserve the history of Saint-Ange-du-Lac. After all, the Chaput family farm had once been the pride of the West Island.

The farm might have been worth preserving, I conceded, but it was gone now and though the deed did include a right of way to the lake through the estate across the road, we'd have to go to court to revive it. The house itself was in no way historic. In truth it was nothing more than an old ramshackle clapboard cottage, a wreck inside and out. It had none of the charm of the old stone farmhouses with their wide wooden verandas and pitched roofs that still dotted the Lakeshore Road, many of them meticulously restored and updated at impossible expense. I would have sold my soul for one of those. But it was affordable.

The day I capitulated was a Saturday, the busiest day of the week in the shop. Charmaine and I had worked straight through our lunch breaks. Thomas was in the back with Gaston, catching up on repairs and doing his best to ignore the crush out front. With three customers on the go I paid scant attention when the phone rang in the workroom. And then his long, willowy torso thrust itself between me and a plump teenager in desperate need of size six satin pumps in a shade called patates frites.

"Imogene, listen. I have to talk to you a minute. Jeanette called. She just heard. There's a developer after the old Apple House. An American. He's going to put in a cash offer on Monday. She said if we're serious we have to make a move today. I told her I'd be right over. What do you think?"

What did I think? The renovation would cost the earth, more than we could imagine, but I wanted a house.

"Do you really want to live there?" I asked for the umpteenth time.

"Don't worry. We can sell if it doesn't work out. And it's close to your parents." He grabbed my hands. "We'll put in a low bid, then they'll have to counter. We can discuss it some more tonight. But we have to do it today."

Over his shoulder I glimpsed Charmaine's face all agog and became aware of an expectant silence in the shop. All at once I was overcome by the ridiculous conviction that everyone would leave empty-handed and never return if I said no.

"They'll tear it down for sure and build some big high-rise. Your parents would hate that," pressed Thomas.

It was a possibility, I knew. That section of Lakeshore was zoned one-family residential, but zoning restrictions were not set in stone. Development was the life blood of city council. At the very least an expensive monstrosity would go up. The thought was unbearable.

"I'll put in a really low bid," he wheedled.

"Okay, but we have to do the kitchen first."

"Yes!" He lifted me up and spun us around on his heels.

There was a soft prolonged hissing sound as if every single person in the shop had exhaled in unison, and then a burst of clapping. Thomas gave me a quick kiss. "I won't be long. All I have to do is give Jeanette a cheque. You can sign later." He was out the door before I could catch my own breath. Swen appeared out of nowhere to join him and I watched them head down the street to the real estate office, Thomas loping along, looking straight ahead, intent on his mission—in silent mode, I could tell—and Swen hustling along beside him, taking two steps for every one of Thomas's.

A few hours later, just before closing, Jeannette burst in and, with what I can only describe as a wild war whoop, plunked an enormous bouquet on the counter along with a pile of business cards.

"You two are the esteemed owners of La Maison de Pomme," she announced. "It was meant to be. You got your bid in just in time. You are so lucky, so, so lucky! I can tell you someone is gnashing their teeth. Thomas, I think you must lead a charmed life."

There were only two customers left in the shop by then, but our folly as I came to think of it was all over town by Monday and for the rest of the week we had record sales. Everyone seemed to know exactly which house we had bought—anyone over fifty had apparently been inside—and they all had advice, though even those people who thought we were being foolhardy seemed impressed by what we had undertaken. "A bold step," Charmaine's father said when he came over from the pharmacy to congratulate us. "Like the walk on the moon."

Looking back, I remember a constant stream of customers in the shop; former schoolmates pumping Thomas's hand; old-timers shaking their heads with bemused incredulity, their wives clutching their bosoms; neighbours from Garden Crescent starting back in astonishment at the news; wild-eyed children recounting Halloween ghost sightings; my father catching his breath before congratulating us; my mother saying, "Once you get it fixed up, you can have a baby"; and Petey, in a yellow hardhat from the St. Vincent de Paul thrift shop, bouncing from foot to foot and telling me he would paint the siding any colour we liked for free as long as Thomas supplied the paint. But always in the background, there was Swen swaggering and laughing, pushing his way past the customers, past me to the back and to Thomas.

The only naysayer was Louise Chaput, who is my best friend in the village, or anywhere else for that matter. The original owner of the farmhouse was an ancestor of hers, and her grandfather, old Papa Chaput, still lived there when I was a child. I remember seeing her there the day of his funeral, hiding under a chair. She had on a long black cardigan buttoned up to her neck with a bright green dress that barely covered her bottom flaring out underneath, and thick brown stockings, the kind they used to make the convent girls wear, bunched up at the ankles and obviously uncomfortable because she kept tugging at them. She stuck out her tongue at me. I remember it distinctly, though she denies it. She's never been one to beat about the bush, has Louise. She thought we were nuts to buy Maison de Pomme and she said so, both to me and to Thomas, which made things awkward for a while.

Louise is Catholic and French of course; she grew up in the

village, but she was sent to a private English boarding school in Montreal so we were both outsiders in a way. When I met her properly, the winter Thomas and I were married, she was working at the local library, which in those days operated out of the draughty old Kinsmen clubhouse in the municipal park across from the water filtration plant. The book collection was bilingual, with French and English at opposite ends of the one-room building, separated by a waist-high shelf of encyclopedias and presided over by Louise.

Wandering in one lunchtime, I found her perched on the checkout counter, a sandwich in one hand and a book in the other; her stocking feet, which barely reached halfway to the floor, poked out from under a long, flowered skirt of Indian cotton. Her heels thumped unevenly against the flimsy wood-panelled front of the counter.

"Puis-je vous aider?" she asked, or something to that effect. Her words were muffled by a mouthful of sandwich. I was silent for a moment, formulating my request in French, but before I could speak, she switched to English. "Oh, sorry, you must think I'm an awful pig, but I'm on my lunch hour. How can I help you?"

"I was looking for something simple to read in French. I've just moved into the village," I said, faint-heartedly opting for English.

It was a common enough request, I'm sure, in the aftermath of the Quiet Revolution, but her eyes, which were dark and enormous, seemed to pop out of her head. She gulped convulsively and put a hand to her mouth. I stepped forward in alarm, wondering if I could manage the Heimlich manoeuvre, but she recovered herself and waved me away.

"Omigod, I know who you are!" she burst out. "You must be Imogene Jackson, or, no, sorry, I mean Imogene Laviolette. You married Thomas! I've had a crush on him forever. You can't imagine the number of shoes I've bought there, a new pair practically every month. I haven't even worn half of them. I've spent a fortune, but he's never even noticed. He hides in the back all the time. And I thought it was just because he was shy."

"Sorry, I didn't realize," I said, feeling myself blush. The possibility that I had a rival had never occurred to me.

"No, no, don't be sorry. I'm just being silly. I'm much too short for him anyway. Really, I'm thrilled for you both. I'm so glad you came in. I've been dying to meet you. I need someone to talk English to."

"I'm supposed to talk French," I said apologetically, still poised to take flight.

"Yes, of course. But you can't talk French all the time. You'll go nuts. We can take turns if you like. Just as long as we talk. Nobody my age ever comes to the library. Hardly anyone comes in at all. You're my first customer today. Banging my feet on the desk is the only form of conversation I have." She thumped her heels sharply against the counter to illustrate her point and jumped to the floor.

"You must think I'm an idiot," she said, clapping a hand to the side of her head. "I wouldn't blame you. Actually, I am an idiot. I haven't even introduced myself. Louise Chaput, idiot librarian." She held out her hand and I shook it gingerly. "Honestly, I'd be glad to get together sometimes. I'll give you lessons if you like. Or we can meet once a week and just chat. We'll call it Club Franglais. Oh, I'm so glad you came in. I'll find you something to read right away." She slipped into a tiny pair of bright red sling-back pumps with at least four-inch heels, the vamps intricately embroidered in gold thread, handmade obviously. I'd never seen anything like them in the shop.

"Actually I got these at the Asian Emporium, but don't tell Marie-Josephine," she said with an impish grin.

"My lips are sealed," I promised and we both laughed. We've been friends ever since.

After Thomas died, she made a point of stopping by the store on her way home from work. One afternoon I was in the back, sorting through a mound of boots and shoes awaiting repair, wondering whether Gaston would ever find the time to start on them or if I should call up their owners, when the bell chimed and in breezed Louise. Charmaine was out front clearing up after a session with the famously impossible Therrien twins, who have a precocious sense of style, an indulgent mother, and impossibly narrow feet. I saw a look pass between them and then Louise sauntered over and leaned on the counter.

"Imogene, why are you still here?" she demanded, straight to the point as usual. "I thought you were taking the afternoon off."

"I have a business to run," I retorted.

"Well, you're not running it," she said bluntly. "You're in the way. Think of Charmaine. She's run off her feet. She has enough on her hands managing the store. She can't be looking after you too."

It was, it turned out, the very same box of shoes I'd been sorting through the day before and the day before that.

Early Risers

Petey was inconsolable over the loss of his job. For a week he moped about the house rehashing events with each of us in turn. At night when he had exhausted even Tillie, he kept us awake shouting at Swen in his dreams. It wasn't just being fired that upset him, though that was bad enough. He'd had his heart set on helping to fix up the farmhouse; it was his memorial to Thomas and now he felt he was letting him down.

"Should've been me," he said one morning as I dozed in bed trying to ignore his nattering. "Then you an' Thomas could be in the house."

I snapped awake. "Don't be silly. Nobody would want that."

I got up then and padded to the bathroom, appalled by the anger in my voice and biting my lip to hold back tears.

Thomas was killed by a drunk driver, blind drunk or so they told me, an alcoholic with several previous citations and, no doubt thanks to Swen, not a little marijuana in his blood along with the alcohol. Petey is a reformed alcoholic himself in a minor way. Once, years ago, with the help of Rupert and Charley, who should have known better, he got tanked up with beer and took off all his clothes and peed on the Dunsters' lawn. He was caught in the act by Darwin Dunster, who was outside at midnight with a flashlight, checking his mousetraps, according to Charley. My brother hasn't had a drink since, though that doesn't mean he's not tempted. He expects to be rewarded in heaven, he told me the other day, like Thomas.

He's made up a paradise for Thomas and I can see it's an alluring vision. It's a great big workroom with a fancy computerized sewing machine that runs all by itself, an adjustable chair on wheels, bowling pennants suspended from the ceiling, rich-guy customers, and a brand-new, bright red taxi with Laviolette & Fils on the door. I like to think of Thomas in Petey's heaven, cruising over to the Bowlerama in his taxi and designing exclusive footwear for Petey's rich guys, not to mention myself. I'd get rid of the bowling pennants, but I haven't told Petey. It's not a subject I want to get him started on.

My parents coped with his nightmares in their usual way, mugs of warm Ovaltine all round at midnight and every hour on the hour after that if need be, and long mornings in bed. I lay awake agonizing about the future and longing for the familiar comfort of Thomas's hot, lanky body pressed against mine. He was a deep sleeper and, except for the occasional twitch, rarely budged the whole night, though he talked endlessly in his sleep, a low, incomprehensible muttering with periodic pauses, rather like a telephone conversation. He had no memory of it in the morning.

"Ordering eggrolls," he would say if I teased him about it.

No matter what time I finally dropped off, I was wrenched awake at five every morning by a vision of Thomas lounging in a blue and white deck chair, his fingers wielding a joint, his half-hearted protest pounding in my brain.

"What's the hurry? I just want to finish this."

I got into the habit of taking Tillie for her morning constitutional before returning to bed. It was the best time of day to be out, since the street was deserted. I had a horror of meeting the neighbours, who either passed by with a nod, looking embarrassed, or else, under the assumption that misery loves company, felt obliged to leap into the abyss and inquire how I was doing. I had a kind of condolence phobia, I suppose.

Every step beyond the front door was a trial for Tillie, who was stiff with arthritis in the morning. I kept her out just long enough to stimulate her digestive system. Once she had done her duty, we could both spend the rest of the day lounging about indoors. One morning we had been all the way to the corner without result and were passing the chemical green expanse of the Dunsters' front lawn for the second time when she started sniffing and circling in an unmistakable way. I skulked ahead along the sidewalk, tugging on the leash, hoping to persuade her into the long yellowing grass that marked our side of the joint property line. My parents had warned me that Rita Dunster was an early riser and there was a telltale crack in the living room curtains that I hadn't noticed earlier. We had reached a stalemate when we were both startled by the raucous rattle of a poorly tuned engine turning over. A minute later there was a honk and Swen swerved across the road and pulled up beside me in his rusty black pickup.

We hadn't spoken since the funeral. He hadn't come near the shop and I had made a point of avoiding him. He had sent a huge, garish wreath of yellow gladiolas the day after the accident and every day after that for a week. He wasn't the only one to send flowers of course; by the day of the funeral the shop was overflowing and the delivery boy began leaving bouquets outside on the sidewalk, arranging them in a semicircle under the window in an impromptu shrine. They were there for weeks, wilted and brown, tripping up customers and forcing passersby into the street until one afternoon I looked out and saw the men from public works clearing them away. It was such a relief, I wondered why I hadn't done it myself. But they had barely begun when Swen charged out from the alley behind the IGA and started shouting and gesticulating wildly. I couldn't make out his words but his meaning was unmistakable. The men retreated into the truck and drove off. They must have come back under cover of darkness or very early one morning because a couple of days later I looked out the window and noticed that the sidewalk was clear again.

There was no possibility of avoiding Swen now. He rolled down his window and drawled, "Hey, Jackson, what's with your brother?"

"What do you mean?"

"I gave him a job, eh, I felt sorry for him—I wanted to help him out—but he's not responsible. He had some guy over, checking the place out."

"He was trying to help," I said stiffly.

Swen rolled his eyes to the back of his head and let his jaw drop. "Oh sorry, Swen, sorry. I was only trying to help," he said in a slurred voice that was meant to be an imitation of Petey's.

My brother had long ago learned to turn aside from such crude taunts, but I was out of practice. I took a deep breath and forced myself to speak slowly, but I couldn't stop my voice from rising. "For your information the man he had with him was a professional exterminator. He was from Dunster Debug and he was trying to do you a favour."

"I don't care who he was." Swen stuck his head through the window, his chin jutting out. "I told Pete, no visitors. I'm the one doing the favours here. I call the shots. He's got to smarten up if he wants to keep a job." He smacked the palm of his hand on the outside of the door.

"Petey spent a whole week cleaning that place up for you and you haven't even paid him!"

"He has to learn to do what he's told."

"Oh, right." Coming from Swen, this was the purest hypocrisy. "Well, I hope he's learned not to work for someone like you again. How'd you get to be living there anyway? Doesn't look like much of a landscaping business to me." I gestured at the bed of the pickup, which held a motley collection of gardening equipment, an old gas mower, hedge trimmers, two rakes, several rusty spades, and a plastic snow shovel, all of garage sale vintage.

His face reddened. "I been trying to help you. Thomas and me, we were like brothers, eh. We did everything together." His voice choked and for one terrifying moment I thought that he was going to cry. His grief was real, I knew that, though I hated to admit it. "We had plans, you know," he went on, his voice thickening. "He wanted to go partners with me. We were going to really do something with that house. It's historic, eh, but what do you care about stuff like that?" He opened the door suddenly and put a foot on the running board.

I stepped back in alarm and tripped over Tillie, who, having done her business, had flopped behind me on the sidewalk. She stood up with a cowardly yelp and backed away.

"I don't know what you're talking about. Thomas would never have gone partners with you," I said as calmly as I could. "I wouldn't have let him." My heart was racing. It was a mistake to respond or even to take him seriously, I knew.

His face hardened. I saw the knuckles of his left hand whiten against the black door frame of the truck. He let loose a gob of spit that landed at my feet.

"Bitch!"

He drove off with the seatbelt dangling and clanking against the running board. Fifty yards down the road, opposite Finney's old place, he stopped and got out and went to the rear of the truck and pushed down a rake that had jolted upright and was threatening to fall out. For a moment he stood staring back at me. My stomach heaved. I looked around for somewhere to be sick, anywhere but the Dusters' pristine lawn. I couldn't seem to move. Then I felt a hand on my arm.

"I wouldn't have anything to do with that man if I were you. I don't hold with spitting," said a gravelly voice.

It was Rita Dunster in her slippers and dressing gown, a long, rumpled blue garment patterned all over with horses and riders galloping off every which way. I supposed she must have sewn it herself. Her hair was wound up in those fat pink foam rollers left over from the sixties, held in place by a dark brown hairnet.

"Is he a friend of yours, dear?"

"No. But I know him," I conceded. We watched Swen climb into the truck and drive off, seatbelt still dangling.

"You'd better come in."

Still shaking, I followed her around the side of the house to her back door. It was years since I'd been inside. A musty odour emanated from the basement stairs, overpowering the heady scent of furniture polish familiar from childhood visits. In the kitchen, counter, table, and chairs were all heaped with plastic piping, tangled knots of fine copper wire, steel wool, and old-fashioned wooden mousetraps. She led me through to the dining room, where the table was strewn with newspapers and unopened mail.

"Now you sit down, dear, and I'll get you some breakfast." She disappeared to the kitchen.

I perched on the edge of a chair, wondering how soon I could get away, and distracted myself by studying the family photograph gallery that took up most of one wall. In place of honour was a large black and white photo of a youthful Darwin Dunster, Charley's dad, in his Queen's Scout uniform, with Rita beside him in her cowgirl outfit. Surrounding them on all sides were pictures of Rupert and Charley in Cub Scout uniforms, Halloween costumes, or Sunday best, posing with various relations. The most recent photos were all of Rupert: Rupert in cap and gown graduating from McGill, Rupert receiving his law degree, Rupert in his Vancouver law office, Rupert leaning on his new car, and even Rupert looking jaunty in a Dunster Debug uniform and cap, which by all accounts he had moved to the other end of the country to escape. According to Charley, he's obsessed with a board game he's invented called Pounce. It features a three-dimensional board, battery-powered mice that run along a track, and a marauding Disneyesque cat that pops up and spins and pounces. He's looking for an investor to stake him.

I was searching for another photo of Charley when Rita bustled in with two instant coffees and a plate of soda crackers, the kind they hand out in restaurants in individually wrapped packets.

"You want to keep your strength up," she said, shoving aside a pile of papers and sliding the plate toward me.

I hadn't had a soda cracker in years and never for breakfast, but it was exactly what I felt like eating. Soda crackers, I remembered, had been a staple in the Dunster household throughout my childhood. I was peeling the little red strip off my third packet of crackers when there was an energetic thumping on the stairs. I caught a glimpse of Charley's startled face as he thudded into the kitchen and then retreated out of sight.

"Come and say hello to Imogene, dear. I've saved you some crackers," his mother called after him.

The response was a furious hiss. "For heaven's sakes, Mother, not now!"

I listened for his tread on the stairs and then stood up to leave. There is something mortifying about grown children living at home, I thought, whatever the reason might be. It's unnatural, a catastrophe for everyone involved. There was Charley sleeping in his old room, sneaking about the house in his father's pyjamas with the Dunster Debug crest embossed on the breast pocket, forcing himself to eat soda crackers that I happen to know he hates, all because he was getting divorced. He's perfectly capable of looking after himself. Why wasn't he renting an apartment? He should have known better than to move home, especially with a mother like his. And so, I supposed, should I. There I was, after all, fending off endless mugs of Ovaltine, sleeping or rather not sleeping in my childhood bed, and moping about the house all day like a moronic teenager. Come home and you'll feel better. Everything will be all right. That had been the gist of my parents' message. But everything was not all right, and there was no point pretending it was.

One Potato, Two Potato

On the farmhouse verandah Madame Chaput sits on a green ladder-back chair, peeling potatoes into a bucket that is set on a footstool between her knees. The peelings fall at her feet, spreading out around the chair in unruly brown waves, curling over her stumpy ankles and lapping at the sagging hem of her dress. Her bum, encased in brilliant blue flowers, spills over the edges of the seat as she leans forward, cutting and peeling with a paring knife that flashes a warning in the pale spring sun. She is keeping guard and she will sit there peeling her endless supply of potatoes until the watchers abandon their lookout post behind the stone pillar or until she turns into a potato herself. Already she is starting to look like one, for though it is barely April and the children are still weighed down with winter jackets, Madame has pushed back the sleeves of her dusty-brown cardigan, exposing the lumpy winter-white flesh of her arms.

"Round people do not have the cold feeling," observes Finney, who is in a position to know since the three women in his family are all short and fat like Madame. His sisters go about the house bare-armed and sometimes bare-legged even in winter. Finney himself is all skin and bone because of the pneumonia and he needs a belt to keep up his pants no matter how much meatball soup or cherry pudding cake he devours. Having no natural insulation of his own, he wears a thick red Nordic sweater under his Canadian jacket and a wool hat with flaps that fold down over his ears and that he never removes even when he is safely out of his mother's sight.

It is the way of the world for men to be thin and for women to be fat, Finney says. He admires Madame's ample and familiar shape and her strange obsession with potatoes. In his opinion his own mother, who is otherwise perfect, does not cook nearly enough potatoes, and though he has begged her to many times, she never makes french fries, which she dismisses as vulgar, poor people's food and no part of a respectable diet, Canadian or Swedish. He has confided to his Canadian friends his disloyal suspicion that she doesn't know how.

Imo's mother never makes french fries either. It's too much trouble, she says, but sometimes on a good day, when she has the use of the car, she and Imo drive over to the chip wagon beside the tavern in the village and ask the french fry man, who is tall and thin with a grey face and a smudgy tea towel tucked into the top of his trousers, for two orders of patates frites and he cooks them right there in the back of the truck. Imo likes to watch the explosion of bubbles as he plunges the square wire basket into a vat of hot oil. Leaning into the cloud of steam, he grabs hold of the long wire handle and shakes it again and again until the bubbles leap up and tumble over the rim and roll along the handle toward his fingers. Just in time, he lets go and steps back. When the chips are done, he lifts out the basket, shakes it one more time to drain off the grease, and then, without spilling any, tips the golden cubes, still sizzling and spitting, into two little cardboard boxes, and they eat them sitting in the car with vinegar and salt for lunch.

"French people eat french fries every day. That's why they talk so funny," says Rupert, whose own mother has declared more than once that she wouldn't touch a single crumb from the chip wagon, not even if her life depended on it.

The children consider this statement in silence. Rupert's logic is indisputable because the fact is that every day around suppertime the aroma of potatoes cooking in hot grease wafts out the kitchen window of the farmhouse, enveloping passersby in a warm tantalizing mist, floating into their nostrils, seeping into the tiny invisible pores of their skin, and, Finney says, creeping under the earflaps of his hat, filling his throat with saliva, and making him dizzy with hunger so that he is almost too weak to walk to the mailbox with his letter for Sweden in time for the five o'clock pickup. And everyone knows that even Finney's father, who has lived in France where proper French people live, could not understand a word the farmer said when he came with his tractor to pull the car out of the mud, not even when the farmer spoke English.

"Sometimes it is okay to eat french fries, I think. I have told my mother this, but she has not listened," says Finney, shaking his head.

"Maybe once a week," suggests Charley in a hopeful voice.

"Yeah, maybe," concedes Rupert. "But not from the chip wagon."

"We will make them ourselves," says Finney. "It cannot be so hard."

Finney, it seems, has a plan. For two weeks now he has been studying French after school with a special tutor. It's easy, he says, no harder than English, which he has conquered in a single winter. Already he can rattle off lait, buerre, oeufs, crème à fouetter, and the milkman understands him perfectly. Before the summer is out Finney intends to raise a white flag over the farmhouse and make peace with Madame in her own language. No more raids, he will promise her, on the condition that she teaches him how to make french fries. Surely she will not refuse such a generous offer. And then Finney in turn will show his friends and they will have a feast at the fort. The older boys will be in charge of the cooking. Charley will collect wood for the fire and Imo can peel the potatoes.

"It's a good job for a girl, I think," he says, smiling benignly.

Imo does not smile back. It's a long business peeling potatoes. Madame has been at it for nearly an hour and she hasn't even begun to slice them up. Better to stick with the chip wagon. Better too, she thinks, to make peace right away, but she knows that won't happen for a while. Every day something new appears in the farmer's makeshift dump: a broken crutch, a fishing rod, a pile of old tires with a fat inner tube on top, and only this morning a glorious pink bathtub on claw feet. Finney and Rupert have a list, nearly a page long and still growing, of the things they must have for their fort. At the top of the list, half-hidden now behind the bathtub, is the big black witch's cauldron to make the fries in. Rupert wants to take the tub too but most likely it's too heavy to lift. With a pang Imo remembers the beautiful pale green dishes stacked in the cabinet under the verandah, but she doesn't want them, not really. She doesn't want to go back to the farmhouse at all, not even if she could have a Victrola, but she would never say so out loud, not with Charley crouching beside her still longing for his toboggan even though it will soon be summer and what use will a toboggan be then?

All at once Finney groans. Rupert has jabbed him in the ribs.

"She's getting up. She's getting up," hisses Rupert, pounding a fist into his open palm and jiggling up and down. Rupert is never still. Even in church he taps his feet on the floor, drums his fingers on the pew, and bumps up against Charley, poking and pinching him until his brother pokes him back and they both get in trouble. In bed at night his arms and legs thrash about and in the morning his head is always at the wrong end. He talks in his sleep too, long garbled sentences that make no sense to Charley though Rupert maintains he is just too dumb to understand. It's like he has a snake inside him, Charley says, slithering up and down looking for a way out.

Or maybe a mouse, thinks Imo. At the Dunsters' house it is the mice that cause all the trouble. No matter how many traps Darwin Dunster and his sons set out, there are always little black droppings in the basement and a nasty smell at the back door. Once when Imo was sitting on the back step with Tillie, waiting for Charley, the door blew open and Tillie jumped up with a woof and bounded right inside and snuffled at the closed door of the hall closet. It was a mouse probably, Charley told her later in secret because he's not supposed to talk about it. The next day, which was Saturday, Mr. Dunster borrowed a spade and a pickaxe from the contractor and dug a trench along the outside wall where the mice come in and filled it with poison cheese pellets; one bite and a mouse will have a heart attack and die. But then it rained and the trench filled up with water and the milkman slipped in and got a soaker right up to his knee and when he pulled out his leg a mouse jumped out of his trouser cuff. So now the trench is covered with a board that bends in the middle when you walk on it and at each end there is a stick with a little red warning flag. Every morning there's a tiny corpse floating in the water. Charley has offered to show her but she doesn't want to look; it makes her feel creepy. When she calls on her friend, she walks around the other side of the house. The milkman doesn't like walking on the board either; he won't go around the back at all and Mrs. Dunster has to leave the empty milk bottles at the front door like everybody else.

"She's getting up!" hisses Rupert again, on his feet now and hopping from one foot to the other.

From their lookout post behind the stone pillar, the children watch as Madame's broad white shins slowly rise out of the brown sea. There is a sudden turbulence as she picks up a broom and sweeps the peelings off the edge of the verandah to the billy goat, who has been waiting all morning among the rusty washtubs and broken bicycles, chewing on a vacuum cleaner hose.

"Here comes a taxi. I bet she's going out," says Rupert as Madame picks up the bucket and disappears inside the house. "Come on, let's get the cauldron now. Quick, before she comes back." But the taxi only honks and drives by without stopping.

"Someone else is coming," says Charley.

Imo strains to see. In the open doorway, as stiff and still and thin as a post, stands the old grandfather, Papa Chaput. He has been ill for days, so ill that he nearly died. Like Finney he has had pneumonia. "Lanumonnie," the farmer called it when he came with his tractor to pull the milkman's truck out of the mud. The danger has passed, he said—the doctor no longer comes every day on his motorcycle—but most mornings the old man refuses to get out of bed. His leg, the one that isn't there anymore, has been aching, and when the pains come in the middle of the night, he cries out and wakes up the farmer and his wife, Madame. When a person's leg is chopped off, it keeps on hurting until they die and maybe even after, Rupert says. There is nothing anyone can do.

The old man steps onto the verandah and walks with short jerky steps, like a wind-up grandfather, thinks Imo, to the overstuffed platform rocker. His body cracks in the middle and slowly sinks from sight until all that is left of him is the tip of a blue beret and his artificial leg sticking straight out from the chair, the ankle glinting in the sun. Imo wonders if he knows she is there, crouched behind the stone pillar watching him, or if perhaps, from the padded depths of the rocker, he is spying on her. She picks at the scab on her elbow to make sure she is awake. In her dreams, the old man limps around the farmhouse yard, poking through the piles of cast-offs searching for his leg that is still in the culvert, water-logged now and swollen, jammed in tight by debris and spring mud and blocking the flow of water. The farmer's field has turned into a lake that even the goat dares not cross, and every night in Imo's dreams Papa Chaput stands at the water's edge and calls her name.

Dreams come from inside you, Imo knows that, but the things that happen in them are all mixed up. They are like a puzzle, her mother says; you have to put the pieces together to see what the picture is, but they aren't real because when you wake up the pieces scatter and all that is left is a funny sad feeling. But feelings are real even if you can't touch them, and Imo has a feeling that she and Papa Chaput have been dreaming the very same dream.

Dr. Campeau

It was nearly nine by the time I left the Dunsters that morning and to my relief Swen's truck was nowhere in sight. Apart from one small lone child straggling off to school, the street was deserted. At home my parents were still in bed and Petey's snores reverberated through the house. I went into the kitchen and made myself a cup of coffee that I couldn't bring myself to drink. I sat at the drop-leaf table watching the squirrel running up and down the lightning rod, jumping back and forth from the roof to the bird feeder, all the while chattering furiously at a flock of starlings.

It was two weeks since I'd fled the village, and Charmaine phoned morning, noon, and evening with questions about overdue bills, hold-ups at customs, misplaced repairs, and what to do about the arrival of an entire shipment of size twelve men's snow boots. Since I refused to answer the phone, she had consulted my mother, who unaccountably encouraged her to order six dozen reindeer hats with battery-illuminated antlers from a wholesaler's catalogue that had arrived in the mail.

"Well, they sound very cheap to me. I'll certainly buy one for Petey, I'll buy two if you like," my mother defended herself when I objected that half the shops in the mall would be selling the same thing for less than we were paying wholesale. "Oh, for heaven's sakes, Imogene! What was I supposed to say? If you don't want her to order them, then you'll have to tell her yourself."

"Why don't you just take over the whole business?" I snapped.

"I think I might have to."

"Good. Maybe then I can have some peace!"

She left me alone after this exchange, but the next day when I still refused to come to the phone, she told Charmaine to close the shop. I could hardly complain, but we couldn't stay closed forever. Sooner or later I would have to go in and start sorting things out. But not yet. I had an appointment with Dr. Campeau at ten. I didn't want to go, but I'd already postponed twice and the results of my various tests were in.

I had emerged from the accident with no obvious injuries, the only apparent after-effect being an overwhelming fatigue. For days I had cocooned myself in sleep, ignoring phone calls, avoiding visitors, and refusing to take part in decisions about the funeral or to communicate in any meaningful way with my family or Louise, who all took turns watching over me. Only when my designated guardian had left for the night did I emerge from the bedroom to gorge on one of the casseroles that mysteriously appeared in the fridge day after day and that I consumed with scrupulous precision in reverse alphabetical order.

My body ached all over and I found it impossible to focus my thoughts. If I did manage to rouse myself and go down to the shop, I couldn't follow a conversation at all if people were speaking French, though at the time I thought it was because they were muttering. I remember noticing that our customers were all behaving oddly, talking in strange exaggerated whispers, out of respect for Thomas, I supposed in my groggy state. Their words, when I could make them out, didn't make sense but then I hardly listened. I was in a world of my own.

I'd resisted my mother's urging to see a doctor until a swollen toe sent me shuffling over to Dr. Campeau's office in Thomas's slippers without an appointment or even a preliminary phone call. He's a sweet man, Dr. Campeau. Some people consider him a bit of a joke, long past sixty and still riding around on his motorcycle, an old Harley he's had forever, and still flying a tiny threadbare Canadian flag—an original from the sixties—off the back. Sometimes it seems as if he's the only French-speaking federalist left in Saint-Ange-du-Lac. Not that any of the locals seem to care. In the extremity of illness they turn a blind eye to politics.

"Language is not important," he told me when I married Thomas and moved to the village. "Allophone, francophone, anglophone, these categories are all nonsense. The old days with English in one neighbourhood and French in another are finished. Why bring them back? We must learn to live together. You are one of us no matter what language you speak. We must forget about sovereignty and separatism. We must become a nation of families." He became impassioned as he spoke; his face seemed to puff and his eyes, which were usually half closed, started open. A nation of families. It's a nice thought, positively utopian in fact, and all his own as far as I know.

He had heard about the accident of course and when I told him I hadn't been given a physical examination or admitted to hospital, he was skeptical at first, then aghast, and finally furious. He ordered a barrage of X-rays and blood tests, and insisted that I check in with him regularly while I waited to see a neurologist.

"You never know, you might have to sue," he warned me when I refused, on some misguided principle that now escapes me, to see any kind of therapist.

There was no one to sue as far as I could tell since the other driver had also died, but he was adamant. "These days there's always someone to sue," he insisted. "You might even decide to sue me. Already you have a case for negligence against the hospital. It's better to be prudent."

When I admitted what must have been obvious, that my hard-earned fluency in French had vanished, that I could no longer pass the time of day with my customers or decipher the headlines in *La Presse*, he forbade me any strenuous exercise and recommended patience. It's a temporary after-effect and not uncommon apparently. A transitory stress reaction is what he called it, likely to wear off in time. I didn't believe him. There'd been a story in the paper about a woman who had fallen from a high-rise balcony and walked away without a scratch, only to collapse and die three weeks later in the middle of a family gathering. I couldn't get it out of my mind.

He was on the phone when the receptionist ushered me into his office that morning, speaking in rapid French with great animation. He held up a hand in greeting and gave me an apologetic smile. I plunked myself down on a chair across from his cluttered desk and studied a framed abstract painting on the wall above his head: randomly shaped blobs of yellow red and blue arranged in a ragged horizontal, overlapping each other in muddy hues, the latest creation from his grandchild. He was talking to her now, judging by the lilt in his voice. The only word I could make out was Lolo, which I knew to be her nickname. He's an old-fashioned sort, Dr. Campeau, fond of babies and children in general. He didn't spend nearly enough time with his own, or so he says.

He hung up quickly and leaned across the desk, his face still glowing from his conversation.

"I have wonderful news," he announced without preamble. His dark eyes glinted at me from under a pair of dark shaggy eyebrows that as a child I had found intriguing and somewhat alarming.

I smiled politely, assuming he was referring to himself.

"My dear, there's nothing wrong with you. You are going to have a baby!"

For a split second I thought he was speaking French. I looked at him blankly. "What do you mean, a baby?" I asked.

He broke into a grin. "A baby. You're going to have a baby!"

I shook my head. "I don't think so." I didn't see how I could possibly be pregnant when I felt hollow inside.

"The result is certain, my dear. Your tests are fine. There's nothing at all wrong with you except the concussion. Possibly that is still affecting you. But the nausea, the fatigue, this is because you are pregnant."

I put a hand on my abdomen, but there was nothing there.

"This is a shock of course, after all that has happened," he added when I didn't reply.

A baby was something that Thomas and I had planned together. It was why we wanted a house. Thomas had even squirrelled away a piece of goatskin to make booties. There was enough for a hat and mitts as well, he'd assured me, though I hadn't paid much attention. He had already sketched a design with tiny bells on the hat and coloured beads on the mitts. I couldn't possibly do it alone. I didn't want to.

"There must be a mistake," I said.

"There is no doubt, my dear." Dr. Campeau's grin widened.

I was beginning to sweat. "But there'll be something wrong with it!"

"No, no, everything is fine. You are both healthy." He gazed at me expectantly, waiting for his words to sink in.

He didn't understand. It was Thomas I wanted, not a baby. My mind raced, searching for a way out.

"This is a gift," he said gently, his smile fading. He sat back in his chair and chewed on his thumb, visibly puzzled by my reaction.

"I don't want it," I mumbled, staring at my feet.

He sighed and his eyes seemed to sink into his head.

"My dear, you have suffered a terrible tragedy. You are grieving. You must give it some time. We must let nature take its course. Your body is very strong. You will have a healthy outcome. I have no doubt of it."

"You can't be sure. Look at Petey. Nobody can be sure of anything," I burst out. It felt like a scream, but my voice came out in a whisper.

"But, my dear—" he broke off and began to shuffle the papers on his desk.

"I can't have a baby," I said, gripped with panic.

"No, no." His voice rose but he stopped himself and continued with a sigh. "I will refer you to a counsellor. Thérèse will book an appointment for you."

"I don't want to talk to a counsellor."

"But you must." With what seemed a great effort he raised his eyebrows and gazed at me sadly. "You have suffered a terrible tragedy. You must not have another one. To end the life of a child, a little girl perhaps . . ." He paused, at a loss. "You will have no one."

"We don't know it's a girl," I mumbled, taken aback.

"No, of course. At this stage we cannot be certain if it is a boy or a girl, but we know that it is alive. You are both alive. And that, my dear girl," he told me, "is a miracle."

A miracle? It felt like a curse to me.

An Old Man with One Leg Tries to Fly

At first the leg won't budge. It is jammed deep into the culvert with only the toe of the shoe sticking out, and when Imo tugs on it, the whole shoe comes away in her hands, exposing a metal pin that is too short for even her small fingers to grip. Charley jabs at the compacted mud with a piece of rebar from the construction site. Biting on his lower lip and grunting fiercely with each thrust, he shoves the long metal pole into the mud and then pulls it out with a deep, heavy sigh. He didn't want to come, not really. He's not supposed to fool around in the water or go near the culvert at all but already he has a soaker and his new trousers are wet halfway up to his knees.

Imo scrabbles at the mud with her bare hands, prying out sharp bits of gravel and tiny shards of china until she makes a little space around the shaft. Grabbing hold of the leg, she yanks as hard as she can. There is a sucking sound and it comes loose with a whoosh, punching her in the chest and knocking her backwards into the marsh grass.

She lies there in breathless amazement, watching a fat white cloud drift across the unexpected expanse of blue sky. Cold water seeps through her jacket, shocking her skin; a rotten smell invades her nostrils and looking down, she sees that her baby finger is bleeding but she doesn't cry. With a grunt Charley pulls her up and together they peer into the hole left by the leg. The culvert is half full of brown water laden with debris but they can see right through to daylight at the other end. Charley leans into the opening and, one after another, pulls out a bicycle pedal, a chair leg, and a tin potty. A gob of mud falls on his neck, splattering down his back, and when he backs away, they see that water is flowing freely, rushing at their boots. Laughing, they jump aside and struggle up the bank, rolling the leg ahead of them because it's heavier now and slimy from being in the culvert and hard to grab on to.

Across the road over by the stone pillar Finney and Rupert are making plans to build a raft to float across the lake that has formed in the farmer's field. They seize on the leg for something they call flotation. They offer Imo part ownership and a chance to sail on the very first voyage and then a whole week's loan of Finney's new bicycle, which will be arriving from Sweden any day now, and, lastly, special membership in the boys-only fort. But it will take forever to build a raft and Imo's dreams will not let her wait even one more day. Intent on her mission, she gazes down at the lake, wondering if it is too deep to wade across, and sees that the water is flooding into the culvert.

"We're taking it back. She had a dream," Charley explains.

"You're not allowed to go there, Charley Dunster," says Rupert angrily, as if the dream is all Charley's fault.

Imo hardly hears them. She kicks at the leg to start it rolling and sets off down the bank after it. Charley hesitates briefly, then follows.

"I'm telling," Rupert shouts after them. "You're not allowed near the water."

"Tell, then. I'm telling too," Charley shouts back.

"You're kicked out of the fort then. For good."

"It is possible to drown, I think," calls Finney in his deliberate voice.

But you can't drown in a field and already the grass has begun to reappear.

Taking turns dragging the leg behind them, Imo and Charley trudge along the receding shoreline, their boots squelching in the wet grass. The goat, discouraged by all the water, has taken refuge under the apple tree and snorts only feebly. In the farmhouse yard, Imo picks her way through the detritus of old tires and discarded furnishings. The Victrola has fallen to pieces and the bowed front of Charley's toboggan bulges out from under a mountain of bottles and old newspapers. She peers into the gloom under the verandah and a huge black and white cat with a checkerboard face springs out with a hiss from under the stairs. The smell of cat pee catches in her throat. Behind her Charley gives a high-pitched hiccup.

"Let's just lean it against the pillar," he suggests.

"No, we have to put it back or else he won't know where to find it."

"He'll find it easier if we leave it where he can see it," points out Charley.

"No, he won't."

"Yes, he will."

"He won't," insists Imo, though she suspects her friend is right. "Anyway, I don't care."

"That's stupid."

"What'd you come for then if I'm so stupid?"

Their bickering is interrupted by a gruff cough. They turn, prepared to run from the goat, but there, at the bottom of the stairs wearing his blue beret and still in his pyjamas though it is already afternoon, is Papa Chaput. One faded blue-and-white-striped leg flutters uselessly in the breeze and Imo sees that he is leaning on a crutch. His face is wrinkled and brown like the water in the culvert and there are tiny rivulets running down his cheeks. His eyes light up and his mouth opens.

"Adélie," he croaks. He raises his free arm in a wave, then lowers it again and lifts the crutch, planting it on the ground in front of him. His pyjamas billow out and the empty leg swells with air so that it seems as if his body is whole again, as if he is about to rise up like a blue-and-white-striped carnival balloon and float away into the clouds. But he remains earthbound and, leaning heavily on the crutch, he lurches toward them.

"Adélie."

"Come on, let's get out of here," says Charley in a wavering voice.

Imo stands rooted to the ground. The old man has stepped out of her dream; he has come for his leg. He doesn't understand that it is swollen from being in the culvert and that he can't use it just yet, not until it has dried out and the shoe has been replaced.

"Run!" Charley pulls on Imo's arm, his voice shrill.

But there is no need to run because Papa Chaput has dropped his crutch. His arms rise past his shoulders and he is transformed into a huge ungainly bird flapping its wings in preparation for flight. Then his body tilts forward and his hands reach out to Imo and she realizes that he is falling. She steps forward to catch him and her hands meet his. He leans against her and they sway together, crumpling slowly to the ground. As they fall, his face brushes hers and she inhales the scent of camphor and stale cigarettes. Then she is lying on the wet grass, her body pinned beneath his good leg, his two hands clutching hers.

"Get up, get up," hiccups Charley.

But the grandfather is not filled with air. His body is dense and heavy like a bag of cement from the construction site and, though his eyes are open and staring, he seems to be asleep.

"Get up, get up!"

"I can't. He won't move. I'm stuck." Her voice sticks in her chest and the words come out in a whisper.

"I'm not supposed to be here," says Charley, half-crying now. "Come on, Imo. Come on. Get up."

The grandfather's grip tightens.

"Help me," Imo cries in a whisper.

But now the only sound is the hoarse rattle of the grandfather's hot breath in her ear. Charley has vanished. Probably he has run home scared. Soon the goat will come sniffing around and then what? A goat will eat almost anything, a rotten potato, a tin can, an old mattress, even the laundry off the line. Maybe even a child. And then she hears the thud of feet on the verandah stairs, fists pounding and banging, banging and pounding, and now the harsh metallic screech of the screen door, and Madame's sharp, scolding voice letting loose a torrent of incomprehensible words.

Va t'en is the only phrase Imo can make out. It means "Go away," and she has heard it many times before.

And then Charley's loud, hiccupping scream, "Papa!"

The tirade stops. "Papa?" Madame's voice is puzzled and faint.

"Papa," Imo shrieks into the silence, a single, panicked imperative hurled into the air from somewhere deep in her gut.

The old man groans and sighs, a long shuddering exhalation, and his body shifts. Now he is no longer heavy. The cement inside him has melted away, but still he does not let go of her hand for if he does he will float away. She is his anchor.

"Imogene, Imogene," whispers a new voice.

She opens her eyes to see a face bending over her, a man's face with a beaky nose and dark eyes and bushy eyebrows. It belongs to Dr. Campeau from the village. She wonders if he came on his motorcycle.

"You're a very brave girl," he tells her. His voice is French but she understands him perfectly. "You have done a wonderful job. Papa has gone to sleep and now we must put him to bed. We'll try not to wake him up, eh."

Imo turns her head. The old man is lying beside her; his eyes closed, his face grey. Except for their hands, their bodies are no longer touching.

"Try to relax," Dr. Campeau tells her, and she discovers that her hands are clenched. Her fingers uncurl reluctantly. "That's a good girl. Let's get you up now. Can you stand up for me?"

One leg is numb, and when she tries to stand, it collapses beneath her. She looks down to make sure it's still there. Dr. Campeau carries her up the stairs and sits her in the rocking chair. Charley is already there, hunched over on a footstool with his head in his hands, crying like a baby because he is in trouble. Madame brings them each a glass of brown liquid. Charley gulps his down, slurping noisily, but Imo knows better than to drink water from the culvert and anyway she isn't thirsty.

Madame stands over her, insistent. "Please, you must drink."

Imo takes a sip, but only to be polite. Bubbles go up her nose. She snorts.

"It's Coke," says Charley with a laugh. He belches loudly.

Imo tips back her head and swallows. The bubbles rise up in a burp and she laughs too. They both laugh; they laugh and swallow and burp and laugh again and then her mother is there and she starts to cry.

A Tangled Spool

One day, having watched Swen rattle off in his truck, I decided to walk Tillie down to the lake and the muddy stretch of shoreline that nowadays passes for a public beach. As we passed Maison de Pomme, I heard a short sharp yip and, peering through a gap in the cedar hedge, saw a black dog flopped on the grass, a puppy by the looks of its outsized paws, but already huge. I supposed that Swen must have adopted it from the pound, though, having seen him fling stones at stray dogs in the village, I couldn't imagine him as a pet owner. The puppy stood up when it saw me and wagged its tail in a tentative way.

"Hello, pooch," I greeted it.

The response was a warning rumble. I stepped away hurriedly, but Tillie, who had squeezed between my legs for a better look, growled back. There was an explosion of snarling. Gigantic suddenly, the puppy reared up and lunged at us but was brought up short by its rope, which was attached to a stake in the lawn. Tillie and I retreated to the far side of the street, pursued by frenzied barking that continued long after we were safely inside the house.

It was a guard dog, a female and part Rottweiler, Petey informed me a few days later in an awed voice. Her name was Lucifer, Lucy for short.

Not realizing that the animal had replaced him, he took to hanging around the farmhouse, trying to befriend her in the hope that Swen would hire him back. Lucy was outside day and night, barking at anything and anyone except Petey bold enough to use the sidewalk. And once she had started, she carried on for hours. Within the week, residents of Garden Crescent had taken to walking on the far side of the street to avoid setting her off, but cats and dogs and local wildlife felt no such compunction. A big mackerel tabby cat from up the road regularly flaunted its freedom by sitting on the walkway to the house, just out of reach, washing itself with elaborate deliberation. And when they weren't raiding my father's bird feeder, the grey squirrels, who considered every yard their own, teased Lucy unmercifully by running back and forth along the branches of an old maple that overhung the yard.

At odd times, usually in the late afternoon, Swen would take Lucy inside and then an almost religious hush would fall over the neighbourhood, an all too brief respite before the street erupted with lawnmowers, excited children, and teenagers toting their boom boxes. I think every household on Garden Crescent put in a call to City Hall, but nothing came of these complaints. And then one Saturday morning, goaded, Petey told me later, by the tabby daring to pick its way along the top of the hedge,

Lucy uprooted her stake and bolted out of the yard and down the road after the intruder. The cat sought refuge in a tree a few doors down and Lucy ran round and round the trunk barking and leaping at the lower branches. Half an hour later, having barked herself out, she discovered that she was free and set out to explore the neighbourhood.

For the next two hours she loped from yard to yard, rooting through garbage pails, digging up flower beds, and stopping to sniff at every bush or fencepost she came across. From our vantage point on the front step Petey and I watched her uproot one of Rita Dunster's precious wooden tulips and bury it again in the middle of the lawn at the exact spot where Tillie had done her business a few days earlier. Despite the havoc she left behind, a wandering, telltale trail of plastic, paper, tin cans, bones, coffee grounds, vegetable peelings, and fast food cartons, it was hard to begrudge Lucy her freedom.

Petey, seeing a chance to redeem himself with Swen, wanted to lure her home with a piece of sirloin steak my mother was defrosting for supper.

"It's worth it," he protested when my father objected with unaccustomed ferocity to giving up his dinner.

"No one with any sense would go near that animal," my father snapped. "It's a vicious beast; it can't be tamed."

"Can too be tamed," insisted Petey, but he surrendered the steak and stomped off with his lower lip jutting out.

In the few hours that Lucy was free she never left the street. About three o'clock in the afternoon, she was galumphing down the middle of the road with the stake, which appeared to be a flimsy plastic tent peg, trailing at the end of her rope, a large pizza carton in her mouth, head and tail held high, apparently heading for home when Swen's truck turned the corner and pulled up in front of the farmhouse. Swen jumped out and started toward her, slapping his thigh and calling out "Lucy!" in a loud imperious voice that carried right down the street. She stopped in her tracks when she saw him and stood with her head cocked to one side, her feet slightly splayed and her tail between her legs, wagging feebly. He was within arm's length of her when she turned and bounded across the neighbouring yard and took refuge under the verandah, a low, sagging do-it-yourself affair that years earlier had been tacked onto the front of the house by the owner, old Mr. Connibear, a widower now and famously antisocial.

Swen followed but halted a few yards away from the verandah and stood in the middle of the Connibear lawn, legs apart, knees bent, snapping his fingers and whistling and calling out "Lucy" in a voice that was alternately threatening and cajoling. There wasn't a peep from Lucy, who wisely stayed out of sight behind the wooden lattice that enclosed the lower part of the porch. Only the tent peg, which had snagged on a post, betrayed her presence. After a while, Mr. Connibear came out and started haranguing Swen, and a crowd of children and adults, Petey among them, gathered on the sidewalk and began offering advice.

Some twenty minutes later they were joined by the dog catcher, a small man with a nasal voice who was generally unpopular in the neighbourhood. Possibly for the first time in his career, his arrival was greeted with a cheer. He got out of his van and sauntered round to the rear, where he opened the double doors and took out his dog catching gear, a long stick with a voluminous net attached at one end, rather like a butterfly net only larger, and rumoured to be of his own invention. He stood on the sidewalk, surveying the scene before advancing slowly up the Connibears' walk, holding the net behind his back. As he neared the steps, Mr. Connibear shouted something and pointed toward the lattice. In the same instant Swen leapt forward and, in one smooth motion, dove under the verandah. His head, shoulders, and upper torso disappeared into the small opening and his disembodied legs and buttocks encased in tight white jeans lay stretched out like an afterthought on the grass. Moments later his legs contracted and he backed out on all fours, dragging Lucy by the collar, the pizza box still clenched in her teeth.

Grabbing the rope with his free hand, he stood up and began whacking her across the back with the tent peg over and over again. She yelped once and was silent. He stopped finally, dropping the peg and finishing off with a boot to the ribs. He dusted himself off, swiping energetically at the grass stains on his pants, then without so much as a glance at the dog catcher or any of the onlookers, he ripped the pizza box from Lucy's mouth and dragged her across the grass, through a gap in the hedge, and out of sight. Almost immediately she began to yelp.

The crowd, who had looked on in stunned silence, stirred. Several people started toward the farmhouse, but the dog catcher waved them back and stepped into the yard himself. The yelping stopped. Minutes later he returned to his van. He sat in the driver's seat for a few minutes, writing in a notebook, and then drove off. Gradually the onlookers dispersed, all except Petey, who remained on the sidewalk, staring at the farmhouse until Tillie and I went to fetch him for supper. I had to jog his arm several times to get his attention.

"Not fair, Imo. She was only having some fun. Swen doesn't understand," he said in a desolate voice.

"No," I agreed. "He doesn't know a thing about animals. But you have to come now, Petey. It's time for dinner. Mum's cooking the steak and you have to feed Tillie."

He came in the end, but he couldn't manage his supper, and after a few bites left the table and went upstairs to be sick in the bathroom. It was a noisy performance and being Petey he didn't think to close the door. We sat in painful silence until it was over.

After that none of us felt like eating; I found it impossible even to look at my plate. Finally he whistled for Tillie, who emerged reluctantly from under the table, loathe to abandon the coming feast of leftovers. She lumbered out of the room, casting longing and reproachful glances back at us.

"Didn't that Swen fellow use to be a friend of yours?" demanded my father when we heard Petey's bedroom door slam closed.

"What are you talking about?" I sputtered. "I know him, that's all. He was in the orphanage with Thomas. I never said he was a friend. I've never had anything to do with him if I could help it and I don't think Petey should either. I told you already he might be a drug dealer. I . . ." I could hear my voice rising and forced myself to stop speaking. In any case, there was no point continuing. My parents were staring at me in that expectant way they have, as if I was responsible for Swen and could somehow make him disappear. We sat in silence until the all too familiar strains of *The Beach Boys Greatest Hits* floated down the stairs, the volume rising until the bass pounded against the ceiling and, inevitably, Tillie started to yodel.

"Oh, Petey, not this again," said my mother, pulling off her glasses and pressing her fingers to her temples.

"One of these days I'm going to break that bloody machine," said my father.

But before either of them made a move, the music stopped abruptly and Tillie's howls faded.

"But why is he living in the Apple House?" demanded my mother. "I thought it was going back on the market."

I sighed. "It's nothing to do with me anymore. We made an offer, that's all. But it's annulled." I had made it clear to the lawyer that I wanted to withdraw our offer; if necessary I was prepared to lose the deposit. He had assured me that, under the circumstances, this was unlikely to happen but warned that it might take months to sort things out. In the meantime, he supposed the house could be rented. Standing empty it would only be a target for vandals. He was right of course. But Swen, of all people!

"I suppose he must be paying rent," my mother commented.

"I have no idea."

"He should be sent packing."

"You can't evict someone for beating a dog," my father pointed out.

"I don't see why not. Maybe Imogene should talk to Jeannette," suggested my mother

"Really, Ireney, it's nothing to do with Jeanette. She's a real estate agent. It's in the lawyers' hands now. Imo's just told us."

My mother stood up and started clearing the table. "You run along now, dear," she said to me. "Your father and I'll do the dishes. You need your rest."

I went to bed early but awoke around midnight, feeling nauseated and hungry at the same time and obsessing about the termination. I had an appointment to see a counsellor in the morning and I wondered what she would ask. I pictured a sharp-faced woman with dark hair asking me penetrating personal questions, trying to catch me out. It was my decision, I told myself. I didn't see why I should discuss it with a stranger.

I had tried for years to get pregnant. I should have been in a state of bliss, enraptured at the thought of a tiny Thomas growing inside me—I had no doubt it was a boy. The truth is that Thomas was always keener than I was. I think he needed a link to the past, a child who would embody the spirit of its grandparents and reveal to him who he was and where he came from. But it was his presence I longed for; I cared nothing for mythical ancestors. In some part of my mind I knew I was being irrational but I couldn't help feeling that if only I wasn't pregnant, Thomas would be back in the workroom, stitching up a pair of loafers for the Man With The

Wide Feet, and I would be out front peddling flip-flops and running shoes to Madame Poulin's great-grandchildren or else up at La Dolce Vita having lunch with Louise.

My parents would be over the moon at the prospect of a grandchild, my mother especially. And Petey would be thrilled to be an uncle. He's always loved babies. My earliest memory is of lying in my crib with his face bending over me. My mother let him hold me the day she brought me home from the hospital and she had a hard time getting me back. For half an hour he sat on the couch with me in his arms, both of us perfectly still, neither making a sound. She had to watch him like a hawk because he was so clumsy, but he held me every day after that.

A child is for life. Living with Petey had taught me that and I couldn't imagine a world without him in it but I could hardly contemplate living with myself. How could I bring up a child? And it wasn't a child at all, I told myself, not yet.

I could hear Lucy howling. It was a lonely sound, half moan, half wail and full of longing. What would happen to her if Swen moved out? Back to the pound, I supposed. More than likely she would be put down. Petey would be desperate to rescue her. I got up finally to close the window. The street lights had gone off at midnight and I could barely see to the edge of the yard. All at once I longed to be in the village, where the lights were never turned off though I had often griped about light pollution. The window sash stuck briefly, then slammed down with a crash. I returned to bed but now the room felt stuffy and I could still hear Lucy howling. I felt like howling too.

There was a thump on the door and Petey stuck in his head.

"You okay, Imo? You can have Tillie," he said gruffly and closed the door again.

Tillie padded in and scrambled onto the bed and flopped against me with her head on my pillow. She gave me a perfunctory lick, heaved a sigh, and instantly fell asleep. I lay awake, breathing in her doggy smell, comforted by the familiar pungency. Long nights with Petey had accustomed her to her role as a sympathizer. She was the household stoic, more familiar with human tears than canine sorrows. A wet pillow had no meaning for Tillie; tears were salt water and nothing more. She snuffled gently in her sleep. I snuffled back. She wouldn't think it ridiculous to cry about a lonely dog and I refused to cry about anything else.

A few days later a truck pulled up at the farmhouse and unloaded an enormous roll of heavy wire mesh and a pile of metal posts.

"It's a fence. Must be for Lucy so she won't run away," declared Petey.

Sure enough, that afternoon I saw Swen outside with a couple of semi-delinquent boys from the village. One of them was holding a spool while the other unrolled a string along the outside perimeter of the hedge. Swen stood at the corner, clipboard in hand, supervising. They were aligning the postholes, I supposed; their efforts were thwarted by Lucy, who kept bounding through the hedge, snapping and biting at the line and trying to run off with it. The boys, clearly bored with the proceedings, kept raising and lowering the string to tantalize her. It broke eventually and while they were tying it back together, she ran round in circles with the spool until it was empty and the contents in a tangle on the sidewalk.

Petey, who was helping Charley clear out his mother's basement, carrying out boxes of old Dunster Debug equipment and piling them up on the sidewalk for the city's special biannual pick-up, couldn't keep his eyes off them. He lingered longer and longer in the driveway and several times walked round the corner past the farmhouse on the pretext of mailing a letter. By the end of the day the mailbox must have been overflowing with tattered, dusty brown envelopes stamped Dunster Debug.

"It *is* for Lucy, so she won't have to be tied up," he reported when he got home, slurring his words and hopping from foot to foot with excitement. "She can run around the yard all she wants now and she won't get in trouble. It's the right thing to do. Swen's sorry he hit her. He's not going to do it again."

"Oh, really."

"He promised. And anyway," Petey added triumphantly, "those other guys aren't coming back. I'm going to help."

"I don't think Mum and Dad will want you to work there again."

"I can do what I like." He crossed his arms and stuck out chin.

"They might worry, though," I suggested, and his whole body seemed to sag. He chewed on his lower lip.

"It's okay, because I'm doing it for Lucy. She needs me," he declared at length. "Swen needs me too. I'm a good worker. He said so."

The next morning he was up at the farmhouse helping Swen put in the posts, and the day after they installed the fence. It was an ugly thing, about five feet high with gaping hollows at the bottom where the ground was uneven, more suited to a works yard than a suburban neighbourhood. I wondered how long before it occurred to Lucy to jump over it or else to tunnel underneath, but Petey had no such qualms. He came home exultant, flashing a twenty-dollar bill.

"Swen paid me. I told him to, just like you said. I'll be working regular from now on. I have to feed Lucy and I'm going to train her too. It's a real job!"

The Old Man Goes to Heaven

There are four black taxis parked along the road in front of the farmer's house, and a dented grey car with a spare tire mounted on the rear bumper backed right up onto the grass with its front wheels on the sidewalk. Blocking the gravel driveway that leads around the side of the house to the field is the big white delivery van from the IGA, wrapped round and round with dusty black crepe paper streamers. Imo runs her finger along the crinkly strips. They feel dry and powdery like her mother's hands before she rubs in the cold cream.

"Come along. Don't dawdle," her mother says now. "You'll get your dress dirty."

"Don't care."

Chasing one another around the broad trunk of the elm tree are three black bicycles, and halfway up the stone path to the front door, leaning into the flowerbed, is Dr. Campeau's motorcycle. It has a fat black leather seat and silver fenders spattered with mud, and rising up from the handlebars on a silver pole is a little rectangular mirror so that he can see the cars coming up behind. Imo stands on her tiptoes, but her eyes don't reach the mirror. If she wasn't wearing a dress, she could climb on the seat in a jiffy.

Her mother tugs at her hand. "Don't dawdle," she says again.

Imo would dawdle forever if she could. *Dawdle*. She likes the sound of the word. It makes her think of water, tiny waves dipping up and down in the lake, or lapping at the sides of a bowl of chicken noodle soup, the noodles slithering around and around on the bottom, eluding her spoon, slipping up the sides and flopping over the rim onto the table. Or Papa Chaput in his old overstuffed chair on the verandah, rocking back and forth all day, dawdling, but she doesn't want to think about that, and that's not what it means, not really, not what the grown-ups mean by it anyway. It means taking a long time to get ready when you have to go somewhere, like this morning when she didn't want to put on her yellow dress, the one with the scratchy brown smocking and the short puffy sleeves that leave a red ring on her upper arms because she has grown too big. There was a tearing sound when she pulled it over her head and another one when she took it off again so that her mother could let down the hem, and now there's a hole in the armpit big enough for her fist, and even though it's already spring and she's wearing her heavy winter parka, she can feel the cold air coming in. The wind is blowing right up inside her dress, tugging at her panties, which are stretched and floppy and slipping a little bit, making her bare legs all goose bumpy because her knee socks have fallen down inside her gumboots.

Her mother is not wearing a coat at all, only her good black dress and the beautiful black shawl that came from India and nylon stockings inside her gumboots. Tucked under her arm, wrapped first in wax paper and then in aluminum foil, is a date–nut loaf for Madame because Papa Chaput was her father-in-law and now he has fallen down dead. It's nobody's fault that he died, her mother says, and especially not Imo's. She's not to feel bad because after all he was old and tired and ill and now he has gone to a better place up in the sky called heaven. Imo is relieved that it's not her fault, and she's glad that Papa Chaput is no longer sick, but she's not so sure he has gone to heaven. In the night, after she has fallen asleep, the old man lies down beside her with his good leg pressed hard against hers so that she can hardly move and he won't go away until she screams and wakes herself up. It isn't really Papa Chaput, her mother says; it's only Tillie taking up too much room on the bed, but Imo doesn't believe her. It never happened before and Tillie always sleeps on her bed when Petey is away at school. She wonders if Papa Chaput visits Madame too. She has made a card for Madame with a drawing of the old man in his rocking chair with his blue beret poking over the top and now she and her mother are going to pay their respects. It's a way of saying goodbye, her mother says, and it will make Imo feel better. She has promised they won't stay long, only for a minute, just long enough to hand over the card and the date–nut loaf. They won't dawdle.

Imo didn't want to come. She would rather stay in her room for a week, like Charley, who should have known better than to trespass on the farmer's property even if it wasn't his idea. He should have been a gentleman and stopped Imo from going there too. Serves him right, Rupert says. He's mad because he and Finney had to stop building their raft. Finney's father made them take back the wood they stole from the construction site, only it wasn't stealing, not really, because now all those boards are in the slash pile waiting to be burned.

Charley has written Imo a letter on his mother's good pink notepaper and dropped it out his bedroom window to her in a pink envelope. He's sorry that he is not a gentleman, he has written in smeary blue ink, but he hopes she still wants to marry him and he'll buy her a ring and a box of chocolates as soon as he has saved up his money. So far Imo hasn't written back because Finney wants to marry her too. She is the only person he knows who has touched a dead person and he thinks she is very brave, braver than his sisters or any Swedish girl he has ever met and it is in his heart to marry a girl like her, though he would prefer it if she could speak Swedish. He has invited her over to play in his basement, where there is an empty wooden crate from Sweden big enough for two people to sleep in. They can live there together, he says, and his mother will make pancakes whenever he tells her. Imo would love to live in the crate, which has a real door and two windows with blue curtains, but she doesn't think she could ever learn to speak Swedish. And anyway she is not sure she wants to get married at all.

There is a singsong sound coming from inside the farmhouse as if the whole house is full of birds. Imo's mother has to knock three times before the door is opened by a lady with a bright red mouth and a high bouffant hairdo like someone in a magazine except that she is fat. The lady's mouth drops open when she sees them and her arms fly to her breast with a hollow grunt.

"La Petite!" she exclaims. It is Madame.

Imo holds out the card, which being homemade is not in an envelope, and for no reason at all Madame bursts into tears. She bends over and crushes Imo in her mashed potato arms so that Imo's breath sticks in her chest and then without even asking she pulls off Imo's boots and lines them up beside a row of overshoes, each pair stuck together with a clothespin like at Sunday school. Taking hold of her hand, Madame leads her away from her mother to a room filled with men and women perched on hard wooden chairs, all of them dressed in black and jabbering away at each other in French like crows on a telephone wire.

"La Petite," Madame announces in a hoarse voice from the doorway. There is a sudden hush. All eyes turn to Imo and there are echoing murmurs of "La Petite." Imo waits for her mother to explain that her name is Imogene Jackson, to say that they have only come to drop off the date–nut loaf and that they can just stay for a minute. But there is no release from the damp squeeze of Madame's hand and she is plunged into a shifting forest of soft thighs, bony knees, scratchy trousers, and broad fleshy shins imprisoned in taut nylon mesh. Trouser cuffs and black boots, puffy ankles and stumpy high-heeled shoes extend in front of her like giant tree roots in the jungle; then, one at a time, draw back to let her pass until only a small black patent leather shoe blocks the way. Attached to the shoe and poking out from under a chair is a long skinny leg encased in a thick brown stocking. A black-haired girl with a bright green dress hiked up around her bum stares out at Imo.

"Louise," says Madame in a stern voice and leg and shoe disappear under the chair. Louise sticks out her tongue, but before Imo can do the same, a hand reaches out to touch her arm.

"Mademoiselle Imogene. We meet again." It is Dr. Campeau in his black leather motorcycle jacket. He shakes her hand gently. "And how is my brave girl today?"

Imo shows him the red mark on her palm where the grandfather's nail dug into the skin. He examines it carefully, sketching a circle around the tender spot with his long index finger. "This is a badge of courage," he says gravely. "In a few days it will be gone, but you must always remember what a brave girl you are, and I will remember too." His black eyes crinkle around the edges.

If she was really brave, she would ask for a ride on his motorcycle, but she doesn't feel brave at all. Her hand tingles and spit rises in her throat. She gulps it down and nods. Looking back, she sees her mother standing in the doorway talking to the farmer, but then a fat man with a cigar in his hand stands up, blocking her view. Then Madame nudges her forward again and they make their way toward a long table draped with a white cloth that hangs all the way to the floor. At the near end of the table there are two photos in stand-up frames. One shows a young man in an army uniform; Imo knows it must be Papa Chaput before he went to war. In the other photo the same young man is standing in front of a wedding cake with a lady in a long dress. The rest of the table is filled with food, plates of ham and orange cheese, a big-bellied brown casserole for baked beans, a fancy cut-glass bowl of green jelly, and plates and plates and plates of date–nut loaf, already sliced and buttered.

Madame places Imo's card between the photos and then she hands her an empty plate. Imo understands that she may have whatever she wants to eat, but she isn't hungry, not even for the jelly, which is full of little bits that might be shredded cabbage. Instead she points to the row of bottles at the far end of the table and Madame uncaps a giant-sized Coke and fills a glass. She hands it to Imo, patting her on the head with her free hand as she does so, and the Coke splashes over the rim a little. Then she disappears around the far end of the table into the kitchen.

Holding the glass in both hands, Imo flattens herself against the wall. She can see her mother over by the front porch; the fat man is waving his cigar at her and the smoke is curling up round her head to the ceiling. The girl in the green dress, who is still under the chair, sticks out her tongue again. Imo slurps at her Coke, smacking her lips between gulps to show she doesn't care, and when the glass is empty, she fills it up again from the giant-sized bottle. It spills a little and now there is a puddle of Coke on the floor and all of a sudden she has to pee.

Leaving the glass on the table, she goes into the kitchen, where the two ladies from the wool shop in the village are making sandwiches. The plump one with the funny bulges is brushing melted butter onto squares of white bread and the bony one, who is thin and sharp like a knitting needle, is chopping up hard-boiled eggs. They are wearing long black floppy dresses that they knitted themselves. Everything they wear is made of wool, and you can go in their store and order anything you want—socks, skirts, sweaters, stockings, hats, even underwear, Charley says—and they will knit it for you in any colour you choose. His mother is going to order a red toque for him next winter. In the shop the ladies sit side by side behind the counter, their knitting needles clicking, but today they are seated across from each other at a table that looks just like a restaurant booth, with long, high-backed padded seats and a jukebox against the wall at the end. The bony one makes a clicking sound when she notices Imo and the bulgy one pats her on the head. Imo watches them for a while in case they put a quarter in the jukebox but most likely they don't have any money with them because they carry on talking and making sandwiches. And Imo can't wait for long because she is in a hurry to find the bathroom.

She wanders through the kitchen, past the screen door that opens onto the verandah, and back into the front hall. Her mother is no longer there but from somewhere in the house she hears the gurgle and swoosh of a toilet flushing, and then, down a dark passage where the bedrooms must be, she sees the fat man coming out of a doorway, holding his cigar behind his back. She squeezes past him and enters the same door. But it is not the bathroom at all, it's a bedroom, and even though it's the middle of the day, the curtains are closed. And there, right in the middle of the room, in a long wooden bed with high sides, all dressed up in a silver blue suit, is Papa Chaput waiting to go to heaven. His hands are folded on his chest and his legs are stretched out straight in front of him with a bump in the middle at each knee and two shiny black shoes at the end with the toes pointing up to the ceiling so that no one, not even God, could tell that one of his legs is missing. And maybe it's not because over in the corner, leaning against the wall, is a fat metal cylinder with a shoe attached at the bottom, glimmering in the light from the crack in the curtain, his aluminum leg. And right next to it, balanced on a little peg because the shoe is missing, is the wooden one. Someone has cleaned off all the mud and polished the wood so that you can hardly tell it's been in the culvert. He won't need it in heaven; Imo knows that. He won't need the aluminum one either. In heaven he will have his real one back. Maybe he has it already. His silver-blue suit shimmers in the dim light, blue for the sky and silver for heaven. Slowly, hesitantly, she steps into the room, one foot after another, until she is close enough to touch his shoe, but before she can reach out there is a gasp behind her.

"What are you doing in here?" demands a high-pitched, scolding voice that is at once frightening and familiar. "I've been looking all over for you." It's her mother.

"I have to pee," says Imo. But it is too late.

Ginger Ale

I had scandalized Dr. Campeau, I knew that, but I had some idea that if I jumped through all the right hoops, he'd understand, and I needed someone to hold my hand. I understood he didn't approve of abortion, but then no one in their heart of hearts approves of the actual bloody act, no woman especially, least of all those who suffer through it. How could we?

His daughter was a single parent at age eighteen. In those days, not so long ago, when most pregnant teens were banished on pretence of furthering their education to live with an imaginary aunt in another town, the baby was invariably handed over to an adoption agency. But Dr. Campeau's daughter stayed at home in full view of the village throughout her pregnancy. She and her parents brought up the child together. So I should have known better than to assume he'd ever approve, but I wasn't really thinking. I've known him nearly all my life and he's seen me through more than one childhood crisis. I needed him, where he's always been, on my side.

The counsellor he referred me to worked out of the regional office of the CLSC, an umbrella organization that takes care of Quebecers from cradle to grave. It's a few miles north of the tracks, up past Louise's expensive new library and the even more expensive Hotel de Ville, a monument to Saint-Ange-du-Lac's proud status as a city, beyond the English high school, the French high school, and innumerable little strip malls, right at the edge of the concrete wasteland of the industrial park. It's a one-storey cement block building plunked in the middle of a field of spiky yellow grass that serves as an overflow parking lot and a dumping ground for derelict cars, a sorry end for what is quite possibly the last bit of farmland remaining on the West Island. It couldn't be more out of the way, but presumably the land was cheap and there's a shuttle bus every half-hour from the big shopping centres along the Trans-Canada Highway, the assumption being perhaps that anyone, no matter what their state of health, can get themselves to a shop, or else, as Charmaine's father and most of the village merchants maintain, that shopping centres will make you sick.

The location suited me perfectly, since I had no intention of confiding my plans to my family. I had some vague idea of announcing, well after the fact, that I'd had a spontaneous miscarriage. I prepared the ground for this deception by casually announcing to my mother that Dr. Campeau had scheduled more tests.

"Shall I come with you?" she asked immediately.

"No, no, I'm fine. Maybe next time, if there's a problem," I said, pricked with panic by the look of concern on her face.

The counsellor, whose name was Collette, looked about sixteen, though she must have been older, but in any case far too young to be giving advice or guiding anyone through a crisis. She was a thin-faced, small-boned young woman, ensconced behind a large, uncluttered desk that filled most of the small bare counselling room. She was reading what I assumed was my file when the receptionist announced me.

"Dr. Campeau has recommended you for counselling. You have requested a termination," Colette stated without preamble in heavily accented English.

I sat down, biting my lip nervously but somewhat reassured by her tone, which was neutral and even a bit tentative.

"I understand that you have been in an automobile accident. I am required to ask you some questions." She glanced down at the file again. "Dr. Campeau has written that you have had a severe concussion and the possibility of brain damage. The extent of this damage is not known—" she paused, then corrected herself. "Not that we have evidence." I realized that she was reading straight from his notes, translating as she went along. She continued in a halting voice. "The trauma has been complicated by the tragic death of the husband. The language has been severely affected. However it is possible to make a full recovery. It is a question of time only. Patient has concern of fetal deformity." She looked up and stared at me for a moment, as if searching for a third breast or an extra ear, then continued, "Also anxiety and severe morning sickness, resulting in weight loss, moderate to severe."

I gave a start. I had seen myself in the mirror, gaunt and hollow-eyed, but it hadn't occurred to me that I'd lost weight.

"If the circumstances were otherwise, you would want to keep this baby. I am correct?" she asked when she had finished reading.

Well, yes, obviously, if circumstances were otherwise, I thought. That was the whole point. I nodded.

"And you are capable to make such a decision?"

Again I nodded, and she flushed. I realized that she was as intimidated by my age as I was by her position of authority. Evidently she had no intention of trying to talk me out of anything.

"In this situation there will be no problem to refer you. I must inform you that if you do not wish to have the termination, there are many families wanting to adopt a baby. Your child can have a good home." She continued without waiting for a reply, "I just have to fill up this form and you can make an appointment for the procedure. The receptionist will arrange it for you now, before you leave. You must do this in person. Today." She stood up and handed me a single sheet of paper which she had signed at the bottom. "I wish you the best."

I felt a fluttering in my chest but cleared my throat and croaked thanks. In the foyer, which was crowded with people, I dutifully handed the form to the receptionist, who appeared reluctant to accept it.

"The earliest appointment for a termination is two months from today. I can tell you that right now," she announced in booming tones. I flinched, but no one even looked up.

"Two months?" I whispered, aghast.

"That was as of yesterday morning. It's probably longer now."

"I don't think . . ."

"If you can't wait that long, it's better to go private. I can give you a list of clinics. It's simpler in the end if you can manage it financially. You can avoid all this nonsense. I don't know why she didn't tell you that right off but she never does. It's better to get it over with, really. Otherwise you'll have to go back to your doctor and see if he can get you on the emergency roster." She glanced down at the form. "Dr. Campeau, is it? I can't imagine your chances would be very good." She pulled a sheaf of papers from a drawer and handed them to me. "It's up to you, dear."

"So a clinic would take me right away?"

"Less than a week. And you'll be in and out the same day."

I shuffled through the papers without actually taking in any information. My head was beginning to swim. I wondered if I was going to faint. "Which one should I go to?"

"That's up to you, dear. There's only the one in Montreal. You must have seen it on the news. You should read the leaflet before you make the appointment."

I took the papers with a shaking hand and retreated to the car. Until that instant I had avoided thinking about the actual procedure. I had expected the counsellor to try to talk me out of it and when she couldn't to shepherd me through the process. I was on my own with it all and the prospect was daunting.

I ran through a list of questions in my mind, determined to be practical. I had no idea how much a private clinic would charge, but whatever the amount, I supposed I would have to manage it. I wondered if I could insist on a general anaesthetic. That way I could forget I had ever been pregnant. But I would be too groggy afterwards to go home on my own. Someone would have to pick me up from the clinic, which meant there was no possibility of pretending I'd had a miscarriage. If only I could ask Louise. It would be easy enough for her to take a late lunch and pick me up from the clinic, but she had some absurd idea that my pregnancy was a gift from God, my saving grace. "It will redeem you," she had said when I finally confided in her. I hardly knew what she meant—she had never been particularly devout—but I knew I couldn't burden her with this decision, let alone ask her to participate.

All I knew of private clinics was what I had seen on the news: protesters waving placards. What if someone waved a placard in my face or tried to block my way? And what if the cameras were rolling that day? It was unthinkable. I knew I would run away. I reminded myself that I was making a reasonable decision, but the whole point of going to a counsellor was to explore my own feelings, and I hadn't done that. Did Dr. Campeau have any idea to whom he had sent me?

I was shaking uncontrollably by the time I arrived home. My mother was in the living room, but I went straight upstairs without greeting her and flung myself on my bed. She followed me up and hovered in the doorway. "Is everything all right?" she asked in a tentative voice.

"Not really," I admitted, staring at a long V-shaped stain on the ceiling that had been there as long as I could remember. My father had painted it over more than once but it kept reappearing. Cheap paint was the problem, according to my mother.

"Oh, honey, what's wrong?"

"I'm pregnant," I said in a low voice, fixing my eyes on the ceiling.

"You're pregnant! But that's wonderful." Her voice echoed around the room.

"I'm not going to keep it." I clenched my fists to control the shaking but could not mask the tremor in my voice.

"Is something the matter? Did the test show something?"

"I just don't think I should have it, that's all." I closed my eyes, willing her to leave me alone, and she was silent for so long that I thought she must have gone away in shock and disgust, but when I opened them, she was leaning over me, her grey eyes peering worriedly over the rims of her glasses.

"What did Dr. Campeau say?"

"It's not up to him."

"Yes, but what does he think you should do? You must have talked to him about it."

"He sent me to some woman up at the CLSC." I turned my head away but forced myself to continue, squeezing the words out one at a time. "She thinks that, considering the circumstances, it's a perfectly reasonable thing to do. She told me to make an appointment."

"For an abortion?" My mother seemed bewildered rather than shocked.

"It's called a termination, and I have to go to a private clinic because the waiting list is two months long. Actually I might have to borrow some money."

"But you must go to a proper hospital." She sounded panicked now.

"A clinic is better than a hospital," I explained with exaggerated patience, my body under control finally. "The doctors know what they're doing. They do it all the time. That's all they do." An appalling vision of protesters waving placards and chanting rose to my mind again, but it was preferable to seeing my mother's face so I kept my eyes closed.

Silence again.

"I think you should talk to someone, a counsellor of some kind," she said at length

"I just told you. I did. She thought it was a good idea."

"Yes, but a real counsellor, a psychologist."

"Someone who will talk me out of it?" I felt the blood rush to my head and clenched my fists again. Why wouldn't she go away?

"Someone who will help you think it through. I know this has been a terrible time for you, but I don't think losing a baby will make it any easier."

I sat up then, my heart thumping. "That's what Dr. Campeau said. How could either of you possibly know what will make it easier? I don't want to talk about it anymore. I haven't made the appointment yet anyway."

"No, of course. You rest now." She backed away but stopped at the door. "I'm off to the village to do a bit of shopping. We're nearly out of bread. There's just enough for Petey's lunch. Is there anything you need? Shall I get you some ginger ale?"

"No, nothing. I'm fine," I said, knowing she would probably buy a whole case. Ginger ale was the panacea for every childhood illness.

I listened to her retreating footsteps with a combination of relief and shame. Faced with the most adult of problems, I had reverted to childhood petulance. But I had told her at least. I comforted myself that the whole thing would be over soon. At most I might have to wait a week, according to the receptionist. I had intended to call the clinic as soon as I arrived home, but knowing I would burst into tears if I did it just then, I decided to wait a day.

Too restless to doze off or to read through the sheets the receptionist had given me, I lay on my back, staring at the ceiling, becoming convinced that the stain was growing larger, which was ridiculous but ominous all the same. I could hear my mother knocking about in the kitchen, rattling things, a sure sign that she was agitated. Then the back door slammed as my father came in from the garden. I listened to the murmur of their voices floating up through the hot-air vent. No doubt she was telling him everything. He would be listening uneasily, frowning intently while he heated a can of soup, mushroom most likely, stirring constantly in obedience to the instructions on the tin, then carefully pouring the contents of the saucepan into a bowl and sitting down at the drop-leaf table with napkin and spoon and maybe a piece of cheddar.

I heard my mother leave at long last and stood at the window watching the car drive up the street. She tooted at Petey as she went by the farmhouse. He had tied Lucy to one end of what looked like our clothesline (which had disappeared a couple of days earlier) and was making her walk up and down the yard, training her to sit or stay or some such thing. The rope was much too long to allow him any control, and Lucy seemed to think it was a continuation of the game with the string because she kept charging at it where it sagged in the middle and trying to run away with it. After a while I noticed Swen standing in the doorway. Contemplating his little empire, I thought sourly. The yard was more of a mess than ever. Leftover metal posts and a role of wire fencing were piled against the foundation of the house in a haphazard way and the gaps in the hedge seemed wider than ever and the grass practically non-existent.

I waited until I heard my father go into the living room, where I knew he would doze off, and then slipped downstairs to the kitchen. I was starving and not for a bowl of soup. Opening the fridge, I foraged through anonymous plastic containers, ancient bottles of condiments, and a surprising amount of wilted lettuce in search of the leftover roast beef. I found it eventually on the top shelf right in front of my nose inside a crumpled cylinder of foil that held a single soggy roast potato, a large bone, and a great deal of fat and gristle. I was standing in the middle of the kitchen, gnawing on the bone, when Petey clumped in.

"What happened to the roast beef?" I demanded. "It's all gone."

He peered at the package. "Not all gone, Imo."

"I can't make a sandwich out of that. It's all gristle. What'd Mum do with it? Do you know?"

"I took some for Lucy," he said, reaching past me into the fridge for the peanut butter.

"You gave it to Lucy," I echoed in disbelief. "What am I supposed to eat?"

He shuffled his feet. He could see I was upset but he had no idea why. It was understandable, I suppose: I hadn't touched the meat at supper the night before. Why would I want any now?

"Sorry, Imo," he said contritely. He was well practised in apologizing. "You want a peanut butter sandwich?"

I sighed. "No, thanks. I feel like roast beef. It's the only thing I wanted." I said plaintively. "I didn't get any last night."

He stared at me, his forehead furrowed with concern. "Here," he said, holding out his sandwich. "I put jam on it."

I took the sandwich with ill grace, knowing it was a mistake, and bolted the first half, then rushed into the bathroom and stood over the toilet, fighting back a wave of nausea.

Petey followed me in. "You going to throw up, Imo?" he asked from the doorway. "I throw up sometimes," he offered when I didn't answer. "When I'm nervous, you know. And then I don't do things right. I got something you could have. Make you feel better. Like medicine. Here."

I looked up reluctantly. From his pocket he produced a neatly rolled joint, slightly crumpled but otherwise pristine. "You can have this."

It was a magnanimous gesture, I realize, looking back.

"Make you feel better, Imo. Honest," he said.

"Where did you get it?" I demanded, though I thought I knew full well.

"It's good, Imo. Good stuff. You don't have to worry. It's pure, really pure."

I was about to refuse but put out my hand instead. Considering my own plans, I could hardly get on my high horse about smoking pot.

"You have to smoke it outside, Imo, down at the lake or something. Don't tell Dad, okay," he said earnestly.

"Okay. Thanks, I'll keep it for later," I promised him.

Going to Church

I stood in the hall outside the downstairs bathroom and contemplated Petey's gift. For once I was tempted—at the very least it might settle my stomach. I could head down to the lake as he had suggested or, better still, I could light up in the privacy of the apartment. Oblivion beckoned. Why had I been such a wet blanket all these years?

"Half the village is high on something Sunday mornings and it's not just a cloud of incense. Look at that old bag across the road, La Pantouffle. Sure, she goes to church, but the second she gets home she's into her snuff. Everyone needs to relax once in a while." That was Thomas's response when I protested one day, not for the first time, that he was wasting another precious Sunday morning getting stoned.

It was true about Madame Poulin. For reasons known only to herself she never closes her curtains. We'd both seen her in the act, or just afterwards, sneezing with gusto. Once in a while was fine as far as I was concerned. I had indulged myself, though only rarely. It wasn't really the smoking I objected to; it was Swen.

He called for Thomas on Sunday mornings whenever he was in town. In summer they would head down to the tiny gravel beach where Thomas kept his chaloupe, and if they were too lazy to put it in the water, sit on its upturned hull, smoking and reminiscing about the bad old days at the orphanage. In winter they would commandeer an empty ice fishing hut and hole up inside with not even a token fishing line between them. Going to church, they called it, because they invariably met up with friends and neighbours on the way to or from mass, though fewer and fewer as the years went by, to Father Trepannier's sorrow. I never went with them, preferring to catch up on chores or else to take my coffee back to bed and nurse my resentments until Thomas returned with a conciliatory six-pack of doughnuts to tide us over until we joined my parents and Petey for Sunday dinner.

After Joseph died, Thomas and Swen started spending their Sunday mornings in the old downstairs apartment. I was welcome to join them, Thomas said, but it was clear that Swen resented my presence at least as much as I resented his. Monday mornings, if we hadn't aired the place out, there would be a lingering odour of pot, what Thomas referred to as le beau bouquet. By then there were rumours about Swen, that he was peddling hard drugs, maybe even about Thomas, though I never heard them, so it was safer to smoke out of sight.

Swen came and went from the village at irregular intervals. He had no job that anyone knew of but he rented a room from

Madame Poulin, so he must have had an income from somewhere because there would have been no question of not coming up with the rent. Why she put up with a layabout like Swen remains a mystery. Her own grandchildren worked at one or other of the family businesses from the age of twelve onward and were required to toe the line in every respect. Possibly she got a vicarious thrill out of his shiftless lifestyle or perhaps he was meant to be an example to her grandchildren of how not to behave. But then the whole village put up with him, including me.

One Sunday afternoon, a couple of hours before we were due to go over to my parents, I wandered downstairs looking for my old green sandals that Thomas had promised to resole and was startled to hear Petey's voice coming from the little back kitchen. He sounded odd and rather dreamy, not like his usual self. Assuming that he had stopped by on his way to do an errand for my mother, I poked my head in the back. There they were, all three.

Thomas, his bare feet and ankles sticking out of a pair of ancient baggy cotton trousers that had once belonged to Joseph, was tilting back on one of the old wooden chairs, his long legs propped on the table and his hands clasped behind his head, fingers lost in his unruly mass of straight black hair that he hadn't had cut in ages. His mouth was shaped in an O and he was blowing a perfect smoke ring. Swen was leaning against the open door of the old armoire, pressing it back against the wall, oblivious to the stress he was putting on the fragile hinges and laughing derisively. Plainly, he had been up all night because his eyes were bloodshot and his shirt, which was bright pink as usual, was wrinkled and sweat-stained. Between them, squatting on a fitting stool from the shop, like the monkey in the middle, was Petey with an open bag of chips on the floor beside him and a joint gripped tightly in his fist. His mouth hung open in admiration, his eyes following the progress of the smoke ring as it rose, elongating and thinning but never breaking the circle until it bumped against the ceiling and dissolved. I had made Thomas promise never to let my brother smoke with them, not even a cigarette.

"Petey! What are you doing here?"

All three heads turned toward me. There was a groan from Swen.

"I'm cool, Imo," Petey told me, waving his joint to prove the point.

"No, you're not cool, Petey. You better go home. You're not supposed to be here."

"Hey, Jackson. He's a big boy now and he said he's cool," said Swen.

"I'm not talking to you."

"I'm cool, Imo, honest."

"Mum called, Petey. She's been looking for you. She needs you home right away. Now," I said, blurting out the first lie that came to mind. "And she wants you to pick up some ice cream."

"I bought chips, Imo."

"She wants ice cream, Petey. Ice cream is cool too."

"Ice cream is cold, Imo." He giggled.

"She wants you to shoo. She's the shoofly lady," said Swen.

"Mum wants you home," I repeated obstinately, aware I was getting nowhere. "We're supposed to go over early."

"Okay." Thomas brought his feet to the floor with a crash. "I guess we have to go. Maybe see you later, eh," he said lazily.

Swen pushed away from the wall. The door of the armoire shifted but didn't swing closed and I saw that one of the hinges had pulled loose from the old wood. "So long, sucker," he muttered as he slouched out the back door.

Thomas was bemused when I told him later that I had invented the phone call from my mother.

"Why not let your brother smoke a joint once in a while?" he asked mildly. "What can happen? I'll keep an eye on him."

"That's not the point," I told him, still furious. "He has enough strikes against him. He doesn't know when to stop. He'll turn into a zombie if he starts smoking pot."

"A zombie? Like me?" Thomas let his head flop sideways and with his eyes closed and his arms outstretched began to stagger about the room, bumping into tables and moaning theatrically.

It was impossible not to laugh, but I wasn't going to back down. "No, of course not like you. Petey is different; you know that."

"So let him be different. It's not his fault. He couldn't be a zombie if he tried. He's too busy all the time trying to be normal. You and your parents never leave him alone for two minutes. You set all these impossible standards for him. He just wants to be one of the guys. Give him a break, eh."

"It's not that simple, and you know it. It's better not to get him started on something like that. It's one thing if he gets it from you. What if he tries to buy it from someone else, or off the street? He's vulnerable."

Thomas shrugged. "Okay, okay, so I won't give it to him anymore. It was the first time anyway."

We were late for dinner in the end because Petey fell asleep and there seemed no point trying to wake him up. I never mentioned the incident to my parents, knowing it didn't reflect well on Thomas. Instead I concocted a story about some last-minute repairs for The Man With The Wide Feet. But I did give Petey a lecture the next day and convinced myself that I had nipped things in the bud. Thomas would keep his word, I was sure, but Swen had no scruples.

Now here I was being led down the garden path by Petey of all people. I was still standing in the hall, debating what to do with his gift, when my mother came through the front door.

"I'm glad I caught you. We need to talk," she said in a low, urgent voice, fixing me with her gaze.

I shoved the joint in my pocket, feeling caught out. "I was just on my way to the shop. I promised Charmaine I'd make out a cheque for her."

"Charmaine can wait," she said shortly.

I followed her into the living room and sat down across from her. We contemplated each other in silence. Her glasses were slipping down her nose in a way I had always found endearing, but her mouth was set in a thin line and I could see her jaw working, an old habit she had of grinding her teeth when she was upset about something or if she'd run out of cigarettes. She had given them up a couple of years earlier but she looked like she needed one now; her face was grey. I suspected she sometimes snuck off behind the garage to indulge when Petey was being particularly unreasonable. I could hardly blame her.

"This business about an abortion. You're in no state to decide something like this. You must talk to someone."

"It's a termination," I corrected her. "And anyway, there's nothing to talk about. For god's sake, Mother, I'm twenty-nine years old. I can make up my own mind."

"Well then maybe you should just listen."

I sighed and gritted my own teeth.

"I've never told you this. I've never told anyone, not even your father. There was no reason for either of you to know." She paused and brushed a hand across her face as if removing a cobweb, then shook herself and continued. "After Petey was born, and we realized that there was something wrong, we made the decision not to have any more children. The doctors told us his condition was an accident of birth, not anything hereditary, but they hadn't been much help up till then so it seemed safer not to take a chance." She paused again and gave a kind of a low sighing moan. "Your father and I were both determined not to send Petey to an institution, and I knew it was going to take all my time and energy to look after him. But then of course I got pregnant again. With you. I felt ill from the very first week. I was convinced there was something wrong. I'd been perfectly healthy with Petey. The doctor pooh-poohed it, told me I was being foolish, but I knew I couldn't—" she stopped and corrected herself. "I knew I shouldn't go on. I tried to miscarry, but it didn't work."

I was stunned. "You wanted to end your pregnancy! With me?"

Her voice rose. "There was no possibility of what you so blithely call a termination in those days."

"So what did you do?" I asked hesitantly, not sure I wanted to know.

"To begin with I douched like crazy and when that didn't work, I rode my bicycle into a tree and broke my leg."

I knew that my mother had broken her leg while pregnant with me. It was a family legend, always narrated with humour though I understood that it had been a difficult time. "You can't argue with an inanimate object; just ask your mother," my father used to say when I lost my temper over a toy or puzzle. She had hobbled around on crutches for weeks, her leg encased in a full-length cast, beset by morning sickness that went on much longer than usual and barely able to cope with the obstreperous, developmentally delayed Petey, who could still barely speak.

"You crashed your bicycle on purpose?" I asked, half-horrified, half-admiring.

"I think the doctor had his suspicions."

"What did he say?"

"He said that pregnant women had no business riding bicycles. Only a selfish beast or a criminal would take a risk like that. He told me it was a miracle I hadn't miscarried and that I should stop feeling sorry for myself and start thinking about the baby. He was a horrible man. I never liked him, but he arranged for a nurse from the VON to come in every day for an hour until the cast was off. I suppose nowadays I'd be given a pill. You mustn't think I'm sorry I had you."

It had never crossed my mind that I might not be wanted or needed. As a child I had thought of myself as the epicentre of the family, my mother's indispensable assistant when Petey was home, her comforter when he was away at school. At the age of five, coached by my father, I learned to take her a cup of tea in bed in the mornings when Petey was away at school; there was no possibility of anyone sleeping in if he was home, not even for the dog. It occurred to me now that a cup of tea from a five-year-old couldn't have been much comfort to her. Had she even wanted tea? Nowadays she drank coffee in the morning. I had a vision of her on her hands and knees, working her way up the stairs with a cloth and a bowl of water, scrubbing at a line of slopped tea stains that led to the bedroom.

Petey was another matter. By the time I could speak in sentences, I considered myself his mentor, a sort of older younger sister who could interpret the world for him. I still did, I realized. But that was the edited version of events—selective memory at work—because as I grew older I had resented having a retarded brother. I couldn't count the times I had refused to let him play with Charley and the gang, though they never objected.

In the end it had been too much for her and they did send Petey to an institution, though not permanently. It was an expensive decision. Most of his classmates were less capable than he was and rarely saw their families, but it was the best they could find for him. The Bastion Training School for Retarded Boys, it was called, and he had hated everything about it except the uniform. He hated that too when he learned what it meant to have the word *retarded* embossed in bright red letters on the back of his jacket. But he held no grudges. When it was all over, he was just happy to be home for good. I had no doubt he would have been happier if he'd never gone at all.

"Maybe it would have been better if you had miscarried," I muttered.

"Don't be stupid. That's not what I'm trying to say. I can't imagine life without you." She leaned over and put a hand on my arm, but I shrugged it away.

"What *are* you trying to say?" I demanded angrily.

She sat back and eyed me in silence, pressing her lips together as if deciding whether to continue. Finally she spoke. "That doctor I went to was a nasty man—I never went back to him after you were born—but he was right. It's time for you to stop thinking about yourself and start thinking about your baby. It's Thomas's baby too and I don't have to tell you how much he wanted a child. He would want you to have it. You're not the first person to become a single parent and you won't be the last. You know we'll help. Please understand what I'm saying. You have to think this through. Please." She stood up and left the room without waiting for my reply.

I sat for a while, trying to make sense of my mother's revelation. She'd been a good mother. I'd had a happy childhood; no more difficult than anyone else's; fed and clothed and loved, at least I had felt loved, which I supposed was all that mattered. Had she actually ridden her bike into a tree in a desperate attempt to miscarry? It seemed preposterous. Surely she was exaggerating. I could ask my father, but perhaps she really hadn't told him. Lucky him, I thought grimly. Certainly it was the last thing I wanted to know. I felt enraged. How could she? And what was the point of telling me now? The world had changed. The decision was mine to make and I had already made it, I told myself.

Plowing Under

The apple tree is up to its armpits in mud. The field is rising. The water has drained away and the long yellow grass has flattened and disappeared under loads of fill. Hour after hour, all day long, trucks laden with boulders and gravel, trailing stinking black smoke, rumble around the corner and down the road to Finney's house, where they turn and lurch down a rutted dirt ramp into the field, gears grinding harshly in protest. They wheel in a wide circle, engines snorting and farting while a man in a red hardhat with a clipboard in his hand waves and shouts and jerks his head, spewing out a stream of words that no one, not even the workmen, can understand. Ignoring the thrust of his angry thumb, the trucks rear up and dump their loads at his feet, forcing him to stumble backwards and wave his clipboard, and then they lumber back up the ramp and roar away, faster now because they are empty and in a hurry to fill up again.

The contractor is going to build two new houses in the field and even though they're not even started yet, those houses are bought and paid for already. A family with a little girl, the exact same age as Imo, is going to live in one of them. The farmer will be gone by then and the farmhouse will be empty. Already the one-horned goat has been taken away snorting and kicking in the back of a pickup.

It'll take all summer and at least a thousand loads of dirt to fill the field to the top of the bank, and each time a truck thunders by, the houses shake on their foundations and the windows rattle. It's a godawful din, Imo's mother says, and a good thing that Petey is away at school because he can't bear any kind of commotion and especially not loud noises unless he's the one who's making them. Tillie won't go outside at all. Yesterday she spent the whole day in the cupboard under the basement stairs, and when Imo coaxed her out for her supper, she left behind a yellow puddle on the floor. Imo pretended she didn't see it so she wouldn't have to wipe it up. Finney's mother has threatened to go home to Sweden until it stops; already she is packing and his sisters are packing too. If they leave, Finney will have to go with them. He'll be sorry not to go swimming in the lake with his friends, but he cannot let his family travel without a man. He has a duty.

Mrs. Dunster has bought a fancy new ostrich feather duster from the Fuller Brush Man who came around last week. It cost five dollars, which is a real fortune and too much to fork over for a bunch of feathers on a wooden stick, but she doesn't care because she's going to give the bill to the man with the clipboard. Rupert brought it outside to show them. He brushed it over the wooden tulips under the living room window and said "Presto" and the painted blooms turned bright red and bright yellow again. And then he held it up over his head and did an ostrich dance, kicking up his feet and cavorting around the yard, yelling, "Watch out for Magic Man!" and reeling in wider and wider circles—like a chicken with its head cut off, Charley said—until he danced right out into the road in front of a truck and it swerved into the stone pillar to avoid him. A rock fell off the back right onto his head and nearly knocked him out and the pillar toppled over and rolled partway down the bank. The driver jumped down from his cab and swore at Rupert in French, and Mrs. Dunster rushed out in her cowboy boots and her pink housecoat with the horses jumping every which way and stood on the road with her hands on her hips and screamed at him in English. And then she grabbed Rupert by the arm and told him that if he ever did that again, she would use the duster on him no matter how much it cost and she hauled him into the house and he wasn't allowed out for the rest of the day.

Now the children must watch from across the road. They stand at the edge of Imo's property, craning their necks to see over the bank. A bulldozer is pushing the loads of fill out into the middle of the field and spreading it around. "If there's anything you don't need, just toss it over the bank," Charley says. This morning the farmer towed an old hay wagon with rickety wooden sides out past the apple tree and the place where the stream used to be until he was nose to nose with the curved steel blade of the bulldozer; then he stood up on the tractor seat and jumped across into the wagon and started heaving cardboard boxes over the side. They burst as they hit the ground, disgorging boots and socks, and a bucket of potatoes with long white tentacles—enough to feed a whole family for a year at least—until Madame tramped over to the apple tree in her gumboots, waving her arms and shrieking to make him stop, but by then the wagon was empty.

"He's going to buy all new stuff with the money from the contractor," declares Rupert. "He's throwing out everything in the farmhouse and it's all going to be plowed under. Everything. Even the old man's leg, maybe even Old Gramps himself." He hops around in a circle on one leg, pretending to be Papa Chaput and then he falls down and lies stock still, with his eyes closed to show he is dead.

"It is not a time to make a joke, I think," Finney says gravely. "It is better to give these things to the poor people."

But the farmer is not leaving everything behind because out in front of the farmhouse, filling the whole driveway, is a van with a gaping black hole in its side. And at this very moment two men in dirty brown overalls are carrying furniture up a wooden ramp into its shadowy interior. Imo has seen them. This morning when she walked by on her way to the mailbox, there was a long blue couch with a sag in the middle sitting on the lawn and the men were carrying Papa Chaput's old rocker down the front walk. Standing in the open doorway, with the farmer's red-and-black-checked shirt over her blue-flowered dress and her beautiful bouffant hairdo all flat, was Madame, calling to them in a cross voice because the stuffing was coming out through a hole in the back and scattering across the grass. A few minutes later, when Imo was on her way home again, there was a long wooden sideboard beside the couch and the moving men were manoeuvring a chest of drawers down the front steps. They carried it right out onto the grass but when they set it down next to the sideboard, the drawers opened and the top one fell all the way out.

Floppy white underwear tumbled out, elephant underwear, Imo thought, bulky blue knitted bloomers, a lady's brassiere big enough for a lady giant and edged with a mile of pink lace, a tangle of stringy grey elastic with a nylon stocking dangling from a little clip, and then an alarm clock, and a picture in a frame and a comb and a hairbrush and a mirror with a silver handle. An oblong wooden box rolled end over end across the grass, right up to the elm tree, and the lid popped open and the contents spilled out in a shower of silver and gold. One of the moving men, the short one with a rip in the knee of his overalls and a cigarette pack sticking out of his back pocket, said "Taberwit," which was a swear word for French people, and the other man, who was tall and skinny, looked over at Madame and raised his hands above his head as if she might shoot him and gave a shrug. Madame started yelling and waving her arms and the short man said, "Taberwit" again and put the drawer back and then they were all yelling and arguing and none of them had noticed Imo.

There, winking up at her from a hollow in the roots of the elm tree was a silver locket on a silver chain. She knew what it was because her mother had one just like it; inside there is a picture of Imo's grandmother, the one she has never met. When her mother dies, that locket will belong to Imo, but it's a long time to wait and maybe she wouldn't need to die ever if Imo could have this one. Slipping behind the elm tree, she stooped down and walked her hand along the grass but just as her fingers closed around the silver oval, the tall, skinny mover held up a pair of frilly pink panties and said, "Ooh la la" in a high, pinched voice, pushing out his lips and twisting them in a funny way. There was a screech from the steps and Madame came charging across the yard, elbows bent, arms churning. She snatched up the panties and stuffed them back in the drawer, all higgledy-piggledy. Then her eye fell on the box leaning against the trunk of the elm tree, tipped on its side and empty, and she plopped down on all fours and started crawling across the grass, grunting and gasping and peering at the ground, plucking each piece of jewellery from its hiding place and holding it up to the sky to check for damage before replacing it in the box: a long, looping pearl necklace, a brooch in the shape of a flower, a copper bracelet. Then the alarm clock shrilled and she raised her head and her eyes looked right into Imo's.

"La Petite!"

Imo turned to run but her feet wouldn't work properly, and all at once she was on the ground with her foot caught on a root of the elm tree, and for a long minute she couldn't breathe because the wind was knocked out of her. Madame stood over her, red-faced and panting. Out of the corner of her eye Imo could see the locket sparkling in the grass where anyone might find it but nobody had. Her fingers closed around it and she raised her arm and held it out. Madame gave a little moan that meant she was glad and clutched it to her chest and then she reached out to help Imo up but Imo was already on her feet and running. A pain like an arrow shot up her leg and she knew for sure her knee was bleeding. Behind her she could hear Madame's voice calling her back but she was all the way home before she stopped running.

Rupert and Finney have a plan. After supper, when the trucks are gone for the day and it's halfway dark, they're going to sneak over to the field and rescue all the stuff the farmer threw away. It's called a salvage operation and it'll be like diving in the ocean for sunken treasure, Rupert says, except they will need shovels instead of flippers. While the farmer is smoking his after-dinner pipe, they will haul everything up the slope on Charley's toboggan, which has escaped the bulldozer and is teetering on top of a boulder. And anything they don't need for the fort, Finney's mother will take to the Goodwill except for the toboggan, which belongs to Charley. But first Finney is going to write a note to Madame in French, explaining what they have done and listing everything they have salvaged. Anything she wants, they will return to her. He won't be able to write it until the day after tomorrow though because he'll need help from his tutor. It will be Imo's job, Finney says, to deliver the note once it is written because, now that she has been to the funeral, she must be a friend of the family. Imo is not so sure. She thinks maybe she was a friend of Papa Chaput because she helped him when he was dying, but she doesn't want to be a friend of the farmer, not ever, and it's too late to be friends with Madame because you can't be friends with a person if you tried to steal her locket even if that person doesn't know it.

She's not going on the salvage operation either because she has to walk stiff-legged and even now, hours after lunch, bubbles of dark red blood ooze up through the gauze bandage whenever she bends her knee. It's only a scrape, her mother says, and it's bound to be better in a day or two. There's no need to be dramatic. But Finney thinks she might require an amputation and Charley is keeping a sharp eye out for Papa Chaput's leg, the aluminum one, just in case. The very second he sees it, he has promised to go after it even if he has to dive right in front of the bulldozer. It will be too big for her now, of course, but she can save it for when she grows up.

Imo doesn't want to think about growing up; she doesn't want to think about having an amputation; and she doesn't want to stand around watching the bulldozer either, not if it's going to take all summer. And she doesn't see why the contractor has to build a house over the apple tree when there are so many other empty places. If a little girl does move in, she's never going to speak to her, not ever, not even if they were born at the exact same minute.

It's hours and hours till the farmer has his supper, and she's fed up with waiting. She wishes she could crawl into the cupboard under the stairs and snuggle with Tillie but she can't because of the yellow puddle. The trucks roll back and forth in clouds of dust and charge down the ramp to dump their loads with claps of thunder. Slowly the belly of the field is swelling. The apple tree reaches toward the sky and waves its pale green arms but she doesn't wave back.

Alligator Skin Pumps

The first thing you learn when you work in a shoe store is that just about the whole world has difficult feet. The list of ailments is long and revolting: hammer toes, claw toes, heel fissures, creeping fungus, fallen arches, plantar warts, fasciitis, corns, calluses, bunions, and great fat watery blisters that burst, leaving behind raw red patches of skin and occasionally an unsightly yellow stain inside a brand-new shoe that is immediately relegated to the sale table. Most people blame their suffering on poorly fitting shoes. In my experience at least they rarely consult a doctor. Mostly they grin and bear it. Better to cut a hole in a hundred dollar shoe to ease a bunion than to allow some old sawbones to cut off one's toe.

Even Marie-Josephine, who wore sensible shoes all her life, had a hard time walking the half-mile to church because of a broken toe that had never been set. Joseph had a severed ligament curled up like a worm at the base of his big toe, and Madame Poulin shuffles around in her pink pompom slippers because she's too embarrassed to show the doctor her ingrown toenail though she has no qualms at all about showing it to me.

Swen was no exception. According to Marie-Josephine, he had the flattest feet she'd ever seen and a chronic case of athlete's foot. He acquired most of his footwear at the store, not out of loyalty but because she gave him a huge discount. After she died, Thomas fitted him out with discontinued stock for free on Sunday mornings. There would be none of that now, I promised myself as I let myself in the back door of the shop, Petey's joint stowed safely in my pocket. Surely he would have the sense to stay away.

The workroom was deserted. Gaston, who starts early, had gone for the day, leaving behind a jumbled heap of unfinished repairs. Charmaine was out front dealing with a customer. I could see the curve of her back as she bent over to fit someone. Her cheerful voice, friendly but deferential, carried into the workroom, no doubt the same old patter about the style or fit of the shoe at hand. I couldn't make out a single word.

"Remember, French is not your mother tongue. It will come back over time as your brain recovers from the shock," Dr. Campeau had assured me. But how could he possibly know? And how long would it take? If I moved back to the village now, I would be living in a foreign country. Almost everyone in the village speaks English of course; there would be no problem communicating, and in the summer at least half our customers are English tourists. But the language of everyday life, of rumours and confidences and love, is a peculiar variation of archaic seventeenth-century French, interspersed with modern-day English.

I slipped into the alcove and lowered myself into Marie-Josephine's old blue platform rocker. It was the shop itself that was antique, I thought, surveying the workroom. Thomas had hung on to all the old equipment. The day of the accident he had been tinkering with a last made by Joseph's grandfather. An adopted son he may have been, but no one could deny he belonged.

Closing my eyes, I leaned back and allowed myself to imagine that it was Marie-Josephine out front chatting with a friend and listened for the eruption of her infectious, full-throated laughter. I could hear the harsh rattle of Joseph's ancient sewing machine, his hoarse chuckle as he joked with Thomas, and the background babble of the old black and white TV mounted on the wall. I understood then that it was not they who had left me; I had deserted them.

That first summer, the summer of my green sandals, Petey calls it, I could hardly tear myself away. Thomas and I, oblivious to anyone but ourselves, spent our evenings hanging out in the shop, eating takeout meals in front of the TV. More than once we fell asleep and awoke to a snowy blur on the screen long after the station had signed off.

I can remember pedalling home along the Lakeshore Road at three in the morning by the light of a three-quarter moon, with Thomas loping beside me, breathless and panting, his hand on the saddle to slow me down. If I surged ahead, he would fall to his knees yelling, "Loup Garou" and howl at the moon, forcing me to turn back and ride around him in wobbly circles, giggling and just out of reach. More often than not I slept in the next day.

One morning I wandered into work an hour late and was confronted by Marie-Josephine, who was standing in the foyer arms akimbo.

"You are unwell?" she demanded.

Over her shoulder I caught a glimpse of my lover in the workroom doorway, unshaven and bleary-eyed, his hair still tousled from sleep. I looked away, repressing a grin. The floor by the bay window was piled with shoeboxes. We were having a sale, I remembered belatedly. It was to start that very morning and I had promised to come in early to make a display.

"Oh my god, the sale! I forgot." Clapping a hand to my head, I made a dash for the window and began opening boxes, pulling out shoes willy-nilly.

Unimpressed by my theatrics, Madame Laviolette stepped over to the door, rattling her keys. "It's too late for that now, Imogene. Come, please."

Startled, I followed her up the outside staircase to the apartment, where she sat me down in the dining nook that overlooks the street. She stood across from me, leaning on the back of a chair, breathing heavily, winded by the short climb. I waited nervously for her to speak.

Only a week earlier I had been seated in the same chair, gorging on cassoulet, impressing them all with my linguistic prowess, or so I thought, by naming each ingredient in French as I speared it with my fork. Now I sat biting my lip afraid I was about to lose my job. It hardly seemed fair to blame me for our affair, as if I was the scarlet woman and Thomas the proverbial babe in the woods, though I was an idiot to have stayed so late.

"You must set a date for the wedding," Marie-Josephine announced without any preamble when she had caught her breath.

I gaped at her, too astounded to even blush.

"If you carry on like this, we will lose too much business. People will go to that shopping centre and then how can we afford to pay you? It's too much for me now with my heart." She put her hand to her bosom in the characteristic gesture she used when arguing with Joseph or reviewing the accounts.

Thomas and I had known each other for nearly four months by then, but not once had it occurred to me to consider his parents' point of view, or anyone else's for that matter. I had a high school friend who had moved in with a fellow student from McGill. Living in sin, we called it then. Neither of their families would speak to them, but the resulting scandal had no effect on anyone's livelihood.

Marie-Josephine lowered herself into a chair. "It's no good to pretend," she said wearily, clasping her hands together on the table in front of her. "Our Thomas is an artist. It is in his soul. He should have taken his scholarship to study at Beaux Arts but he wants only to make shoes. To have a son who will carry on with the shop, this is wonderful for us of course." She sighed. "Only he doesn't understand so much about the finance, eh. Already in a few months you have learned more than him."

She wasn't going to fire me. She wanted me to stay, to marry her son. I stared down at my sandals; the delicate pale green leather was already scuffed but they were still the most beautiful shoes I had ever owned. I felt breathless; my heart thudded in my chest.

"He will do it if you tell him, Imogene."

I stood up, knocking over my chair, and fled down the stairs only to find my passage blocked by a knot of eager bargain hunters waiting for the sale to start. Rattling the doorknob and scowling was Madame Poulin. She would hang about trying on shoes while other customers twiddled their thumbs and more than likely she would leave without buying anything; I knew that already. But once she had put in an appearance, half the village would follow. And if she spied something she considered a real steal, her children, grandchildren, great-grandchildren, and any number of nieces and nephews would arrive en masse. I knew that too. She was old and grumpy and impossible to please, but she owned half the village. It was vital not to keep her waiting. I pounded on the door and eventually Joseph appeared in his leather apron, a bright red high-heeled shoe with a broken heel in hand. Clearly puzzled to find the door locked and me on the outside, he let us all in.

For the rest of that day I concentrated on selling shoes. I went straight home after work and spent the evening holed up in my room. Agonizing. I wanted Thomas; I had no doubts on that score. But to be proposed to by someone's mother—it was mortifying.

The next day in the shop we tiptoed around each other. I suspected that Marie-Josephine or perhaps Joseph must have cornered Thomas as well—maybe even proposed to him on my behalf—and assumed that we would get together that afternoon, which was Wednesday and half-day closing, to discuss things in private, maybe even have a laugh at their expense. But just before lunch he left to drive taxi for his cousin, who had, quite conveniently it seemed to me, come down with pneumonia. Thomas filled in for him that evening as well and every night for the next two weeks.

By Friday of the second week, we were barely nodding at each other in passing and I had made up my mind to quit. I was putting on my coat, working up my nerve to announce my decision to Marie-Josephine before going home, when he grabbed my arm and hustled me out the back door into the front seat of a waiting taxi.

"Where to, mademoiselle?" Thomas grinned, making no move to kiss me.

It was all I could do not to throw myself in his arms. I pressed myself against the back of the seat instead.

"Does your cousin know you're driving people around in his taxi without turning the meter on?"

"It's not his anymore."

"Whose is it then?" I asked, feeling the blood rise to my cheeks. Thomas appeared not to notice.

"It's mine. He sold it to me cheap"

"Why would he do that? Is he going out of business?" I asked, fighting back tears.

He took my hand and squeezed it. "I told him I needed it for my honeymoon."

Having made the decision to marry, neither of us could bear to wait. We opted for a small wedding. My mother and Marie-Josephine campaigned for a larger, more traditional affair, but as Thomas warned me whenever I wavered, that would have meant inviting half the village, including La Pantouffle and her tribe, as well as months of planning and inordinate expense. In the end my father offered to host a party for us the following summer and we compromised on that.

So we were married one afternoon just before Christmas, in a small, informal ceremony in my parents' living room, a justice of the peace presiding. It was strictly the immediate family, which meant my parents and Petey and, at my mother's insistence, Rita and Darwin Dunster, because "they have known you all your life and what would they think?" And of course, Swen.

Marie-Josephine, who never once referred to our little talk, was ecstatic when we set the date. She insisted on treating all the guests, even the Dunsters, to new shoes: Italian loafers for the men and low black alligator-skin pumps with gold buckles, also Italian, for the women, except for mine, which were made by Thomas and were a deep red to go with a long paisley wool dress I insisted on wearing.

After the ceremony we had a little party with fancy sandwiches from Woolworth's and a cake made by my mother. By the time we had finished the toasts, everyone was tipsy. Marie-Josephine produced an ancient, scratchy album of fiddle music and, having organized Petey to act as disc jockey, insisted on dancing with my father. My mother, meanwhile, took off a shoe to show Joseph her bunion.

"Madame, this is not a bunion; it is a serious offence to the foot," he said gravely. "You must ask my son to make you some shoes."

"Or some new feet," suggested Swen with a high-pitched giggle. Having showed up half an hour late, sporting grubby white jeans and the same rumpled shirt I had seen him in the day before, he was making up for lost time at the drinks table.

I gave Thomas a not-so-gentle nudge. "Come on. Let's get out of here." We were to spend the Christmas week at a ski resort in the Laurentians, a gift from my father, who had expected to fork over for a lavish wedding. A two-hour drive in the dark stretched ahead of us and the weather report predicted snow.

The others followed us out, all brandishing odd shoes supplied by Marie-Josephine from a collection of unclaimed repairs, both Petey and Swen clamouring to come with us, I remember, Petey hoping for a chance to drive, I suspect, and Swen out for a good time as usual. They chased us down the road, chucking shoes that were supposed to have been tied to the bumper. Halfway to the corner, Thomas slowed to a crawl and steered with his knee while he wiggled into his gloves. They caught up with us then and Petey thumped on the trunk with a shoe. Swen tried to open the back door and finding it locked, reached in through my window just as Thomas speeded up again. I rolled the window up quickly, trapping his hand and forcing him to run along beside the car. I suppose I was a bit drunk too because I remember feeling exultant at the sight of his pale face at the window, his eyes large with indignation, his mouth working frantically, the words muffled by the glass. It only lasted a moment. Hearing his panicked cries, Thomas braked and I came to my senses and released him, but I don't think Swen's ever forgiven me. I can hardly blame him. When I leaned out the window to wave as we rounded the corner, he was standing in the middle of the road, clutching his hand, staring after us, the first snowflakes swirling around his shoulders. Even now, years later, I can still hear him screaming out, "Thomas!"

Sitting in the back of the shop that day, trying to make sense of my mother's revelation, still determined to terminate my pregnancy, I seemed to hear it again and was jolted back to the present.

Charmaine was arguing with her customer; their disagreement had been escalating ever since I entered, I realized now, but I had been too preoccupied to notice. Peeking round the corner of the alcove, I saw her face in profile, red and flustered. It's easy enough to embarrass Charmaine, but she grew up helping in her father's pharmacy and is never ever rude to a customer. Even now she appeared more anxious and apprehensive than angry.

I stepped over to the counter, hoping to diffuse the situation. The floor was a confusion of open boxes with shoes scattered about. Standing by the window, in a pair of white and silver runners with an expensive fluorescent swoosh along the side, was Swen. He was wearing the inevitable white or once-white trousers and a bright orange T-shirt, the kind made of that cloth that changes colour in reaction to body heat. There were dark blotches under his arms and around his neck. He was rocking backwards on his heels, his hands in his pockets, his mouth set in an expression that was half-grin, half-sneer.

"Is there something the matter?" I asked.

They both turned toward me in surprise.

"This gentleman would like to put the shoes on his account, but I cannot find his name in the book." Charmaine held out the little leather-bound ring binder in which we recorded the names of customers who paid on instalment. It was a courtesy we extended to pensioners, contemporaries of the Laviolettes for the most part, and sometimes to families in financial difficulty, though it was simpler to offer them a substantial discount.

Swen took a step toward me. "I'm a friend of the family, aren't I, Jackson? We have an arrangement."

I wanted to deny it, to send him packing, but I felt breathless and leaned on the counter unable to speak.

"Tell her, Jackson," he said, jerking his head toward Charmaine. "Her brother, Pete, works for me. I gave him a job. I'm in landscaping now. No one else is going to take a chance on him, you can bet your life on that. He's not an easy guy to work with. We have an agreement, don't we, Jackson?" He leaned back on his heels with a triumphant smile.

I opened my mouth but could only stare at him in confusion. It wasn't just that he would fire Petey if I refused. He would involve him in something criminal, something more than the occasional marijuana cigarette, if he hadn't already.

"You can make an exception just this once," I told Charmaine.

"Yeah, write my name in your little book and send me a bill. I haven't got time to hang around. I got business. She knows where I live." He turned and swaggered out the door without waiting for a reply.

Charmaine was close to tears. "I'm so glad you came. I didn't know what to do. He was here for nearly an hour," she explained when the door had swung closed. "He tried on everything." She gestured at the boxes. "And those ones he picked are very expensive. Almost a hundred. I told him I would put them aside and he should come back later when you were here but he didn't want to do that. I know he is your friend but a real friend does not ask for a favour like that."

"He was Thomas's friend, not mine," I said grimly.

"He's living in the old farmhouse you bought."

"It's not my house anymore."

"But why did you give him the shoes? I don't think he will pay."

Why indeed? Why indeed? I couldn't explain.

A Legal Opinion

Once Charmaine had left for the day, I went upstairs and called my mother to tell her I'd be spending the night in the apartment. There were plenty of leftover casseroles in the freezer compartment of the fridge, I assured her when she offered half-heartedly to send my father over with a plate of supper, and it would be a waste not to eat them. I think we were both relieved not to be facing each other across the dinner table. I pulled out an anonymous crinkled aluminum container coated with frost crystals and, having determined that it was some sort of variation on lasagne, stuck it in the oven. I was only going through the motions. I probably wouldn't eat more than a couple of bites anyway.

While I waited for my dinner to heat up, I sat down at the table with a stack of unopened mail in front of me, trying not to think about Swen. It was several hours since our confrontation by then but my heart was still pounding. In a moment of weakness I had a struck a bargain with the devil and at any second I expected him to reappear. Down on the street I could see a group of teenaged boys gathered around the open hood of a car outside the service station. A few weeks earlier Swen would have been out there joking with them or else chatting up Madame Poulin's great-granddaughter who had just emerged from the late-night dépanneur with the latest addition to the family tree perched on her hip.

The Grande Dame herself was presiding over the sidewalk, wagging her finger at a dishevelled young man with a case of beer in one hand and a hardhat in the other. I wondered if he was her new tenant. She had rented Swen's room the very day he moved to the farmhouse apparently; he would have trouble finding anywhere else to stay if he decided to return to the village. Apart from a modest two-storey apartment building that housed mostly old age pensioners, Madame Poulin had the rental market sewn up and it seemed she had decided he was a liability. According to Charmaine, half the village agreed with her. People had put up with him out of respect for the Laviolettes, I supposed. Thomas had often made light of his foster brother's behaviour, but he wouldn't have been able to dismiss this afternoon's episode. It was blackmail pure and simple, and knowing Charmaine, it would be general knowledge by tomorrow if it wasn't already. People would think I was luring him back with a free pair of shoes, especially if they believed he was living in a house that belonged to me. I felt a surge of panic. Surely Charmaine would set them right about that. But would anyone believe her when half the village had been privy to the purchase?

Jeanette Lauzon, the real estate agent, had come to see me a couple of days after the funeral. "You are absolutely not committed to that house, Imogene," she assured me. "I've spoken to the vendor and she understands the situation. It's a legal problem of course; it'll take some time to release the deposit, but there won't be any penalty. You just have to sign some documents."

Jean-Louis Gauthier, the lawyer who was looking after the estate, had promised to draw up the papers, but I had never been in to sign them or to inquire about the deposit. It occurred to me now, as I waited for the casserole to heat up, that the money must still be in the trust account. It was time to do something about it.

First thing the next morning, after a restless night and a breakfast of cold lasagne, I made a beeline for Gauthier & Fils, which is upstairs above Le Bon Mouton, the old wool shop, owned for years by a couple of sisters widowed in the First World War. It still sells yarn though it now belongs to their nieces. They've expanded the inventory to include cheap fabrics from Asia, pricey handmade quilts, hand-woven blankets, and wool shawls with early Habitant designs.

"Jean-Louis is over at the new office for the rest of the week," the receptionist told me. "But perhaps Monsieur Claude can help you," she added in a bright voice.

Monsieur Claude, Jean-Louis's father and a contemporary of Joseph, had retired a few years earlier, handing the business over to his son with considerable fanfare. Six months later, after a Caribbean cruise, a month in France, and a week at home, he started heading into work again every day—much to his wife's relief and his son's chagrin, according to the gossip mill. He was a charming soul but long-winded, opinionated, and occasionally even interfering. He was a familiar figure around town, and I had often seen him in the shop, chatting with Joseph. Quite possibly we had been introduced, but we had never had a proper conversation.

"I can come back next week," I told the receptionist.

"No, no, he would be delighted to see you. He would love it. He has nothing—I mean, he's not busy today."

Before I could escape, she jumped up and rapped on his door, then disappeared inside. She emerged again almost immediately, followed by an elderly, white-haired gentleman with startling blue eyes. Unlike Jean-Louis, who in summer swanned around the office in Hawaiian shirts and sandals, the elder Gauthier was formally dressed in a light grey three-piece, very fine wool suit, quite possibly cashmere, and a powder blue, flowered silk tie. A pair of gleaming black leather dress shoes that could only have been handcrafted in another era somewhere in Italy or France completed this ensemble. Definitely museum quality, I thought. We shook hands and he ushered me into his office, which was larger than his son's with a panoramic view of the lake.

"I'm sorry, Jean-Louis is not available this week," he said beaming. "My Louis, he's a busy man these days. He came first in his class, you know. And now he's opened a second office over in Dollard, on the very same place where my cousin used to have his farm. He is making his office in the big stone barn where we used to pile the hay, if you can imagine such a thing. Of course he has to be over there every day until it's all organized. So now you have to deal with an old man." He gave me a sly smile. "Please, you must sit down." He sat down himself and leaned forward with his hands on the edge of the desk.

"Tell me, how I can help you, madame?"

Clearly he had no idea who I was. The receptionist had left a file on the desk but he hadn't had time to study it.

"It's about a property . . ." I hesitated, wishing I had insisted on waiting for Jean-Louis. "My husband was Thomas Laviolette. There was an accident," I said at length.

His face clouded with confusion. "Forgive me, madame. I did not realize at first who you were. I knew Thomas from a little boy. Always in the back of the shop, drawing his pictures, making things. For him his work was always his play. This was a terrible tragedy."

I nodded stiffly.

"There is some problem with a property?" He opened the file and began thumbing through. "But of course. There is something from the real estate right here. You will excuse me one second."

I waited in silence, contemplating my feet. I was wearing my old green sandals, well worn and much mended over the years. Thomas was always after me to junk them—a poor advertisement for the business, he said—but at my insistence he had relented and resoled them a few weeks before the accident. "For the last time," he told me.

Monsieur Claude gave a snort of surprise. "That was you and Thomas who bought the old Chaput place. It was big news in the village when Adélie decided to sell. Lots of times she put up the sign and then she changed her mind."

"We made a down payment, but the sale was never completed because of . . ." I let my voice trail off.

He nodded gravely. "Under the circumstances, of course, the deal did not go through. I remember that property very well. It was a farm, you know, not so long ago. Very good land. They grew everything, all kinds of vegetables, potatoes for the whole village. And there was an orchard too. The Apple House, that's what we called it. They had wonderful apples. All gone now." He shook his head. "The developers came in with their cash, you see, and the old man, he sold it, all that land, all those fields, everything except the farmhouse. It was his son Roland who made him do it. Roland, he never liked hard work too much. He wanted to live in the village. Old Papa Chaput, he didn't understand what would happen when he signed those papers. He got sick when he saw the machines digging up his fields. It killed him. That farm was home for him his whole life except when he went in the army. Adélie, she was not so happy either. She didn't want to leave the place where her babies were born."

Monsieur Claude sighed. "It was me that drew up the papers for him. I advised him to wait. 'You are making a big mistake, my friend.' That's what I told him, but he got mad, eh. He said it was none of my business. He wanted his Roland to make his own life, to be happy. Happy!" Monsieur Claude thumped the flat of his hand on the desk. "You know what Roland did with all that money? You know what he did? He drove a taxi for five months. Five months!" He held up a pale wrinkled hand, fingers and thumb spread-eagled. "And then, pfftt, he was gone, just like that. A heart attack." He slammed his hand on the desk. "Adélie, she was left all alone. She should have sold that house but she refused, eh. All these years she rented it out but she never made any repairs. Such a mess." He shook his head. "And now she is old, her nephew, he has told her she must sell." Monsieur Claude leaned forward across the desk. "How come you bought that house? Young people like you and Thomas, you have a good business, you don't need to live in a place like that."

I shifted uncomfortably in my seat. "We wanted a house," I said weakly.

"You were expecting children perhaps?"

"No, no children," I said more sharply than I had intended, shaking my head violently. "I grew up on . . ." I tried to think of the French name for Garden Crescent but all my mind could dredge up was club sandwich. "My parents live down the street," I offered. "The farm was still there when we moved in."

His eyes lit up. "Ah, so you remember the farm."

"I remember Papa Chaput too," I said, glad of the change of subject. "He had an artificial leg."

"Yes of course, a child would be impressed by that. Louis too.

He liked to copy the way the old man walked. He was too little to understand what he was doing." He studied my face. "Ah, so you grew up there on that street. You are English of course. I remember now when Thomas was married—so quick, all of a sudden to a girl from the development, an anglophone. Such a scandale. That was you."

Unaccountably after all these years, I blushed, though Monsieur Claude appeared not to notice. "But you are the one, the child who was there when the old man died. La Petite Anglaise. And you came to the house the day of the funeral. I was there too."

I nodded though I didn't remember him.

He sat back, lost in memory for a moment, then shook his head. "But that is not why you have come. There is a cheque here, a refund for your down payment."

"I've changed my mind," I said. "I want to keep it."

"You want to keep Maison de Pomme?" He blinked several times. "But why, my dear? It will be too much for you, a lady alone. The years are not kind to a house like that. It's not safe, that place. You cannot want to live there."

"Not really," I admitted.

"But of course, you will stay in the shop. That is the sensible thing. It is part of our history, almost as old as the village. All my life I have bought my shoes at Laviolettes'. Joseph brought these in for me especially." He rolled his chair out from behind the desk and thrust out his feet for me to admire. "He ordered them from New York, but they came all the way from France, eh. A whole shipment just for me. Ten pairs. I had to promise to buy every one. These are the last."

On closer inspection, I saw that the shoes, though gleaming, were worn out. The soles looked paper-thin and the vamps were deeply creased and cracked along the outer edge. On their last legs, I thought, stifling an unexpected and alarming urge to giggle.

"You must forgive an old man. My son tells me I don't know when to keep my mouth shut. But what is it you are going to do with this house if you're not going to live in it?" He sat back in his chair with his hands clasped under his chin and gazed at me expectantly.

I stared back at him blankly. I hadn't thought beyond evicting Swen, and I had no idea how I was going to do that. What made me so sure I would be able to stand my ground when only yesterday I had turned to jelly and handed over an expensive pair of runners free of charge? And I had no doubt that Swen would follow through on his threat to involve Petey in something criminal if I called the police.

"You are hoping to sell again, to make a profit perhaps?"

I shook my head and found myself blinking back tears. It was impossible. I would never manage it on my own. What was I thinking of? I would be in debt for the rest of my life.

"Now, now my dear, I have upset you. It is a difficult time. This matter is none of my business. It is up to you of course." He produced a box of tissues from a drawer. "Please, it is not necessary to explain."

But I needed to explain. The words poured out of me. I told him everything, about Thomas and Swen smoking pot on Sunday mornings, about Swen living in the farmhouse, trading on his friendship with Thomas to exploit Petey, paying him off with marijuana. Monsieur Claude listened intently, looking nonplussed but rapt at the same time. I was making his day, I could see that, but I couldn't stop.

"Now, now, my dear," he murmured when I dried up at last. "Please. You mustn't worry. I am familiar with this Swen. He's a bad apple, that's for sure. It's well known in the village. But this is not your fault. To buy a house, this is not a solution."

"If I own the house, I can evict him," I explained. "And if I don't, everyone's going to think we're collaborating," I added with a sniff.

"No, no. You are not responsible for this. I'm going to phone Adélie. She's an old friend. It's her house and it is her job to send him away. You are not to upset yourself anymore, please." He picked up the phone and spoke to the receptionist, tapping his fingers impatiently on the desk while she searched for the number. She must have put him through because a moment later his fingers stilled and he broke into a smile. "Adélie?"

There followed a long, animated, incomprehensible conversation in French, accompanied on his part at least by constant shifting in his chair, vigorous shaking of his head, and the occasional slap of his palm on the desk. It seemed to go on forever. I sat in my chair, dry-eyed now, feeling the lasagne turn over in my stomach each time his hand smacked the desk and fighting off an urge to lie down on the rug.

He hung up at last and turned to me. "That fellow is a caretaker. She doesn't like him too much but he said he was a friend of Thomas and he was interested to buy it himself. I told her, this Swen, he is a bad fellow. He has caused lots of problems for the village and especially for you. She remembers you, eh, from when you were a little girl. She is very sorry for your trouble. So now she is going to make him leave. Today, she said. She will tell him today." Monsieur Claude beamed at me, delighted with his success. "So, my dear, you don't have to buy that house at all. You must take your cheque straight away to the bank. Now everything is fine, eh."

It was too good to be true of course, but I did as he suggested.

The Checkerboard Cat Comes Back

Tillie has a bee in her bonnet. Her shoulders are hunched and she keeps ducking her head and pulling the wrong way against the leash, making choking sounds. She won't go past the farmhouse. Imo keeps telling her there's nothing to be scared of. The farmer and his wife have gone to the village in a taxi and they are never coming back. Their belongings are packed up tight in the moving van, waiting in the driveway for the men in dirty overalls to haul them away. All that's left is an old corn broom on the front stoop and two empty milk bottles.

But Tillie doesn't care about that. She wants to be with Petey. He came home from school last week and she trails him everywhere, even to the bathroom. At bedtime they snuggle together under the covers and he sneaks her cookies and Brussels sprouts and everything he didn't eat at supper. Yesterday they went hunting for dinosaur bones over in the swamp where Finney found the cow skull and the farmer used to throw his garbage. All Tillie found was an old boot, but Petey discovered Rupert and Finney's hideout and they were both inside. It's only a torn tarpaulin that got run over by the contractor's truck, held up by a bunch of sticks, so he lifted the flap and crawled in. They yelled at him to go away but his knees got stuck and he stood up and knocked down all the sticks. The tarpaulin caved in and everyone got smothered. Tillie gave Finney a nip. Rupert called Petey a big bozo and jabbed him right in the belly button with a stick and there was blood. Petey ran home bawling and he couldn't stop until Ireney let him have a whole bag of marshmallows from the cupboard over the fridge.

Mrs. Finney said it wasn't nice to give so much distress to a good boy like Petey when he was just starting his holiday and Mrs. Dunster told Rupert the hideout couldn't be a secret anymore and they better let Charley in too. Now they're having a meeting for boys only and afterwards there will be a ceremony with special badges. Charley is making them now with silver foil from an old cigarette packet. When he's finished, they're going to have a fire and roast marshmallows. Imo's not supposed to know but Petey blabbed everything.

She doesn't care. They will only be getting their bums wet sitting on the swampy ground and anyway she has her own badge from the cereal box, made of real tin. Down the hill on the road to the village there's a hollow stump where she can have her own fort. She's made a sign that says NO BOYS ALOUD in bright red crayon. And if Tillie ever quits gagging, they can fetch a green china mug from under the farmhouse verandah and maybe the little three-legged stool that's lying upside down on the grass to keep her bum dry. It will be just her and Tillie and the little girl who's going to live in the new house when she comes if she's not a sissy, but she'll have to fetch her own mug. The house is empty so it won't be stealing but she'll have to hurry in case somebody else moves in.

Houses are never empty, Finney says. They are full of the spirits of all the people who ever lived in them no matter if those people are alive or dead. Finney's grandmother who stayed behind in his old house in Sweden has written to say that she misses her family very much but they must not worry; she can feel their spirits. His two grown-up sisters cried like little babies when his father read out the letter at supper, and his silly old mother watered the soup, but Finney is happy because now he knows for sure and certain that when he goes back to Sweden, a part of him will stay with his friends in Canada.

Spirits are invisible, but you can tell they are there because they slam doors and make the floorboards creak. Sometimes you can feel them as they swish by, and if you open your ears and stand like a statue, you might hear the chirping and whistling of their spirit voices which are not like their real voices at all since they are made of air. At this very moment Papa Chaput might be down from heaven searching for his leg. After the moving van has left, Finney has it in mind to hide under the verandah and listen for the thumping and clumping.

Tillie's ears are pricked and her hair is bristling. A kind of singing is coming from inside the farmhouse. Imo holds her breath. The front door opens and there, wearing a blue kerchief to match her dress and filling the whole doorway, stands the real-life Madame Chaput. Calling and crooning, she bends over and places a green china bowl on the stoop.

"Minou, Minou."

And there is the cat with the checkerboard face slinking out from the dark under the stairs because it climbed a tree when it was time to go in the taxi. Tillie is tugging at the leash again. Her tail is an arrow and all of a sudden Imo is on the ground, a hot burn on her hand and a pain like a needle in her knee, and she can't move. There is a shriek of breaking glass and an explosion of snarling and caterwauling and when she peeks through her fingers, she sees the corn broom poking and jabbing at a whirling confusion of tails and fur on the stoop. And then the Checkerboard Cat shoots high into the air and lands on the doorsill with a yowl and the broom sweeps Tillie right over the edge onto the grass. With a yelp the spaniel scrambles to her feet and scuttles across the yard, her tail tucked in, the leash trailing.

Imo runs too because Madame is shrieking and swooping with the broom.

"Va t'en. Va t'en!"

And now here comes Petey pounding up the road, arms whirling like a windmill. And Charley is chasing after him with a long stick.

Tillie skins right through Petey's legs but Imo smacks up against her brother. His arms clamp round her and they sway together, his chest heaving, his shouts vibrating in her ear.

"Imo, Imo, guess what, Imo?"

Then he steps back and lifts up his shirt. Tucked in the waistband of his pants is the bag of marshmallows and they are for her! Charley's stick has a perfect point for roasting them and she can have it too. He made it himself—there's a gash on his thumb to prove it—and she is in the fort! But hurry! The fire is already started. Rupert and Finney are waiting.

Up at the farmhouse Madame stands at the edge of her yard, looking back at them. She has pulled off her kerchief and now she is scratching her head.

"She had a bee in her bonnet," says Charley.

And it's hard to run because they are laughing.

Eating Cake

After depositing Monsieur Claude's cheque in the bank, I went straight to Garden Crescent, feeling guilty about deserting Charmaine again but too tired to be of any real help in the shop. I found my father in the garden, wearing an old fedora and a pair of floppy hip waders he could only have acquired at a garage sale because he has never been fishing in his life. He was hosing down the side of the house, sending an occasional spray of water toward the roof where the squirrel was running back and forth, chattering at him.

"It was your mother's idea," he said, looking sheepish when I remarked on his getup. "That ruddy squirrel's made a hole in the siding in behind the lightning rod. Looks like it might be a nest. He probably figures he's going to spend the winter there. I thought I might lure Petey home to help me plug it up. You know how he likes to dress up. But all he can think of is that wretched beast. He hasn't cut the Jacobs' lawn for over two weeks. He's going to lose all his customers if he's not careful."

I had seen Petey in the farmhouse yard as I rounded the corner, engaged in a tug of war over the clothesline with Lucy, but I hadn't stopped or even honked, leery of meeting Swen. He couldn't know yet that he was about to be sent packing, but I had no doubt he would figure out whom to blame.

"Well, he won't be going up there much longer," I said grimly. "His boss is about to be evicted."

"How do you mean?""

I related an edited version of my meeting with Monsieur Claude.

"That's all very well," said my father when I had finished, directing the hose at the squirrel, who was hovering at the top of the lightning rod. "But the fellow's not even home. He left last night for a month and he's put your brother in charge. He was over there till all hours yesterday, keeping the beast company. He wants to sleep there tonight."

"It doesn't matter where Swen is. Petey will have to stop hanging out there if the owner orders him to leave."

My father shook his head. "What about the dog? It has to be fed, and you know Petey, there's no way he's going to abandon her to the SPCA, not without a major battle. She's a vicious thing too. Look at her. Next thing you know, she'll take a chunk out of someone." He gestured toward the farmhouse, where Petey and Lucy were still roughhousing. Petey was snaking the rope along the ground and then flinging it in the air for Lucy to jump at. She was barking frantically.

"We could have a family confab," I suggested. Family meetings had been a regular occurrence for a while after Petey's graduation from the Bastion School. They had been suggested by one of the counsellors as a way of encouraging Petey to take responsibility for his actions. We discussed such burning issues as how many times a week he should go to the shopping centre for fries, how loud he should play his transistor radio, and how sick he had to be to stay home from the sheltered workshop. To begin with he had been keen, but the idea that he might take control of his life was an illusion for the most part and eventually he caught on to the fact that we were ganging up on him. The meetings had petered out after a year or so. My mother still organized one occasionally if she thought Petey was heading for a blow-up, but they were casual discussions that took place over Chinese takeout. I couldn't remember the last time I'd been in on a confab, though I was pretty sure they'd had one without me the day of the funeral, probably in an attempt to calm Petey down. I had a fuzzy recollection of feeling nauseated by the smell of egg rolls on his breath.

"Wouldn't hurt to try, I suppose," said my father, turning off the hose and looking doubtful.

"We could do it today, at lunch," I said, ignoring his half-hearted response. "Where's Mum?"

"She's gone shopping. We're having a little get-together this evening."

A groan escaped me.

My father gave me an odd, penetrating look. No doubt they'd had a confab about me while I was off in the village. And so what if they had? It was none of their business, I told myself. But I made a mental note to check for takeout cartons in the fridge.

"I think you might enjoy it if you feel up to it," he said.

"Who's coming?" I asked reluctantly.

"Well, Rupert for one. He flew in last night to talk to Charley and Rita about the business. Seems they've made a decision to sell. It might be a last chance to get your old gang together. But he's only here for three days and apparently things are in a bit of a mess over there so your mother offered our place. Charley's been trying to get hold of Finney."

"Finney? Is he coming?"

"I'm not sure."

It was ages since I'd seen Finney. Halfway through high school his family had moved back to Sweden. He had returned on his own a few years later to do postgraduate work in Montreal; he's a professor of linguistics at McGill now and married to a musician, a French Canadian, but we hadn't kept in touch. An exceptionally bright child, he had fulfilled his early promise; the same could not be said of me. I felt overwhelmed suddenly and wished I had stayed in the village. "I think I'll lie down for a while," I told my father.

"Good idea. Conserve your strength." He gave me another odd look.

A little after four I was roused by Petey. "Imo, Imo, wake up. Guess what? There's a surprise. You'll never guess. Guess what, Imo?"

"I give up," I said, rolling over, happy for once to confront reality. I had been dreaming that Lucy was out in the hall, leaping at my closed door, red-eyed and snarling, but it was only Tillie seconding the doorbell.

"You'll never guess. Rupert and Finney are coming! It's a reunion. They're coming at four o'clock. I had my shower already. You better get up."

The bell rang again, followed by an explosion of barking. "They're here! They're here." He rushed off to answer the door.

Wary of another round of condolences from old friends who were also semi-strangers, I took my time going downstairs and stood hesitating in the hall. I could hear my mother in the kitchen rattling the teacups and Petey's voice, high and excited, rising above a low babble issuing from the living room. "Where's the cat? Where's the cat?" And then Rupert's good-natured response. "Take it easy, man. It's coming. Just give me a minute to set things up."

Peeking in, I saw Charley and my father over by the window in conversation with a roly-poly little man with a white goatee, a friend of Rupert's perhaps; neither my father nor Petey had mentioned anyone else. I looked around for Finney, but he hadn't arrived yet. Perhaps he wasn't able to get away, I thought, disappointed but relieved too.

Petey was bent over with his back to me, pulling variously shaped objects from a black suitcase on the floor and handing them to Rupert. It was his game, I supposed, the one he had invented called Pounce. The board was an elaborate three-dimensional affair, a conglomeration of styrofoam, cardboard, plywood, and duct tape fashioned into a miniature town complete with roads, street signs, sidewalks, houses, trees, and even telephone poles. Rupert was wearing one of his father's trademark blue shirts with the Dunster Debug insignia on the breast pocket, to please his mother perhaps. Rita Dunster was perched on a straight-backed chair from the dining room, watching intently. She looked ready to pounce herself, I thought. Rupert glanced up and noticed me hovering in the doorway.

"Hey, Imo, you made it. Pete told me he yelled at you to wake up but you were snoring too loud to hear." He grinned his old provocative grin. "You're just in time. The games are about to begin."

"What happened to Finney?"

There was a burst of laughter from the window corner. "I think maybe he got old and fat," said the roly-poly man, striding toward me smiling broadly.

"Finney?" The boy I remembered had been the tallest in his class and morbidly thin, towering head and shoulders over Rupert, who'd had a late growth spurt at the age of eighteen. But the voice was unmistakeable. "Finney?"

"You haven't changed one bit. You're the same girl I remember," he exclaimed, clasping my hand in both of his. The face began to seem vaguely familiar. He was his mother without the accent, I realized. "Charley has told me of your bereavement," he said in a hushed voice, putting a hand on my arm. I stiffened immediately but he seemed not to notice. "Such a terrible tragedy. If I had known of it, I would have come to the funeral. Old friends should keep in touch and you are such a very dear, very old friend. You and Charley and Rupert, and of course Petey, you were my first Canadian buddies." He dropped my hand and threw his arms round me. I found myself hugging him back. After a moment I pulled away.

"I wanted to marry you. Do you remember?" he asked, his hands still on my shoulders. "What a bold girl you were, not at all like my sisters. But you wouldn't have me. In those days Charley was your man. I couldn't understand it." He chuckled. "I was a male chauvinist, that's what Gabrielle tells me. I've told her all about you. She's so sorry she couldn't come, but the children have their piano lessons this evening and they must not miss them. They're preparing for the conservatory exam. My wife lives for music, my children too."

How odd if I had married this funny little man, I thought; our children would be tone deaf, not that there had ever been any question of it, not even at the age of eight.

"But please, you must sit down. Your mother tells me you are not feeling well." He took my arm and guided me over to the couch. "You are expecting a baby, I understand. Gabby was ill with all our babies. She was in bed for months. But they are big and healthy now, two boys and a girl. Your baby will be fine too, I hope."

"I don't know," I mumbled, feeling myself flush. How many people had my mother told? How could she? She was trying to shame me out of ending the pregnancy. I would never trust her again.

Finney sat down beside me and took hold of my hand. "This is a miracle baby, a wonderful remembrance of your Thomas. I regret so very much we never met properly. I remember him well from the shop, of course."

For the second time that day I started to cry, tears of fury as much as anything, but this time I couldn't stop. Finney squeezed my hand. "You are among old friends. It's all right to weep. We cannot choose our feelings," he declared in the solemn tone I remembered so well from our childhood. I looked up with a sniff and managed a feeble smile. The room had gone quiet.

"You okay, Imo?" asked Petey.

I stood up. "I'll be right back."

My mother was in the kitchen, dishing up cake from an enormous roasting pan, her glasses slipping down her nose.

"Oh, Imogene, there you are. Did you see Finney? He brought this wonderful concoction. Isn't it huge? I expect we'll have to send half of it back with him. His mother used to make it apparently. He seemed to think you'd remember."

It was an upside down cake with what looked like cherry filling on the bottom and a thick dusting of icing sugar on top.

"Do you think we should have forks or spoons? I can't decide. It's awfully crumbly."

But I was not to be distracted. "How could you?" I hissed.

"How could I what?"

"You told him. You told Finney I'm pregnant. Who else did you tell?"

She turned toward me, serving spoon poised over the cake, her eyes startled. "Of course I didn't tell him. I've hardly said two words to him since he arrived. I've been in the kitchen. In any case, how could I? When you decided not to come home last night, I thought you might have—" she paused, "made an appointment." Her voice was carefully neutral.

"I went to see the lawyer, that's all," I said, my tone still petulant.

"Yes, so I gather. The only person I told is your father. You could hardly expect me not to," she defended herself.

"Well, Finney knows," I said, still furious.

"I'm afraid he must have mentioned it to Petey. You know what *he*'s like."

Petey! He'd probably announced to the whole street that he was going to be an uncle.

Before I could reply my mother handed me a tray. "Take this in for me, would you, and I'll be along with the tea in a minute."

In the living room, Rupert had finished setting up his game and, under Rita's critical eye, was giving a demonstration. The others had gathered round to watch.

"I don't like mice," Rita announced when Rupert explained what the blocks of wood on wheels were meant to be.

"Well, you can be the cat. Let me just show you how it works first. You move your mouse by pressing the Go button on the remote, like this, see?" Rupert sent a block spinning down the road.

"Looks like it's loaded in favour of the cat," observed Charley.

"What's its name?" demanded Rita.

"The cat? It doesn't have a name. It doesn't matter what its name is, Mom. That's not the point of the game."

"All cats have names. I think it should have a name," Rita insisted.

Rupert rolled his eyes. "Okay, we'll give it a name. How about we call it after Grandma's cat."

"It's dead," said Rita.

"I know it's dead, Mom, but it had a name when it was alive."

"Allison, it was called Allison," said Charley.

"Okay, we'll call this one Allison too. Every time a mouse makes it to the Big Cheese in the middle without getting pounced on, then Allison loses a life. She has nine lives so the mice have to get past her nine times unless they have a lot of babies."

"I don't see what that has to do with anything," said Rita frowning.

"I'll explain it to you later," said Rupert, tipping back and forth on the balls of his feet. "This isn't the real game, Mom. It's just a prototype. Why don't you have a whirl? You be the cat and Pete can be the mouse. How about it, Pete, want to give it a try?" He held out the remote.

Petey took a step back, looking uncertain. He likes games but he takes them much too seriously and it takes him forever to learn the rules. "I have to go out. I have to feed Lucy now."

My father called over from across the room. "I thought you already did that. Surely you don't need to go up there again."

"Have to feed Lucy," insisted Petey. "It's my job."

"You got a job, eh. That's great," said Rupert.

"Have to be responsible," said Petey, beaming.

My father sighed. "Don't stay all night."

"He'll be back as soon as he can, won't you, Pete? We're going to order in some pizza from La Dolce Vita," said Rupert.

When Petey had left, Finney offered round the plates of cake. "My mother still talks about how much you liked her pudding," he said, presenting me with the largest portion. "Last time she came for a visit, she brought us a big jar of lingonberries and she showed Gabby how to make it."

"Really, you mean those are lingonberries, not cherries?"

"It was a misunderstanding, you see. When we first came to Canada, my father insisted we practise our English at dinnertime. And my mother thought *cherry* was the word for lingonberry, because of the colour of course, so she served us up cherry pudding cake. It was only the next summer when the cherries were in season that she realized her mistake. And then for a long time she didn't want to admit it. So now we still call it by that name in English." He hovered expectantly, waiting for me to taste it.

"Do your children like it?" I asked, stalling for time, not sure I'd be able to keep it down.

He laughed. "They're Canadian. They like cherry pie filling out of the can. Do you remember the day I sneaked some out of the fridge and we hid under the kitchen table to eat it?"

I looked at him blankly.

"My mother discovered us and she was very cross because it was supposed to be for dinner, but she was so pleased for me to have Canadian friends that she only said we shouldn't take food without asking first." Finney chuckled. "And then you piped up, 'May I please have another helping, Mrs. Finney? My brother would like some too.' She's never forgotten. Don't you remember? You ate so much she was afraid you would be sick."

I forced myself to take a bite. The cake was pleasantly lemony but rather dry, the taste of the lingonberries reminiscent of cranberries rather than cherries. A dusting of icing powder floated into my nostrils, making me sneeze, and all at once I was in Finney's kitchen, sitting cross-legged on the cold, glossy blue and white-flecked linoleum, cocooned in the golden glow of the tablecloth that hung nearly to the floor, breathing in the mingled aromas of lemon-roasted potatoes, self-polishing liquid floor wax, and something indefinable that I knew to be the essence of Finney and his family and of that remote place on the far side of the world that I would never see called Sweden. My plate was half-empty before I remembered where I was.

Finney was still hovering. "You mustn't feel you have to finish it."

Grinning, I held out my bowl. "May I please have some more, Mr. Finney?"

Half an hour later, having polished off both Petey's and Finney's portions as well as my own, I sat replete on the couch, avoiding my mother's bemused gaze, and fending off Rupert's urging to challenge Rita to a game of Pounce, when we heard the back door slam.

"Petey?" my father called out. "Petey?"

There was no response, only Petey's heavy tread on the stairs, slow and lumbering. And lopsided somehow, as if he was dragging one foot.

"Why doesn't he come in?" asked my mother. "I wonder if that man has come back."

"I'll go see," I said, jumping to my feet, pleased to let someone else confront Rita.

As I mounted the stairs, I could hear water running in the bathtub. I tapped on the bathroom door. "Petey? It's me, Imo. Are you coming down? We ordered pizza. We got a Hawaiian for you."

The answer was a low moan.

"Okay if I come in?" I pushed the door open cautiously and stepped over his jeans, which lay in a crumpled heap on the floor, the once-white denim yellowed with grass stains.

He was sitting on the edge of the bathtub, stripped to his shorts, with one stockinged foot on the floor for balance and the other in the tub. He was bent over, clutching his calf.

"What's the matter?" I could see blood oozing between his fingers, running down his leg. The water in the tub was swirling with red.

"Petey, are you okay? What happened?"

He looked up, glassy-eyed. "Lucy bit me," he said in a wondering voice.

The Apple House

It was hours before my father called from the hospital. When the telephone rang, we were sitting in uneasy silence contemplating the congealing remains of three extra-large pizzas and watching Rita play Pounce. She'd been at it for most of the evening and was compiling a list of modifications she thought Rupert should make to the board. Relieved perhaps not to be arguing over the fate of Dunster Debug, he appeared to be taking her suggestions in good part. They had all insisted on keeping me company, even Finney, who had reneged on his promise to be home in time to read to his children.

"In this situation it is better not to be alone," were his words.

Too worked up to escape to bed and my usual state of semi-consciousness, I had protested only feebly. I was in an agony of self-recrimination. If only I had consulted Jean-Louis about the farmhouse when Swen first moved in, none of this would have happened. At the very least I should have been more insistent with my parents. Really, I should never have introduced Petey to Swen at all.

In my agitation, I had recklessly downed three slices of pizza on top of the cherry pudding cake, and by the time the phone rang my stomach was churning. The emergency room was backed up, my father reported, and there was no telling how much longer they would be. Petey's wound was not deep but he would need stitches and a tetanus shot—they were still waiting to see a doctor—and once Lucy was caught, they would have to ascertain whether she'd had a rabies shot. Petey was in a panic because he had left the farmhouse unlocked and my father had promised him that one of us would close the gate and make sure the door was bolted. The key was in Petey's blue jacket, the one with the fold-away hood; it was probably still in the bathroom.

"Don't go by yourself. Ask Charley to go with you," he instructed me.

It seemed absurd to worry about securing a house that even the local vandals had begun to avoid but of course that was not the point. I could hear the background babble of the emergency room and pictured Petey hunched over clutching his leg, eyes closed against the chaos around him, rocking himself on his chair, his voice rising to a high-pitched, incomprehensible wail. There was no reasoning with him at the best of times and now his world was falling apart.

His blue jacket was not in the bathroom or in the hall or even under his bed, and I concluded eventually that he must have left it at the farmhouse.

"I'll get it. You stay here," offered Charley when I passed on my father's message.

"I will come along also but perhaps it would be wise to call the police in case this dog attacks someone else," suggested Finney.

"How do you know the beast's not still in the house?" demanded Rupert.

"We don't," said Charley.

There was a short silence.

"I don't care if she is. I'm going anyway," I said, feeling I owed it to Petey.

In the end it was agreed that we would all go, but before we could set off, Rita announced she was too old for shenanigans and was going home to bed. She insisted on packing up the game first and began pulling out wires and randomly stuffing cardboard tubes and oddly shaped bits of styrofoam into the suitcase, at which point Rupert lost his composure and rushed over and began pulling everything out again and rearranging it to his own satisfaction. Plainly it was going to take even longer to dismantle his contraption than it had to put it together. I decided not to wait. Armed with a flashlight and a slice of pizza in case Lucy put in an appearance, I announced that I was going to reconnoitre and headed for the door. I was followed somewhat reluctantly by Charley. Finney, who had been trying to get hold of his wife, said he would wait for Rupert.

There was no sound from Lucy and no sign of her in the beam of my flashlight as we scanned the farmhouse yard, just a couple of overturned garbage pails and a pile of tires. The lamppost on the corner had been broken all summer and the only light was a glow from the kitchen window, tinged with green from an old dishtowel that Petey had tacked up, too dim even to cast a shadow. The gate was unlatched and ajar.

While we waited for the others, Charley paced the perimeter of the property searching without success for Petey's jacket. They appeared finally, Finney with a coil of rope over one arm and a ski pole in the other.

"In case we are attacked," he explained. "It was Mrs. Dunster's idea but it's a sensible precaution."

"So, what's the plan? Where's this monster dog?" demanded Rupert, scanning the yard with his flashlight.

"Gone for good, I hope," muttered Charley.

"We must look for Petey's jacket," said Finney.

"So, let's go in and get it. What are we waiting for?"

"Technically speaking, going inside would be trespassing," said Charley.

"So, let's not get technical. It can't hurt to take a look around."

"One of us better wait outside. Maybe Imo?"

"She could be lookout."

"Why don't we just stand around talking till Swen gets back?" I snapped. In twenty years nothing had changed. The last thing I wanted was to go inside, but there was no way I was going to be relegated to lookout.

"I thought you said he was gone for a month!"

"My point exactly."

Charley put a hand on my arm but I shook it free and started up the walk. "What's the problem? You think someone's going to heave a potato at you?"

By the time I reached the door, I regretted my outburst. I pushed it open and stood in the entranceway, surveying the dimly lit kitchen, my heart pounding. Petey's housekeeping duties did not extend to taking out the garbage apparently; the counter was piled with fast food cartons, and there was a strong odour of dog mingled with rancid grease, and a musty smell from the basement. Underlying it all was the pungent aroma of pot. The others crowded in behind me and someone flicked on the light.

Rupert pushed past me with a short, sharp whistle. "You really put an offer on this place?" He strode around the kitchen, opening cupboards and peering into corners. A huge bag of kibble mix toppled forward out of the broom closet and the contents cascaded noisily onto the floor. "That must be one big hound," he remarked, scooping up the bulk of the spilled mix with his hands and then sweeping what was left under the ledge of the counter with his foot. He sat down at the table and slid over to the jukebox and began pushing in the buttons. "Hey, this thing is practically antique. Too bad it doesn't work. I wonder what else there is around here. Remember all that stuff under the verandah?" He stood up again and walked over to the basement stairs and peered down into the dark. "Might as well check out the dungeon. Where's the light switch? Never mind. I'll use my flashlight."

"Actually, don't bother, Petey never goes down there," I said. But he had already disappeared down the stairs. Finney hesitated, then crossed the kitchen and started down after him. Behind me I heard Charley sigh.

I found Petey's jacket in the living room, slung over the back of a threadbare easy chair with a large burn mark on one of the armrests. It was the only piece of furniture in the room apart from a massive floor-model television. A messy pile of newspaper flyers and unopened mail lay on the rug beside the chair, and bulging black garbage bags lined the walls on three sides. I could guess what they held. Probably Swen had so-called landscaping businesses all over town.

This was a criminal operation and Petey was up to his neck in it. There was no way we could report it to the police without involving him. For the last couple of weeks, he had all but lived at the farmhouse, most of that time outside with Lucy in full view of the neighbourhood. How could my parents have let him carry on? How could I? Get out of here and pretend you never came, I told myself. The men were still in the basement—I could hear their voices—but I'd had enough. Grabbing Petey's jacket, I turned to leave, keeping my eyes on the floor as I skirted the pile of mail.

"It's okay. I found it," I called.

"Found what?"

Slouched in the kitchen doorway, his thumbs hooked into the front pockets of his jeans, his legs extended to block my way, was Swen. "You ever heard of private property?"

My breath caught in my throat and I stared at him mutely, wondering how long he had been watching me. He was wearing his new Nikes from Laviolettes', along with the inevitable sweat-stained pink shirt and a pair of grubby white jeans. He eyed me with casual insolence, his eyes travelling the length of my body speculatively, but his voice had a nasty edge in it.

"What are you doing here?"

I felt a sharp pain in my side and my nausea returned with a vengeance. "Petey left his jacket," I said in a choked voice.

"Yeah, well he can get it himself. He's not supposed to let anyone in and that includes you and your pals. What the hell's going on?"

I considered making a dash for the front door but before I could make up my mind, he stepped forward and gripped my arm. "You got no business here."

I received a blast of beery breath full in the face and my stomach turned over. "Let go of me."

His nails bit into my arm. "Not till you tell me what's going on, eh. Where's your brother?"

"I just told you. I came to get his jacket," I said, struggling to control the tremor in my voice. "He had to go to the hospital. Your stupid dog bit him and now she's run off somewhere. You better go find her before she bites someone else."

"You got no business here," he repeated, but he sounded uncertain. His grip slackened.

"She'll have to be put down," I said, sensing I had the advantage. "Someone's going to call the police on you. They probably have already, so get your filthy hands off me." I was shaking violently now but my voice was under control.

"You better not do that." His face seemed to swell and shrink at the same time, his eyes narrowing and sinking into their sockets, his jaw muscles pulsing.

Where were the others? I was close enough to knee him in the groin or at the very least kick him in the shins but my limbs wouldn't work. I felt the pain again, lower down in my side, and then a wave of fury that I couldn't contain.

"It's you," I told him. "You're the one who's got no business here. I know what you're doing and don't think you're going to get away with it. I suppose you think you're some kind of big-time criminal. Well, maybe you are. Everything you do is criminal if you ask me. You know why Thomas hung around with you? Because he felt sorry for you, that's why. You never felt sorry for anyone in your life. You took advantage of my brother because he has a handicap, you corrupted him just like you corrupted half the village, just like that priest at the orphanage corrupted you!"

"Shut up," he said in a hoarse voice. "Shut up about all that."

But by then I was in full spate. "People try to help you and all you do is sneer at them. You think you're so great but look at you. You spend your whole life smoking pot and scrounging off other people. You can't even pay for a pair of shoes. You know what you are? You're a loser!"

His hand tightened on my arm. "Shut up, bitch. Just shut up."

"No, I won't shut up. Why should I? My brother is up at the hospital because of you. His leg is bleeding all over the place. Does that matter to you? No it doesn't. He could bleed to death for all you care. The emergency room could be swimming in blood."

He gaped at me, his mouth slack, his face darkening.

"You're kicked out of this place, you know. I talked to the lawyer. I told him all about you. You should never have been allowed to stay here in the first place—that's what he said."

"What the hell you talking about, the lawyer? Just shut up. Shut up."

"Shut up. Is that all you can say? Every single Sunday, you and Thomas, smoking pot, stinking up the shop. We never had one Sunday to ourselves. So get your lousy hands off me. Get out of my sight, get out of this house, get off this street. Just get out!"

He dropped my arm and stepped back. I saw Charley's head in the doorway, the others behind him.

"What's going on?"

And then I was doubled over with pain, spewing out everything I'd eaten in the last twenty-four hours. Over my head I could hear a confusion of angry voices, arguing and shouting, but none of it had anything to do with the terrible pain in my gut. I couldn't stop retching.

"What did you do to her?"

"Lay off me, man!"

"Call the police."

"Who is this guy?"

"She's barfing all over my shoes."

"It's the fellow that lives here, the drug dealer?"

"You're trespassing, man. You got no right."

"Must be worth a fortune."

"I live here, for chrissake!"

"Lady, get out of my way."

"What the hell!"

I retched into the silence.

"Mom? Mom, what are you doing here? Put that thing down!"

"Get her away from me."

"Mrs. Dunster, I think it is better if you put down the ski pole."

"That girl is sick."

"Mom, please."

"It's Imogene. What have you done to her?"

I felt a soft hand on my forehead. "It's okay, honey. We'll get you home. You're just a bit sick. You'll be okay. Charley, hand me that jacket. Can't you see she's shaking with cold?"

The last thing I remember is the sound of a siren. At the time I thought it was the police but it turned out to be for me.

Smoke

Most of that night remains a blur, though I never lost consciousness. I remember struggling to stand in the poorly lit kitchen surrounded by pale, shocked faces, my arms flailing as I fended off fumbling hands, conniving voices.

"Madame, madame. Urgence Santé, madame. Ça va, madame? Okay, okay."

I was dimly conscious of Charley telling me to take it easy, of someone, I think it was Rupert, wresting the ski pole from Rita and of Swen's ragged ponytail disappearing out the kitchen door and then I was on the floor, vomiting, immobilized by a wave of pain and feeling myself being lifted, still curled in the fetal position, into the ambulance. I knew only one thing, that I was losing the baby, and I understood that it would be better to die.

By the time we reached the hospital, the spasm had passed and I walked into the emergency room under my own steam, ignoring the protests of the paramedics, who trailed after me with the empty stretcher. We paraded down the hall past a man in a turban rhythmically slamming the flat of his hand against the side of a soft drink dispenser. Beside him an elderly, rather haggard gentleman held out a handful of coins. It was my father, I realized as I swept by. It didn't occur to me to stop.

I carried on right past the admission desk and came to an abrupt halt in the waiting room doorway, repulsed by an odour of vomit. It was eerily quiet except for a high-pitched moaning that I couldn't place and at first took to be a ringing in my ears. Listless bodies slumped on chairs lined the walls, faces ashen in the harsh light. There was a lone empty seat beside a sallow-skinned woman in a yellow sari with a limp child draped across her lap. An orderly in white coveralls was mopping his way across the floor toward me, but before I could flee, the moaning erupted into a shout and in the far corner, half-hidden behind a pillar, I saw Petey rocking hysterically, my mother beside him, one hand rubbing his back, the other waving to get my attention.

As I started toward them, the pain began again, lower down this time on one side. I felt a hand on my elbow. "You must to check in, madame."

"Enceinte," I heard someone say. The room wavered and then I was on the floor again.

For hours I lay on a gurney behind a pale green curtain with Petey beside me on a chair, jabbering non-stop, wanting to know if I was all right, insisting on showing me his stitches and speculating about Lucy's whereabouts. "You think she ran away for good, Imo? She knows she did a bad thing. She could be hiding under

Mr. Connibear's porch. He wouldn't like it though. He might chase her away with the rake. Maybe she's gone back up north. That's where she was born. She could be hiding in the back of a truck. She's got to be brave if she's on the highway. You got to be brave too, Imo. We all got to be brave."

I barely listened. The pain when it came overwhelmed me, leaving me weak and quivering as it subsided, and devastated by the certainty that I was having a miscarriage, convinced I had brought it on myself. I was glad I had Petey to keep me grounded, but I didn't feel brave.

There had been no one to keep Thomas company during that last long night, only the doctors and nurses and the machines with their tubes and wires, beeping, and me in the wretched cubby hole next to the intensive care unit, reading back issues of *Reader's Digest*, chuckling at the jokes and improving my word power. In a state of shock, Dr. Campeau had said. A state of denial is what he meant and I had been in that state ever since, hiding out at home, trying to undo the past when the future was there before me, planning to abort the baby we had made together, the baby he had wanted as much if not more than I had; my mother was right about that. Thomas was gone. Nothing was going to bring him back and he had died without ever knowing he was going to be a father.

I lay on my back hardly daring to move, waiting for the next wave of pain, feeling curiously empty when it didn't come, running wary fingers over the soft mound of my stomach, reclaiming alien territory, afraid the slightest twitch or a rogue thought would set off another spasm, and wondering if by some miracle I was still pregnant. Thomas could have felt no pain, the doctors said—he had never come out of the coma—but they didn't know, not really. He might have heard me if I had spoken to him; he might have been comforted.

A downy-faced intern with curly brown hair offered me a shot of Demerol. "This will help," he said.

"I'm pregnant."

"Not to worry. It can't hurt the baby and it'll do you a lot of good. Just a quick jab."

Faces peeked in through the curtains and withdrew again, my mother, my father, an orderly, a nurse, my mother again; their main and only concern to lure Petey away, but he wasn't moving. None of them seemed to understand that I was losing the baby, least of all the nurses who slipped in and out, tossing out trial diagnoses.

"I expect it's a bladder infection."

"I can see you're dehydrated, dear."

"Presents a lot like food poisoning. I wouldn't advise eating pizza with a delicate digestion like yours, not when you're pregnant."

"There's no bleeding, dear. I expect you'll be fine. You've had a scare, that's all."

"You're awfully thin, dear."

"Do you *want* to lose the baby?"

At long last a small, round, middle-aged woman with a dogged expression appeared and introduced herself as Dr. Elvira.

"Are you still here?" she exclaimed when she saw Petey, who was asleep in his chair with his head resting on the mattress, snoring in a companionable way. She prodded him to his feet and he staggered groggily over to my mother, who was hovering.

"Let's have a look, shall we?" Dr. Elvira said when they had retreated to the other side of the curtain.

"You've passed a kidney stone, dear. I thought that might be it. Your symptoms are classic," she announced when she had finished examining me. "I think I've found it. Here you are. It doesn't look like much, I know." I stared in disbelief at the tiny speck in her outstretched palm. A whole world in a grain of sand, I thought, a world of pain. "It was agony, my dear, I know, but it's over now, for the time being at least. You could pass another one of course. It's quite likely at some point in the future."

I made a conscious decision not to think about that. "What about the baby?"

"Chugging away like a little steam engine. We'll get your doctor to arrange for some more tests just in case." In case what, I wondered but didn't dare ask. "For now the best thing you can do is to drink lots of water. Try to eat something too. You need a little fat on your bones if you're going to grow a baby."

The sun was a pale crack in the grey dawn sky as we left the hospital, all of us exhausted and desperate for bed, and all quiet except for Petey, who was trying to get his head around kidney stones.

"Everybody has kidneys, right, Imo? A dog has kidneys too but not everybody has a kidney stone. Maybe Lucy had one. You think? Maybe that's why she got mad at me. You got real mad at Swen. That's what Charley said. Did you try to bite him, Imo? A dog can't go to the hospital—only people. I never been to the hospital before, right, Mum? Right, Dad? Imo, Imo, you think she'll . . ." He fell silent as we slowed to turn onto Garden Crescent. My father gave a surprised snort and I opened my eyes reluctantly.

A veil of smoke hung over the street. There were fire engines, police cars, and people in uniform everywhere, a long ladder truck parked on the Lakeshore Road, another on Garden Crescent, and in the middle of the street, a squad car with its lights flashing. A ragged collection of dog walkers and early risers milled about on the sidewalk in front of Mr. Connibear's house, spilling onto his lawn and into the road, kept at bay by a harassed-looking police officer who waved us on. As my father nosed the car through the crowd, I saw that the animal control van was blocking the Dunsters' driveway. Rita and Rupert were out on the front step and Charley was on the sidewalk in earnest conversation with the dog catcher.

Petey had the car door open before we had come to a full stop in front of our house. "Lucy! Lucy's in the van! I heard her barking."

My mother reached round and put a hand on his arm. "You mustn't go up there now, Petey. You'll only be in the way. Remember what the doctor told you. He said to give your leg a rest. Let's wait and see what Charley has to tell us."

We climbed out of the car and stood on the sidewalk, gawking at the farmhouse. Petey strained forward, shifting from foot to foot and grunting every time he landed on his wounded leg.

My father wrinkled his nose. "What's that smell?"

"Oh my god." My mother started to laugh.

"It's marijuana! That's what . . ." Petey stopped in mid-sentence and looked down at his feet.

The smell of pot hung over the street, mingling with the acrid smoke fumes, faint but unmistakeable.

"I don't know what's so funny," said my father. "Really, Ireney, it's not a laughing matter."

"No, it's not, is it." She made a hiccupping sound. I saw her mouth quiver and realized with horror that she was close to tears.

My father shook his head. "I think we should go inside and get some sleep. Looks like the fire's under control. They're just clearing up. There's nothing we can do about it anyway."

"No, Dad, wait. Here comes Charley!" Petey wrenched free of my mother's arm and limped up the road, calling. "Charley, Charley, where's Lucy?"

"What happened? Where's Swen?" I asked as they came up to us, Petey breathing heavily now but somehow still talking non-stop.

Charley shrugged. "Who knows? Long gone, I guess. His truck's gone, anyway. He took off when the ambulance came. The fire started a couple of hours ago, at least that's when I spotted it. Well, Lucy did really. I heard her barking and when I got up and looked outside, I saw a weird light in the kitchen window." He glanced at Petey and shrugged again. "Could have been the wiring. It must be nowhere near code. How about you folks?"

"I got twenty-five stitches and a needle too," Petey announced. "Imo had a kidney stone. It went right through her but you could hardly see it."

"I'm fine," I said before he could launch into a blow-by-blow account of the last few hours. "It was a freak thing, nothing to do with the baby, just a coincidence. Sorry I made such a, you know, fuss."

"The emergency room is swimming in blood," said Charley with a wry grin.

"I guess I went a bit crazy."

"No, you were great. Really. A kidney stone—that must have hurt like hell. I'm afraid I have to go now though. Rupert has to get to the airport and my mum's pretty upset. I'll catch up with you later." He turned away and started up the street.

I saw that the animal control van had backed out of the driveway and had turned in our direction. We could hear Lucy barking as it went by. Petey made a lunge toward it but my mother grabbed his arm.

"We'll phone the pound later," she promised. "There's nothing you can do now. Why don't I make pancakes?" My father took his other arm and together they persuaded him into the house.

I lingered on the front steps before following them in. A couple of the firefighters had their hoses trained on the roof but most of the crew appeared to be packing up; the crowd was dispersing. I saw with shock that the verandah had pulled away from the house and collapsed into the backyard. The whole structure would have to be torn down. One of the firefighters was posting a sign on the gate and Mr. Connibear was walking the joint property line, picking up debris that had fallen on his side and tossing it over the fence. There was no doubt in my mind that it was arson. Swen burning his bridges, a last hurrah before he cut and run. It would be worth it if he never showed his face again, but that was probably too much to hope for.

Second Breakfast

"Take it easy, Pete, it's not going to run away."

"Dad, Dad, I never had any dinner last night."

"None of us had any dinner."

"But I'm the hungriest, aren't I? I'm the best eater."

We were sitting at the drop-leaf table eating a second breakfast of scrambled eggs, plying one another with toast and jam and coffee. "Like any normal, civilized family," my mother observed hopefully to the ceiling, though it was two o'clock in the afternoon and, with the exception of Petey, who had been too keyed up to go to bed, we were all in our pyjamas. Minutes earlier he had rushed into the kitchen, reeking of smoke. He'd been up to the farmhouse, looking for clues, but had been sent packing by Mr. Connibear. Periodically his whole body twitched and the hairs on his arms stood on end as if an electrical current was passing through him. I could feel the sparks coming off him. He ate compulsively, working his way through a stack of toast. Tillie flopped at his feet, happily awaiting her share, oblivious to the uncivilized events of the previous night.

"You could eat an elephant under the table at the rate you're going," I remarked not too helpfully.

Petey snorted with laughter, spraying crumbs in all directions. "Betcha I could eat two elephants under the table." He picked up a piece of toast and waved it around elephant fashion, elbow bent to make a trunk, his hand flopping over his wrist. Tillie snapped to a sitting position. It was an old game from our childhood called Elephant Pie. I knew perfectly well that once launched Petey was likely to carry on indefinitely, but the alternative was to spend the next few hours admiring his stitches and exclaiming over the discoloured swelling on his leg or, worse, speculating about the fate of Lucy. For the first time in weeks he wouldn't be spending the day at the farmhouse. It was no wonder my parents had turned a blind eye to Swen.

"Can we just concentrate on what's on the table?" demanded my father. "One piece of toast at a time and chew with your mouth shut, please."

I ate almost as voraciously as Petey. I could feel my mother's eyes on me, hopeful yet questioning. Had I come to my senses finally? Was I back to my old self? Hardly. Nothing was ever going to be the same again, least of all me, I could have told her that, but I was going to have a baby, Thomas's baby, and despite everything that had happened I felt euphoric.

Petey's elbow banged on the table, rattling the dishes; the toast flew from his hand. He made a dive for it but Tillie beat him to it.

My father grabbed his coffee mug before it tipped over. "Settle down, Pete. Really, Imogene, did you have to start him off?"

There was a crash as Petey's chair fell back against the wall, followed by the chime of the doorbell.

"Now what?" grumbled my father.

"Might be Charley!" exclaimed Petey.

My mother got up and looked out the dining room window. "It's the police."

My father groaned and stood up. "It'll be about the fire. I expect they're canvassing the neighbourhood for information."

Abandoning the toast to Tillie, we trailed after him into the hall and crowded together behind him in a ragged semicircle, jostling one another for a view of the door. A young-looking police officer with a razor nick on his chin stood on the step, very stiff and neatly pressed, perfectly turned out in fact except for a white splotch that looked like a bird dropping on the toe of one of his shoes.

"Sorry to bother you, sir. It's about the fire. Quite a conflagration up the street last night. Kept you all awake, I expect. I'm looking for Peter Jackson. I understand he lives here."

We all looked at Petey; my mother put a hand on his arm.

"That would be my son," said my father.

"Officer Connelly, Kevin Connelly. May I come in?" He stepped inside without waiting for an answer. "I understand you do a bit of work at the house up the road, sir," he said, looking at Petey.

Petey, whose respect for people in uniform borders on terror, turned white.

Officer Connelly pulled out a small spiral-bound notebook and flipped through it to a clean page. "We're trying to determine how the fire started, and when. I understand you were up there last night, sir. Was everything as usual?"

Petey stared at him open-mouthed, shifting from foot to foot.

"We were up at the hospital all night. Petey was bitten by a dog," my mother explained.

"What time did this occur?"

"About six."

"I'd like to hear from your son if you don't mind, ma'am. He has a particular connection with the place."

"He's not a firebug."

"No, of course."

"She didn't mean it," Petey burst out, thrusting himself forward.

"Oh for heaven's sakes, Petey!" my father exclaimed.

"No, she didn't. She's sorry now. Her name's Lucy. I'm, I'm training her. It's a real job!"

Officer Connelly took a step back. "I see. This dog, Lucy, she bit you?"

"I got stitches." Petey bent over to roll up his pant leg but the material bunched up on his calf. He stood up again and tugged at his belt.

"Actually I was up there last night after they left, checking on things," I said, jumping in before he could take off his pants. "There was no sign of a fire then. Around eight o'clock, I think."

"And you are?"

Before I could answer Tillie padded out of the kitchen and squeezed through Petey's legs, growling.

"She didn't mean it," insisted Petey.

Officer Connelly took another step back, looking confused. "Which dog was it that bit you, sir?"

"Don't worry. This is Tillie. She's all bark and no bite," my mother told him. "I'm afraid uniforms always set her off. Tillie, shut up, for heaven's sakes. Petey, give her a piece of toast or something, then take her up to your room. Perhaps it would be better if you came in, officer. We were just having coffee."

Officer Connelly stood stiffly by the door, reluctant to leave the sanctuary of the porch even after Petey had dragged Tillie away. Eventually my mother persuaded him into the living room, where he perched on the edge of my father's wing chair with a cup of black sugary coffee. My father gave him an earful about Swen while we waited for Petey.

"Fellow moved in one day and said he was starting a lawn cutting outfit. He hired Petey to help him out but I don't think he ever found himself any customers. I don't know how he paid his rent. He never got around to paying Petey, I can tell you that. He was just taking advantage, if you ask me."

"Can you tell me his name?"

"He did too pay me. His name's Swen and it's a landscape company. He has a truck and everything," said Petey breathlessly from the doorway.

"And he hired you to train his dog?"

"I look after everything when he's away. I'm in charge. Me and Lucy. Nobody's allowed to come near."

"And did anybody come near?"

"No way."

"What about when this fellow Swen's at home? Any unusual comings and goings?"

"No knowing what the fellow was up to," said my father.

"I'd like to hear from your son, Mr. Jackson, in his own words. It's important to hear what he has to say while it's still fresh in his mind. He may be a witness." Petey gaped. "We believe there may have been illegal substances in that house. Do you know what a marijuana plant is Pete?"

Petey nodded, eyes lowered, and chewed on his lower lip.

"Did you come across anything like that inside the house?"

"Not supposed to touch anything. Swen said. He's gone away on a trip now. He's going to pay me when he gets back."

"When's that? Did he give you a date?"

"I guess he might not come back here. I guess he might have to live somewhere else now the house is burned. He's going to pay me though. He promised." Petey looked up, struck by a sudden thought. "I might have to look after Lucy when they let her go. She's at the pound."

"Petey . . ." my father started but stopped himself.

Officer Connelly spoke for him. "Let her go? Not if she's vicious. Not a chance. They'll have to put her down."

"No. They can't put her down. They can't." Petey's face crumpled.

Officer Connelly stood up and glanced around at us apologetically. "I'm sorry. It's too bad, but I doubt there's any possibility of letting her go. If you think of anything else, Pete, anything that might help, I want you to ask your dad to call me, okay. Sorry to bother you, folks. Thanks for your help." He retreated to the door.

Petey stood at the window and watched him drive off.

"We'll phone the pound first thing tomorrow morning, soon as it's open," my mother promised. "I'm sure you'll be able to go and see her."

My father clapped him on the back. "Tell you what, son. Now that you have some free time, I'll hire you to wash and wax the car. You can use the special chamois."

"I don't feel like it. I don't . . . " my brother's voice started to rise.

"Don't start," growled my mother. "Just do what your father says. I don't want you back in this house for an hour, do you understand? I've had enough. I'm going upstairs now and I want perfect quiet."

Petey choked back his moan. We all stared at her in surprise. I wondered if she'd slept at all that morning or if she had lain awake worrying.

"You heard the boss," said my father. "Let's go find the wax." He started for the back door. "Come on."

Stomping his feet in protest, Petey started after him.

I waited for the back door to slam, then followed my mother up, intending to lie down. Tillie was in the hall outside Petey's room, curled up in a ball. She opened one eye and closed it again but made no attempt to move as I stepped past her. Petey's door was ajar and I could see my mother sitting on his bed with her hands in her lap, gazing out the window with a slight frown on her face. As a rule none of us goes into Petey's room without permission. It's his kingdom, the only territory he rules, and a Spartan regime it is, a legacy of boarding school, hospital corners on the bed, pyjamas under his pillow, T-shirts and jeans hanging in his cupboard, and matching socks only in his sock drawer. His various collections are arranged precisely on a bookcase he bought from IKEA with his own money. Seashells of the world hold place of honour on the top shelf, bottle caps in two parallel lines on the bottom, matchboxes, racing cars, and hockey cards in between.

I hovered in the doorway. My mother and I had barely spoken since she'd told me of her own misguided attempt at abortion, her confession as I thought of it. At the hospital we hadn't had any kind of conversation; she'd spent most of her time trying to corral Petey, whose crises had always eclipsed mine. I felt a rush of childhood resentment but pushed it aside. That was all in the past now and I was bursting to share my elation. I cleared my throat.

"Mum. I wanted to tell you."

She turned with a start and her eyes flickered to her lap. I saw then that she was holding a joint. Petey must have left it on his bed. It hardly seemed important now that his supply had gone up flames; she was bound to have found out about his habit sooner or later.

"Half the parents of a handicapped child drink more than they should," she said in a flat voice.

And you might as well have two handicapped offspring, I thought. A wave of guilt swept over me. I loved my brother but what help had I ever been? "You've never done that," I said.

"No, I've never been much of a drinker. Cigarettes are my thing." She turned the joint over in her hands as if deciding which end to light.

"Are you going to smoke that?" I asked flippantly.

"Not right now," she said wearily. There was no hint of a smile.

"I, I thought it was Petey's," I stammered. "He offered me one the other day."

She looked up then; her eyes were defiant. "Yes, well, it's better for me to smoke it than for Petey, don't you think?"

It wasn't really a question. I stared at her in consternation, wondering if she was having a breakdown. "If you're worried about Petey, I'm sure he's all right. I mean, he'll get over Lucy. I doubt if she has rabies or anything like that. It's pretty unlikely around here even if she hasn't had a shot."

"She's had all her shots," my mother snapped. "I made sure of that before I let Petey take her on. I'm not an idiot."

"No, of course. I didn't mean to imply . . ." I paused. She was an idiot to let him anywhere near Swen. We both knew that.

"I'm not in the habit if that's what you're wondering," she said, examining the joint again.

"No, no. It's none of my business," I replied, not at all sure I believed her. Thomas had said the same thing on a regular basis.

"And I suppose what you do with your life is none of mine?"

"That's not true. It is. I value your advice. That's what I wanted to tell you. I . . . I've decided not to have the, you know, I'm going to keep it."

She looked up again. "You're going to keep it!" Her voice choked and I saw that she was on the verge of tears. "Oh, darling, that's wonderful! Thomas would be so pleased."

We left it at that.

A Girl on a Swing

The taxis are all lined up along the road, the drivers bunched together on the sidewalk, smoking while they wait for customers, except for the skinny one sucking on a toothpick who is leaning against the wooden shack where the drivers play cards in winter. He's keeping an eye out for children who try to run a finger through the dust on his car. Imo sidles past with her hands in her pockets and her eyes on the ground so she won't be noticed, but the door of the shack creaks open and a pair of shiny brown shoes with fancy stitching on the toes, like the ones in the window at Laviolettes', step out in front of her, and there, as close as her own hand, puffing on a big cigar, is the farmer.

What has happened to his gumboots? she wonders. Did he dump them in the field? And does Madame know? He had better not wear his good shoes on the tractor, but then she remembers that he won't be driving a tractor anymore because he's no longer a farmer. The long moving van that sat all week in his driveway like a sleeping dragon awoke with an angry rumble and drove away with all his furniture and maybe all his clothes too because instead of his old brown hat, he's wearing a black taxi driver's cap. Beneath the hard, shiny brim his faces crinkles in an alarming way and she can see all his teeth except for the one that is missing.

"Eh bien, la Petite," he says, and before she can duck, his hand reaches out and cups her head. Thick calloused fingers tap softly against her scalp, sending an electric buzz down her spine. Her body jolts forward and back in the same instant, like the car when her mother forgets to put in the clutch, and then she is running, her legs pumping, trying to catch up with her heart that is racing like Tillie's when she hears the vacuum.

Down the sidewalk, past the window of the Bon Mouton where all the little rainbow-coloured sheep have fallen over, past the café and the tavern and Rossy's Five to a Dollar, down the dip past the man who fixes bicycles in his living room, not even stopping to spin the wheel on the gate, around the corner and into the little side lane, along past the house with a rooster on the roof for a weathervane and a real live chicken in the front yard, and on and on until her breath stops coming and her legs slow to a walk and she can't go any farther because she's in a cul-de-sac and a low black wrought iron fence is blocking her way.

Behind the fence is a grey stone cottage with a blue roof that slopes over the verandah, and there on a swing suspended from the ceiling, swooping back and forth like a giant seagull, is the girl from under the chair in Madame's living room. She's swinging wildly, head flung back, bare legs stuck straight out in front of her to clear the railing. She sails halfway across the little yard, so high you can see her yellow panties, and back again, kicking over a pile of empty cardboard boxes. Her feet thud against the railing with a practised jerk, her body straightens, and she leans way out over the edge of the verandah, her arms pulled backwards by the ropes, and stares straight at Imo.

"Allô, I know who you are. La Petite. You want to try it?" she asks, and her voice is still swinging. Without waiting for an answer she flips herself upside down so that her feet are touching the edge of the low-slung roof and her dress falls over her face.

Imo puts a hand on the gate. She could do that too, she's pretty sure.

"Louise," calls a stern voice from inside the house. A shadow fills the screen door and out steps Madame.

Whipping her hand behind her back, Imo turns and starts to run again, fingers tingling where they touched the gate. She can hear her heart knocking as if her chest is hollow; her legs are leaden. Behind her a voice calls, "Allô, la Petite," but she can't stop.

Rubber Boots and Warm Mud

By tacit agreement my mother and I did not pursue the conversation we had begun in Petey's bedroom. An occasional joint, if that's what it was, hardly made my mother a drug addict. Heaven knows, she had her reasons, and having spent the better part of the last two months moping in bed, I was hardly in a position to criticize. The least I could do, and it wasn't much, was to stand on my own two feet again, move back to the village, and get on with my life. Surely the morning sickness wouldn't last much longer, but if it did, I could simply hire an assistant for Charmaine; I would have to do that sooner or later anyway. The thought was at once frightening and liberating.

In keeping with my new responsible persona I offered to drive Petey to the city pound so he could pay a farewell visit to Lucy. He announced on the way over that he wanted to go in alone. Having no desire to witness his distress, and feeling little sympathy for Lucy, I made no effort to dissuade him. He's volunteered as a dog walker off and on over the years. More than once he'd arrived at the shop in tears when one of his charges had unexpectedly moved on. He was gearing himself up for the coming ordeal with a series of ultra-macho deep-breathing exercises he'd seen on TV, whacking himself on the chest and grunting with each exhalation. I anticipated an angry outburst when the time came to get out of the car, but to my relief when a young woman in a lab coat flipped the CLOSED sign to OPEN, he thumped out a final tattoo, then climbed out of the car and headed for the entrance without looking back. I waited until he had disappeared inside and then went on to the shop, where we had arranged to meet later.

I parked in the alley and slipped in the back door, sidestepping a shipment of running shoes and another of reindeer hats. On entering the workroom I was momentarily disconcerted to find only the usual chaos: mounds of broken-down shoes tagged for repair overflowing the worktables, a sea of yellow memos curling across the counter and lapping at the telephone, and the inevitable stack of unopened mail. Nothing had changed, it seemed, except me, but then it was only a couple of days since I'd been in. Having riffled through the mail, bills mostly and a few catalogues, nothing I couldn't deal with later, I scribbled a quick note for Charmaine to say I'd be back mid-morning in case Petey arrived before me. Then let myself out again and set off down the alley.

For as long as I could remember I had avoided the owner of Maison de Pomme. I had seen Adélie Chaput around town occasionally, but we had never spoken. On the rare occasions she had appeared in the shop, I had retreated to the backroom, to the bemusement of Joseph and Thomas. It was certainly not my duty to tell her about the fire. I had no doubt she would have heard already. And I had nothing to apologize for—it was not my fault she had rented the place to Swen—but I felt I owed her a visit. She had known me as a child and according to Monsieur Claude remembered me fondly. She had, it seemed, accepted our offer for that very reason. We were both widows, I realized, but our lives were worlds apart. All this time she had hung on to her memories and resentments, refusing to sell, and now what was she left with? I would not make the same mistake, I vowed as I made my way down her lane. I was going to have a baby; I was moving on.

She lived at the end of a cul-de-sac, a short walk from the shop in a small stone cottage that overlooked the lake, built in 1702 according to a metal plaque on the fence and squeezed in now between a couple of two-storey stucco monstrosities. I couldn't imagine pining for a ramshackle farmhouse on the edge of a housing development if I could live in a heritage house a stone's throw from the lake. There were a few historic cottages scattered about the village, some even older, and all charming on the outside at least. I had pointed one out to Thomas the day before the accident but he had shrugged dismissively. Not one of them had ever gone up for sale formally as far as he knew. If they did change hands, it was always privately and they rarely left the family.

I mounted the three sagging steps to the low-slung verandah and knocked, then waited what seemed an interminable time, wondering if Madame Chaput was still in bed or, like many elderly people, afraid to answer an unexpected knock. The windows were draped with sheers, which made it impossible to see in. It occurred to me I should have phoned ahead or consulted with Louise. At last I heard footsteps approaching. A chain rattled and the door inched open with a reluctant groan as if the whole house was shifting. I found myself towering over a little round woman in a blue-flowered dress.

"Madame Chaput?" The figure in front of me bore no resemblance to the behemoth I remembered from childhood, a Fury enthroned on the back porch of the farmhouse, paring knife in hand and a bottomless bucket of potatoes at her feet.

She cocked her head to one side and eyed me suspiciously.

"You may not remember me, but I'm Imogene Jackson. My husband and I put an offer on your house on the Lakeshore Road. We made a down payment but I had to withdraw it."

She stared at me blankly.

"Monsieur Claude, Claude Gauthier, the lawyer, he was talking to you last week. My husband was Thomas Laviolette. He was killed in a car crash." I paused, shocked by the finality of what I had said. Until that moment the knowledge of my tragedy had gone before me; condolences had been turned aside with a murmur. But now I had spoken the words out loud, committed them to the air, and there was no taking them back.

"Quoi?" she demanded.

"Imo, Imogene Jackson," I repeated, pronouncing each word distinctly. "I used to live on Garden Crescent, in the new development that was built on your land. You lived there too, on the Lakeshore Road."

She stared at me, uncomprehending.

"I remember Papa Chaput," I said in desperation. "I was there, you know, when he . . ." I let my voice trail off. It was a memory I had pushed aside for years.

"Papa Chaput." Her eyes narrowed.

I took a step back. "I just came to tell you I'm sorry about the fire. It's a terrible thing. You must be very upset." What had I been thinking of, coming to see this woman when I couldn't communicate with her? I should have come years ago or not at all. I had nothing to tell her that she didn't know already. But as I turned to leave, she gave a chirping cry and I saw her eyes light with recognition.

"La Petite?" she whispered. She stepped forward and peered up into my face, then reached up a hand to touch my cheek. I held my breath, forcing myself to keep still. A faint odour of Sunlight soap drifted into my nostrils and the air filled with the pungent smell of rubber boots and warm mud. I heard voices shouting, the snort of the goat, feet pounding across the grass; my heart raced. I felt myself sway and leaned against the doorframe for support. When my head cleared, she was eyeing me anxiously.

"Viens, come." Clasping my arm, she pulled me inside and led me into a long narrow room. "You must to sit," she commanded, propelling me onto the couch. Then she disappeared back down the hall.

I stayed where she'd put me, hoping she hadn't gone to call a doctor or worse still an ambulance. The fainting spell or whatever it was had passed, an all too predictable result of skipping breakfast. I glanced around, trying to recall a word or a phrase in French, hoping some object in this room, where only French was spoken, might trigger a latent memory. It was a parlour of sorts, stretching from the front to the back of the house, crowded with uncomfortable-looking hard-backed chairs and end tables dotted with doilies. It had an air of disuse, as if it was rarely entered; the lampshades still wrapped in cellophane, the doilies yellowing with age. A memorial to the past, I concluded, contemplating a collection of family photographs in ornate frames on an old pine sideboard that had been rubbed with green paint. Among them I recognized several of Papa Chaput, one with his son, Madame's husband, whose name I remembered was Roland. Almost certainly the room was kept for formal occasions and the odd, unexpected visitor like me; a waste really, because there was a view of the lake. I could hear murmuring in some other room and wondered if she was on the phone or talking to herself, another hazard of living alone.

She reappeared with a glass of Coke, which she put down beside me on the end table, centring it carefully on a doily.

"Oh, no thanks," I said without thinking. Anything fizzy on an empty stomach would trigger the retching.

"No Coke?" She frowned.

I realized I must have sounded abrupt. "It's the morning sickness," I explained.

"Eh?"

I put a hand to my stomach. "Enceinte," I said, flashing back to the hospital. Out of the endless discussions that had raged around me in French, it was the one word that had penetrated my brain. I had heard it over and over again. "Enceinte," I repeated.

She looked dubious.

I patted my stomach. "Bébé."

Her eyes widened. "Bébé!" She gave a gasp and her hands flew to her breast. I thought she might be having a heart attack, but then she snatched up the Coke and carried it away again.

I waited, feeling foolish, resisting the urge to sneak out before she returned. I could hear murmuring again, louder now. She was speaking to someone, a man most likely because the second voice was lower, her nephew, perhaps. They were discussing me, I had no doubt, trying to fathom what a pregnant woman was doing in the parlour. Why on earth had I come? Certainly not to tell her I was pregnant.

Then she was standing in front of me again, holding a tall glass of milk and smiling anxiously. Behind her in the doorway I could see a pale forehead topped by a shock of white hair. Monsieur Claude, impeccably casual in a black turtleneck, perfectly creased grey slacks, and a pair of beaded moccasins, padded over to the couch.

"Madame Laviolette, it is a pleasure to meet you once more." He beamed down at me.

"I thought I should stop by, you know, because of the fire," I explained, a little embarrassed in case he thought I had gone behind his back in some way but relieved to be speaking English.

"I myself have come on the same errand. It is upsetting of course, but perhaps, in the end, it is the best thing."

"I'm afraid I should never have spoken to you about Swen. I . . ."

He interrupted me before I could finish. "No, no, you must not blame yourself. It's nobody's fault." He wagged a finger at me for emphasis. "This fellow Swen, he's a bad lot. He has disappeared, I understand. We must hope he will not come back." He lowered himself stiffly onto one of the straight-backed chairs, glancing at Madame Chaput as he did so. She sat down beside me on the couch. "Adélie tells me that you are expecting a baby. It makes you happy, I hope."

"Yes, very happy." I blushed.

Madame Chaput took hold of my hand. Her fingers were thick and knobby, from long years on the farm, I supposed, or perhaps arthritis.

"You are living at home with your parents, I believe," said Monsieur Claude.

I nodded.

"Adélie is worried for you."

"Worried? Oh no, it was nothing. It's just that I haven't eaten, that's all." I picked up the glass of milk and took a large gulp. "I'll be fine now."

He glanced at Madame Chaput and I saw their eyes lock. "Adélie has asked me to speak for her. She has a proposition for you." He leaned forward with his elbows on his knees and the tips of his fingers touching. "She would be glad for you to stay here."

"Here? In this house?" I couldn't hide my astonishment.

"She has a room for you if you would like it. She is in the habit of taking a boarder, you see, but it happens that for the last few months she has been alone."

I shook my head, at a loss for words. Madame Chaput was watching my face intently.

"That's very kind, but I have a place in the village already," I said at length.

"You will be living above the shop?"

I nodded.

"Adélie fears it will be too much in your condition. She is worried for you."

Madame Chaput squeezed my hand. "You must to stay here," she said. "L'escalier, c'est périleux."

"She is concerned for your safety," explained Monsieur Claude. "The stairs, they are—"

But he had no need to translate. "Perilous. I understand. It's very kind of her, but I'm sure I'll be fine. It's important for me to go back to the apartment. It's my home."

"Yes, of course. You must do what is best for you."

It was impossible. Surely she must realize that. We were strangers; we couldn't even speak to each other.

"It's a wonderful offer." Reluctantly I turned to face her. My eyes pricked with tears. I blinked them back in case she mistook them for consent.

"C'est très gentil, madame, mais je ne peux pas."

She patted my knee. "Ça va, ma Petite. Tu va y penser."

But there was nothing to think about. I shook my head. "Je ne peux pas." My voice sounded strange in my ears. I had spoken French, I realized.

"Tu vas y penser," she repeated, patting my knee again.

I smiled uneasily, wondering how I was going to get away and if I dared leave without finishing the milk. Just then I heard a commotion outside, footsteps thumping on the wooden steps of the verandah, fists pounding on the door, a hoarse voice shouting my name. For a second I thought it must be Swen but he couldn't know I was here. We all turned to the window. There was Petey, his arms waving, head bobbing from side to side as he shifted from foot to foot, trying to peer in through the sheers.

"Imo, Imo!" he shouted. "Lucy's pregnant! I'm going to have a baby too!"

The Language of Love

My father drummed his fingers on the table. He was doing his best to be reasonable, but on the subject of a second dog, a puppy to boot, he wasn't going to budge.

We were at the drop-leaf table again, having a family confab. The special chop suey, almond chicken, mushroom chow mein, and a double order of egg rolls sat cooling on the kitchen counter in crinkled aluminum containers, awaiting consensus. An angry outburst from Petey seemed more likely, but my brother folded his arms across his chest and leaned back with his lower lip jutting out.

"I promised Lucy," he said flatly.

"You promised Lucy. Oh, for heaven's sakes!"

"Petey, it's not that simple. It's a lot of work having a puppy," my mother pointed out in a tired voice. It was a week since her last cigarette and the strain was showing. "Gone cold turkey," my father had confided to me a couple of days earlier. "She hasn't touched a thing, nothing at all." It seems he knew all along about the marijuana.

"It's a lot of work for me, Mum. Not for you. I'm going to train her. I know what to do. I'll buy her food too. I can pay." Petey bounced in his seat as he spoke, his voice rising with excitement.

"Just how are you going to pay?" demanded my father. "Right now you don't even have a job. And you'll be lucky if anyone on this street ever hires you again."

Most of Petey's regular customers, assuming he would be unavailable, had made alternative arrangements for the coming snow-shovelling season.

"Going to get some new customers. I'm a good worker," Petey declared.

"I don't want another trip to the hospital," my mother warned him.

"Mum, Mum, she's not a biter. I told you. I'm going to train her."

"I don't know why we're having this conversation. I think we should eat." My father pushed his chair away from the table and stood up, his fingers tattooing his thigh.

It wasn't the money or lack of it that was upsetting him. It was the thought of having Petey around the house all day, playing his radio at full blast, jabbering on about Swen and the fire or about Lucy. A puppy would only add to the confusion. And I was painfully aware that my own presence in the house, lolling about in bed, upchucking in the bathroom morning, noon, and night, though that part was over now, would only make things worse.

"I'll hire you," I offered. "I need someone to help me clear out the rooms behind the shop. I'm moving back tomorrow."

There was a startled silence.

"So soon," said my mother, looking doubtful but relieved too. "Are you sure you shouldn't wait a little longer?"

"I'm feeling fine now. I could use some help though. How about it, Petey?"

Petey grinned from ear to ear. "See, Dad."

Physically at least I did feel fine. Still a little more tired than usual, but that was to be expected. I had been dilly-dallying for a week, spending my mornings at the shop and returning to Garden Crescent for a late lunch and a nap. I had hired an assistant for Charmaine and could make my own hours, but there was no longer any need for me to be home and every reason for me to be at the shop.

Truth to tell I was nervous about Swen. Just about everyone in the village had a theory as to his whereabouts. He was holed up in a cabin somewhere in the Laurentians, waiting for all the fuss to die down; the mob had put out a contract on him and he was lying low in Vancouver under a new name; he'd gone to Mexico to live in a monastery. One scenario was as unlikely as another. Charmaine passed on all the rumours whether I wanted to hear them or not. The fellow who owns the garage next to her father's pharmacy let him hide in the washroom for a week before he took off, she had confided to me the day before. That one had the ring of truth.

He left me a memento of sorts, a bulky parcel bundled loosely in an advertising flyer from the IGA. I discovered it on the back step of the shop, the day after my visit to Madame Chaput. It fell open when I picked it up and I found myself holding a pair of Nikes. There was no mistaking the yellow stain and no question who had left them. Shaking all over, I stuffed them in the garbage pail and went inside. Charmaine was aghast when I told her, and after I'd gone upstairs, she fished them out and took them down to the police station. They're evidence apparently, the only evidence they have since everything else either went up in smoke or into the back of Swen's pickup, which hasn't been spotted by anyone since the night of the fire.

My father plunked four plates on the table and began prying open the lids of the takeout containers. "It's very good of you, Imogene. You can use the help, I'm sure, but that doesn't mean we're getting a puppy."

But that was exactly what it did mean, and Petey knew it.

The village is only a mile away, but my parents both came out to wave us off the next morning. Petey, dressed for work in a pair of old jeans and a bright red T-shirt, was beside me in the passenger seat of Thomas's old taxi. My one small suitcase was in the back along with a large care package from my mother, half the contents of the fridge, it seemed. I was about to pull away from the curb when a dark blue van with the words LIQUIDATION, RECUPERATION printed on the side in large white letters turned the corner onto Garden Crescent and parked beside the farmhouse. We watched as four men wearing protective face masks and silver-grey coveralls made of what looked like some kind of space-age material piled out and filed into the house. Moments later two of them reappeared carrying the table from the restaurant booth in the kitchen. A third followed with the jukebox. Petey was out of the car and up the road in a flash.

They had been hired, we learned later, by Madame Chaput's insurance company in the hopes of recovering some historical treasure and recouping their expenses. The salvage operation took the better part of a week and Petey was there every day, along with half the neighbourhood. Madame Chaput's nephew stopped by from time to time with a couple of old-timers from the village, and a woman from the heritage society filmed the whole thing on a nifty-looking Super 8 camera.

I spent that week catching up on paperwork at the shop, refusing my mother's increasingly pressing invitations to dinner, gorging instead on french fries and smoked meat sandwiches from the deli, and, despite my best resolutions, brooding about what should have been. I had put my name on an offer to purchase Maison de Pomme for Thomas's sake as much as my own and I would have put up with any amount of faulty wiring or crooked floors if only I could have him back. That house had dogged me all my life, it seemed. Everything I'd ever had to do with it had ended in disaster. A bad luck place, I'd heard someone mutter the day we put in the offer. I couldn't help wondering if, as a child, I had precipitated some of that bad luck.

"Don't be ridiculous," Louise exclaimed when I said something of the sort to her. "It's nothing to do with you. Papa Chaput was always going to die. He was a sick old man—he couldn't eat, he couldn't sleep, his leg hurt like hell."

She's right, I suppose, though to this day I can't shake the feeling that it was the sight of a grubby urchin clutching a waterlogged wooden cylinder that triggered his heart attack. What a brazen little thief I was, even if I was trying to make amends.

"The place was a dump. You know that," Louise continued. "It should have been torn down long ago. Tante Adélie thought she was doing you a favour, letting you have it so cheap, but you and Thomas could never have lived there, not with a baby. It had to be full of mould. The first contractor you talked to would have told you so. The two of you would be paying someone big bucks to tear it down if only Thomas hadn't gone and died like that."

If only.

She put a hand to her mouth and turned red. "Oh, sorry, Imogene. I don't mean it like that."

I shrugged. "Anyway it's not just the house. I feel bad for your aunt. I have a thing about her, I guess."

Louise rolled her eyes. "She has a thing about you, that's for sure. It used to drive me crazy. She was always talking about La Petite Anglaise. Such a brave little thing." She grinned. "I remember when you came to the house the day of the funeral, I was so jealous, I was nearly insane. I knew for sure you were really a little brat like me. She's a bit funny, you know, my aunt—asking you to go and live with her like that—and Monsieur Claude. You like him, I know, but he's a busybody. He had no business encouraging her. It's a good thing you had the sense to say no."

I drove by one afternoon toward the end of the week. There was nothing to see except a hole in the ground and a set of stairs leading down to the basement. A few old trunks, anonymous canvas bags, and assorted cardboard boxes were lined up along the chain-link fence in preparation for a yard sale the next day, but anything remotely antique or even retro had been carted off to an auction house apparently. Whatever the salvage company couldn't sell was going to be bulldozed, according to Petey, who made a point of keeping me posted. The spacemen, as he called the work crew, had finished for the day. There was a guard leaning on the gate eating an apple and a few people peering through the fence. It was idiotic, but I broke into a sweat at the thought of stopping.

With the exception of myself and Mr. Connibear, who's been pulling rubber tires, bits of metal, and cow skulls out of his vegetable garden for years, the entire neighbourhood lined up at the gate at eight-thirty the next morning. And almost everything, legless bottomless chairs, chipped crockery, broken utensils, was snapped up at two dollars per item or three for five. Petey scored an old toboggan with a few missing slats. He's going to fix it up and take the baby for rides, he says. Charley went along under duress, hoping to dissuade his mother from adding to the clutter in her own basement, but she came away with a crate of mousetraps, for Rupert apparently, to help him with his game. The whole scene gave Charley the creeps, all those memories rising out of the mud along with heaps of rotting canvas and worm-eaten wood, he'll be glad to leave them behind. He and his wife are getting back together, he told me the other day, and now that his mother's agreed to sell Dunster Debug, he's moving back to town. By noon the sale was over, the yard deserted, and an hour later a convoy of trucks rolled in with loads of fill, and after that a bulldozer took over. It started to rain then and by the end of the day the foundation had disappeared and the yard was a sea of mud. At least that's how Petey described it to me.

Charmaine had just put up the CLOSED sign that same evening when Petey pounded on the back door. Before I could open it, he burst in and plunked a muddy burlap bag on the floor. Charley followed, looking sheepish, and they stood over it, grinning expectantly.

"Guess what, Imo? You can't guess. We got something for you."

I didn't have to guess. Sticking out the top was a disembodied leg cut off at the ankle and, just visible, poking through the frayed string closure, was the toe of a shoe.

Charmaine gave a screech and rushed to the bathroom. She explained later that she thought there was a body inside and assuming it could only be Swen's, concluded he'd been dismembered by the mob. For once my stomach stayed put, but I caught my breath, half-choked by the smell of smoke and mildew that emanated from the sack. When I made no move to approach it, Petey undid the string and dumped the contents onto the floor: two artificial legs, one metal, one wood, ten left shoes, a fleece-lined rubber overshoe with metal clips for fasteners, and something that looked like an old-fashioned wooden shoetree with a metal shaft sticking out the top.

"For the museum!" he crowed.

I remained speechless.

"We just wanted you to see. You don't have to keep them," Charley said over and over.

In the end, to Charmaine's horror, I stashed the whole lot in the little bathroom, though I made Petey take the sack away before everything in the shop became imbued with smoke fumes. It didn't seem right to toss them in the garbage.

"Absolutely not," Louise declared when I wondered out loud if I should consult Madame Chaput. "My god, Imogene, she left them behind for a reason. It'd be a nightmare for her. If I were you I'd take them out and dump them in the lake, or, better still, let's have a bonfire and burn them! Papa Chaput wouldn't care. He hated wearing his prosthesis; his stump was always sore. What were they thinking of? You can't want to keep them!"

She was right of course. I didn't want to keep them, and I didn't have to, I realized when I came to my senses. I've arranged to show them to someone from the war museum in Ottawa. The peg leg at least is historic, and with any luck they'll take the aluminum one as well. It's hollow all the way down, I discovered, and was stuffed full of socks until I emptied it.

I'm keeping a few of the shoes for the museum, though it means adding another shelf. For the time being they're in a box on the upstairs landing. I open it every morning to give them a chance to air out. They're everyday shoes, a little on the small side for a man. Papa Chaput was barely five foot four, my father tells me. There's nothing out of the ordinary about them except for the fact that they're fifty years old and have never been worn, though the telltale black droppings indicate they have served a purpose. And it's rare nowadays to find even expensive footwear made entirely of leather. The shoetree is a kind of a wooden clog, hand-carved by the look of the chisel marks. It belongs to the peg leg, I've decided, which is why it never got hollowed out.

It's a couple of months since I moved back to the apartment. The days go by quickly enough but the evenings seem never-ending. I live with the memory of love now. Thomas is everywhere, in the workroom, pulling a pair of pale green sandals from the shelf, tinkering with Joseph's old sewing machine, or whistling through his teeth as he pounds tacks into a pair of alligator skin loafers as wide as they are long for The Man With The Wide Feet. At night I feel his long supple body slipping into bed beside me and in the morning there he is with a lazy smile and two cups of lukewarm tea laced with sweetened condensed milk. I see him in the downstairs kitchen on Sundays, tipped back on a wobbly wooden chair, his hands clasped behind his head, blowing perfect smoke rings to impress Petey, reminiscing with Swen. I try to stop there but the memories keep coming.

Swen in his sweat-stained pink dress shirt sidling through the back door, dropping a joint in my lap and drawling, "Lighten up, Jackson," Swen hauling Lucy out from under Mr.Connibear's porch. I can still feel his nails biting into my arm. He's gone for good, I tell myself; there's nothing to bring him back except spite, and surely he's not foolish enough to show up in the village and hang around peddling drugs again, though Charmaine tells me that the local supply has dried up. How she knows I haven't inquired.

The news of my pregnancy is all over the village. Madame Poulin was in here yesterday, eyeing up my expanding waistline and trying on a pair of Happy-Tread Lace-Ups for Ladies. We got along in Franglais, that halting mixture of English and French so frowned on by the language police, but I didn't manage to sell her anything. I can never predict what's going to take her fancy. A couple of weeks ago Charmaine persuaded her to buy a reindeer hat for one of her great-grandchildren. He wore it to school the next day and started a fad. Just about every kid in the village has one now and some of the teenagers are getting into the act. I told my mother the other day that we've had to order a second batch.

Charmaine thinks we should go in for hats. She's been studying up on marketing and we need a niche, she says. For the spring, she wants to order some cheap baseball caps with Laviolette & Fils printed on them and give them away with each purchase. I'm more inclined to get in a big selection of children's shoes, but there's no reason we can't do both so I've told her to go ahead.

Petey comes over in the mornings to help with the clearing out. I cut him his first paycheque yesterday. It can be a slow process, unearthing the past and then deciding to bury it again. My brother hasn't missed a day, though the dust gets up his nose and makes him sneeze. I think he'd wear a spacesuit if he knew where to get one. We started in Thomas's childhood bedroom. It's full of papers mostly, stacks of old invoices and tax returns from the year dot, odds and ends of discontinued stock, and a whole host of repairs that were never picked up. He came across one of Thomas's old sketchbooks the other day, charcoal drawings of villagers trying on shoes, including one of Madame Poulin crossing the road in a wide-brimmed hat and her pompom slippers, and another of Joseph bent over his sewing machine. I thought of tacking that one up on the wall, but I've decided to have it framed instead.

All Petey talks about these days is babies, and that's fine with me, though some of them are the four-footed kind. He stops by the pound every morning on his way over and plays with Lucy's puppies. There are five in the litter and they look a lot like the Labrador retriever that lives at the top of Garden Crescent. According to the vet, there's no reason to assume any of them will be bad-tempered as long they're well treated. Petey's picked out the one he wants, a female he's christened Lucy 2. He wore my father down in the end, but he still has to explain things to Tillie. Lucy herself has had a reprieve of sorts. Once the pups are weaned and adopted, she's to be sent to live on a farm in the Eastern Townships, at least that's what they've told Petey. He considers himself *in loco parentis.* There's enough love in his heart for a hundred babies, he tells me.

Love is a way of life for Petey; it's what makes his world go round. Sometimes I envy him. French is the language of love, they say. That's Parisian French of course, not the language I learned to speak and to love over all those years. Not Québécois. To me it's a language of loss now, though the words that were locked into some remote part of my brain the day of the accident are surfacing slowly, not all in a rush as I'd hoped. A word or a phrase each day is the most I can manage.

"The heart has to heal first and the head will follow," Dr. Campeau tells me when I complain. "For now you must concentrate on growing your baby." Loving my baby is what he means; I can tell by the way his eyebrows arch. He would never say it outright, but he's afraid I'm going to change my mind again and do something stupid, or else that after the baby's born, I'll refuse to have anything to with it.

There's no danger of that. I can't believe I nearly had an abortion. I want the baby more than my life, though I'm not sure if what I feel is love; more a ripple of surprise followed by a weakness in all my limbs whenever I feel a flutter inside me, and then an involuntary grin, knowing I've fooled the fates.

Babies turn your world upside down, people say. I can believe it. In the night, when an invisible elbow or knee prods me awake, my whole body quivers with excitement; then the disappointment sets in because there's no one to share it, no one to bring me a cup of sweet milky tea, or to roll over with a groan when I get up to raid the fridge. Love is an act of faith, I've decided, a way forward through joy, through grief, through pain. It's the language of life really. Maybe in a few months I'll be right side up again and the baby and I can learn to speak it together.

Madame Poulin's great-grandchildren, all ten of them, wore their reindeer hats to church last Sunday. It was a grand procession apparently. Father Trepannier must have been torn—he has so few attending mass these days—but he stood his ground, insisting they leave them at the door. The children think it's because he doesn't have one himself, so they're all chipping in to buy him one for Christmas. I tried on one myself the other day just for the hell of it, and wouldn't you know it, there was the man of God himself coming down the sidewalk in his holey old boots. He glanced up at the window as he passed and I'm pretty sure I saw him crack a smile.

Now that the dark sets in so early, Charmaine and I stand at the window in the late afternoons before the streetlights come on and watch a wavering line of tiny lights floating down the street. I can't think of anywhere better to live.

Acknowledgments

Heartfelt thanks to my editor, Kathy Page, for her guidance and her insightful reading of the manuscript. I am indebted to Margaret Thompson, Helen Heffernan, Jen Howe, Maureen Moore, and once again Kathy for keeping me company along the way. Their feedback and encouragement were invaluable. I am grateful to Elizabeth Owen Durham for her stalwart support and appreciative reading of an early draft, and to Tirthanker Bose for his warm and perceptive response to the final draft. Thanks also to Pearl Gray, and to Lorraine Gane for that initial moment of inspiration.

GILLIAN CAMPBELL's short fiction has been published in *Grain* magazine, *The New Quarterly*, *The Antigonish Review*, and *creekstones: words & images*. She has a BA from the Université de Montréal and a master's of library science from the University of British Columbia, and for many years she worked as a children's librarian. Gillian grew up on the West Island of Montreal, and now makes her home on the West Coast on Salt Spring Island, British Columbia. *The Apple House* is her first novel.